THE DEVIL'S DRUM

WILLIAM COLT MACDONALD

WHEELER
CHIVERS

This Large Print edition is published by Wheeler Publishing, Waterville, Maine, USA and by BBC Audiobooks Ltd, Bath, England.
Wheeler Publishing, a part of Gale, Cengage Learning.

LIBRARY OF CONGRESS CATALOGING-IN-PUBLICATION DATA

MacDonald, William Colt, 1891–1968.
  The devil's drum / by William Colt MacDonald.
    p. cm. — (Wheeler Publishing large print Western)
  ISBN-13: 978-1-4104-2948-3 (softcover)
  ISBN-10: 1-4104-2948-2 (softcover)
  1. Large type books. I. Title.
PS3525.A2122D48 2010
813'.52—dc22   2010017703

BRITISH LIBRARY CATALOGUING-IN-PUBLICATION DATA AVAILABLE
Published in 2010 in the U.S. by arrangement with Golden West Literary Agency.
Published in 2010 in the U.K. by arrangement with Golden West Literary Agency.

U.K. Hardcover: 978 1 408 49229 1 (Chivers Large Print)
U.K. Softcover: 978 1 408 49230 7 (Camden Large Print)

Printed and bound in Great Britain by the MPG Books Group
1 2 3 4 5 6 7 14 13 12 11 10

CONTENTS

[I]
AMBUSH

For a considerable time there wasn't the slightest doubt that the three-day downpour was responsible for the landslide at Shoulder Bluff where it elbowed to one side the twin tracks of the T.N. & A.S. Railroad, slickly wet in the rain. Fortunately, no wreck took place. The headlight of the freight train's locomotive, cutting a bright beam through the slanting arrows of moisture, had picked out in plenty of time the tumbled debris of earth and rock spilled across the right-of-way, and the engine had been brought to a safe stop. Followed some bitter profanity on the part of the train crew, while the usual precautionary measures were undertaken, flagging signals set out and so on.

Meanwhile, less than a mile distant from the point where the train had halted, two mule-drawn wagons made their way doggedly through the wet night. A stretch of gumbo-like clay wasn't helping the progress

7

any. There was considerable cracking of whips and vitriolic cursing as each team of mules strained against the traces, hoofs tearing at the slippery, mud-churned roadway on a grade approaching Shoulder Bluff. Roadway? There wasn't any roadway. A sort of trail, perhaps, little used nowadays, with sage and greasewood and cactus thriving along ancient wheel ruts. The mesquite grew higher on either side of the old trail, and more than once a wagon had missed the way in the sodden gloom when one of the mules found itself pushing through low brush. Then there'd be more swearing until the wagon was swerved back on the trail again.

The wagons traveled one behind the other, rain beating steadily into the faces of the drivers. Sometimes brakes were jammed on abruptly, and the harness set up a jangling, until slipping animals could once more find a sort of footing. Then, one after the other, they'd lurch on through the dripping night. The teamsters were both lean muscular oldsters, heavily bewhiskered, with battered, shapeless felt hats from which water dripped in an almost continual stream. Their clothing was shabby and at present soggy. Patched breeches were tucked into knee-length flat-heeled boots. Their names were Corny Callahan and Ringbone Pardee, and a tough pair of old roots they were by any standard.

By this time, Corny Callahan, in the lead, had tooled his team to a more level stretch of ground. Calling back something over his shoulder, he pulled the steaming animals to a halt. Ringbone Pardee too halted and after securing his reins, climbed down from his wagon and made his way, slipping and sliding, to the foremost wagon, where Callahan was endeavoring to light a short stubby pipe. In the light from the flickering flame, his keen old eyes looked down with some amusement on his companion. Then he too dropped to the earth. "It's quite the night to be out, Ringbone, me bye." He chuckled. There was a touch of Irish brogue in his tones. "And it's me that's seein' plain ye're not likin' of it."

Ringbone Pardee swore. "What did ye stop fer?" he demanded in aggrieved tones. "We was finally makin' some time —"

"And it's you sittin' on your drivin' seat, takin' of your comfort, that's complainin'," Callahan scoffed. He gestured toward the panting mules. "Is it forgettin' ye are that them kittens is needin' a breather after makin' of that grade?"

"What difference does weather make to a

mule?" Pardee growled. "It ain't no fit night for a human to be out — so black you can't see your face in front of you."

"And why —" Callahan laughed, "— should you be wantin' to scare yourself to death in that fashion?" He cut short a half-snarled retort and went on. "This is nothin' at all, at all. Had you been with me in the old days when we was drivin' of the six-mule high-wheeled freighters, through blizzards and desert heat, ye'd be thinkin' a trip of this kind was play for a child —"

"Yaah! Yaah! Yaah!" Pardee cut in peevishly. "All's you can do is talk of them old days. I'm sick and tired of your guff. I was a damn' fool to take this job with you —"

"It was you that was needin' of the money, you kept sayin'," Callahan reminded. "And when the opportunity come it was of my old friend, Ringbone, I thought on the fir-r-st. It's sorry I am, if the job is not to your likin' —"

"I'll never take another job with you," Pardee said sullenly.

"That is as it may be," Callahan said mildly. "But now that we're into the job, we'd best be carryin' of it through." His old eyes probed the darkness trying to find some reaction on Pardee's face, but it was too dark to see. "Anyway you look at it, the

10

wor-r-st should be over, with the two of us makin' of more downgrade on the return trip. We'd better be startin' again."

"Leastwise, it could stop rainin'," Pardee said disagreeably.

"That would be makin' no difference to us, at all, at all," Corny Callahan said philosophically. "We can get no wetter than we are at the moment."

Pardee swore and said, "You talk like an old fool. Let's be gettin' on." Without waiting for an answer, he turned and sloshed a slippery path back to his wagon. The mules were started again.

Half an hour later the gloom ahead of the teamsters lightened a trifle and it wasn't long after that before they sighted Shoulder Bluff, silhouetted against a faint reddish luminosity. Light gleamed dimly on wet steel tracks and to the right of these Corny Callahan and Pardee sighted the landslide of tumbled boulders and heaped wet earth. Rounding the huge pile they came within view of the train. Red fusees had been placed at the rear of the train and ahead of the landslide across the right-of-way, casting a sort of eerie light over the scene. A spiral of slow smoke rose lazily from the funnel-shaped stack of the locomotive, with its T.N. & A.S. R.R. painted in bold white

11

letters on the side of the cab, showing plainly in the sizzling light of a flare.

Callahan, followed by Pardee, tooled his mules carefully around the helter-skelter tumble of rocks strewn across tracks and beyond into the mesquite and crushed spots of brush and cactus, taking in, as he reined the team this way and that, the two telegraph poles down with their tangled wires snapped against a boulder the size of a small house. Callahan, with Pardee's wagon at his rear, pulled to a halt alongside the locomotive, and raised his eyes to see the conductor, engineer and fireman staring down at him from the engine's cab. No one spoke for a minute.

Then Callahan said gravely, "Would you be likin' me, gents, to hitch on my kittens and be haulin' that billy-be-damned tea-kittle out of the mess you're after-r-r findin' yourselves in —"

"Where the devil did you come from on a night like this?" the conductor demanded. He was a thin middle-aged man with a gold watch chain stretching across his vest. His eyes bugged out.

"And this is no tea-kettle," the overalled engineer said grumpily.

" 'Tis as much good as a tea-kittle would be doin' you in the situation you be findin' yoursilves," Callahan responded genially. "In the old days, now, ye'd not be seein' of no jerk-line freighter hauled up short by a molehill I'm after-r seein' athwart your tracks. A leap and a bound and we'd be after clearin' the top of the mess. It would be takin' more'n a couple of pebbles and a fistful of dirt to be detainin' of us in thim days. Why —"

The engineer felt his ire rising. He was about to speak when the conductor asked, "What you fellows want here, anyway?"

"We're after seekin' Conductor Fraley of eastbound freight train number twenty-four. 'Tis the orders of the station agent at Clarion City we're after-r-r carryin' out —"

"I'm Fraley," the conductor said shortly. "What do you — what's the station agent want?"

Callahan continued, "We've come to relieve you of some of your freight which is bad needed to send on its way, and to tell you a work train to clear the track is bein' sent t'once, and it's been a sore-bad trip for us from Clarion and the sooner we finish the business the better all around. So let us get started." He squirmed around on the driver's seat, to speak to Pardee. "Ain't that right, Ringbone?"

Pardee nodded sulkily without reply and

13

spat a long stream of tobacco juice to splash on the side of the locomotive. The conductor's jaw dropped open. The engineer exclaimed unbelievingly, "But — but how could you get here so soon? This slide just —"

"So soon, is ut?" Callahan gave a scornful laugh. "Soon, ye calls it. And with me and Ringbone a-swimmin' our mules through a pitch-black torrent for comin' on three hours to get here —"

"By God," the fireman pushed into the conversation. "I could have swore that slide hadn't happened but a minute or so before we got here. There was still some small rocks tumbling down —"

"I saw that myself," the engineer interposed. "The headlight showed plain —"

The conductor got into the conversation again: "That must have been some sort of small secondary slide, George" — to the engineer. "This teamster says he was ordered out from Clarion City some two or three hours back. The station agent there sends word a work train is on the way to clear the tracks. Jeepers! If I'd known that I'd not have sent Witt walking that long distance to Clarion —"

"Your brakie can flag down the work train when it comes along," the fireman put in

"He'll be mighty wet by that time, of course."

"I've been thinking," the engineer said. "It's after midnight now. There's been no train through here, eastbound, for nearly eight hours. Must be the eight-thirty-seven westbound discovered this slide and backed up to Clarion City —"

The conductor swore irritably. "All right, they knew about it. Why weren't we flagged down, back there at Arvila? Seems they could have got word to Arvila station some-how."

"Was you after stoppin' at Arvila?" Callahan asked.

The conductor said shortly, "Arvila's just a watering station. Eastbounds don't stop there — just westbounds before they hit that grade beyond —"

"I know that agent at Arvila," the fireman put in. "He's got a habit of hitting the jug while on duty. Might have been asleep when we balled through."

"Which is all neither the here or there, as I'm seein' ut," Callahan stated. "Me and Ringbone is gettin' wetter by the minute. 'Tis settled there's a landslide. 'Tis also settled no work train on this blessed earth is going to clear the way for you the nixt ten hours or more. The drinkin' man at Arvila

15

is not our problem. So would you please be lettin' us have the load we was sent to haul, so's we can be gittin' back to a dry bed and a nip of the creature."

"What in the devil load you talking about?" the conductor asked testily.

Callahan started to answer, then paused and withdrew from within his faded shirt a roll of oilcloth, which had managed to keep reasonably dry the papers he carried. The small square of oilcloth was unrolled and the papers passed up to the conductor. A lantern was held high and the fireman and engineer stood close while the conductor perused his papers. Quite suddenly the conductor swore a violent oath.

"What's wrong, Sam?" the engineer asked.

For a few minutes the conductor could only stutter. Then, with an effort he calmed himself. "This is from the station agent at Clarion City. He got orders from Tyrus Wolcott himself to hire teamsters to come out here and take some of our freight off our hands. Seems said freight is to be taken to Clarion City 'with all dispatch.' That's what it says here. There is to be no waiting for the work train to clear the tracks." The conductor started to swear again.

"You take my advice," the engineer said, "and you'll follow old Tyrant Wolcott's orders to the letter. What's the old buzzard got aboard this train — a shipment of gold bars?"

"Yeah," the fireman put in. "When Tyrant Wolcott snaps the whip, you'd better jump fast. How that mean old skunk ever got to be manager of the Clarín Division, I'll never know."

"Damned if I'll do it," the conductor said wrathfully. "It means opening a car and —"

"Maybe you'd sooner have a sixty-day layoff, Sam," the engineer reminded. "It don't pay to trifle with Wolcott's orders. What's the freight, anyway? Must be mighty precious."

More profanity from the conductor. Disgustedly he said, "Precious your hind leg! Strawberry jam, that's what it is! Strawberry and plum preserves! Peach preserves! All canned stuff, boxed. Down from some company in 'Frisco, consigned to Chicago. Now what in the devil would Wolcott want —"

"You'd best obey orders, Sam," the engineer advised.

"Crazy orders, if you ask me," the conductor snapped. "It goes against the grain to open a car just to satisfy some whim of Wolcott's. I know my business. Opening a car is against company policy unless —"

"Onless," Callahan interrupted, "it's on the big boss's orders. Now you can do as this Wolcott spalpeen says or not, jist as pleases you, Mister Conductor, jist so's you let me and Ringbone have your decision within the next month or so. One way or t'other, we're wantin' to be on our way. Do we get this load to be haulin' back, or don't we? Not that we be givin' a damn. The railroad is hirin' of us and our mules, and the railroad will be payin'. Is it that you'd be spendin' good railroad money to see us haul back and no load at all?"

That settled it. The conductor grouched some more before he reluctantly climbed down from the locomotive cab, then led the way, the two wagons following, toward the end of the train. They passed boxcars, gondolas and loaded flat cars on the way. At the caboose, a brakeman with a red lantern took form. The conductor entered his caboose and consulted papers, then re-emerged. With the brakeman's help, one of the boxcars was entered. Freight was shifted around. A number of wooden boxes — there couldn't have been more than twenty — weighing around fifty pounds each, were divided equally between the two wagons. With the aid of the two teamsters, the work was quickly accomplished. In lifting one box

18

to his wagon, Ringbone Pardee dropped it to the earth. The heavy box struck a chunk of rock and splintered open. The top board of the box came loose. Cans spilled out on the soggy earth. Cursing, Ringbone dropped from the wagon, retrieved all cans he saw, and crammed them, helter-skelter, back into the damaged box. In time the load was stacked on the wagons, Callahan signed a receipt for the freight, and the two wagons once more got under way on their return trip.

Darkness again settled down on the teamsters, as they left the lights at the scene of the landslide behind. The rain had slacked off to a steady drizzle by this time, and the wind had dropped considerably. Realizing they were homeward bound, the mule teams bent stoutly to their task. Loaded as the wagons were, they were making better time now. Once, Callahan twisted around on the driver's seat and called back to Pardee, "Most all downgrade goin' now, my bucko, clear to Clarion."

"Tell me somethin' I don't know," Pardee replied ungraciously. "It's damn' wet either way."

Callahan settled to his driving. "There's the hell of a lot," he muttered, "that I could tell you and you not knowin' of it."

They advanced another half mile with no word between them. After a time, Callahan spoke to his companion again: "Mind ye don't force your team into that big rock, like ye did comin' up," he warned. "It's jist ahead of hereabouts some place. Jist give your kittens their head this time."

A tall upthrust of granite, rising from the soaked earth, loomed up through the darkness a minute later. "Here 'tis," Callahan shouted back as his team swerved to avoid the rock towering above his head. He pushed on past, then, warned by some inner sense, started to turn on his seat. In the abrupt flare of gunfire he caught a brief glimpse of a man and saddled horse, before something smashed violently into his body.

A choked "Dry-gulched, b'Gawd," left his lips as he started to rise from the driver's seat. He felt himself toppling back and back against the boxes in the bed of the wagon, even as one hand clawed at the ancient six-shooter in holster. His yell of warning to Pardee was interrupted by a second explosion, and he knew his warning had been useless.

Then silence. Somehow, Callahan managed to extricate himself from the bed of the wagon and reach the ground. There was a warm stickiness within his shirt now mingling with the wetness of rain-soaked garments. Forty-five in hand, he swayed against the side of the wagon, peering through the darkness for a target. He fired once in the direction where he had first seen the man and horse, but the flame from the gun showed him nothing.

He'd a feeling he couldn't last much longer. Somewhere, behind the tall rock was the hidden assassin. From Pardee's wagon came a long-drawn moan. The thought went through Callahan's head that Ringbone hadn't even had time to draw before being hit. Callahan was growing lightheaded now, his strength was slipping fast. With Irish tenacity he decided to get Pardee's gun and with his own weapon make a stand against the unknown assailant.

Slipping, sliding, he made his way back to Pardee, reached through the darkness to the wagon seat. "You — hurt — bad, Ringbone?"

A groan, then, "Sorry — I — crabbed 'bout this job . . ."

A choked gurgling ended the words.

"Sorry as hell I got you into this, Ringbone." This time Callahan's voice came clearer, but Pardee was beyond hearing.

Consciousness was going fast, but doggedly Callahan strove to turn away from the wagon and face the enemy. He was gasping terribly now, forty-five dangling in right hand. His left hand on one wagon wheel held him in a swaying position. Then came the third shot, smashing through flesh and bone between the shoulder blades.

And Corny Callahan too died.

[II]
A MYSTERIOUS DISAPPEARANCE

The heat of the day hadn't yet made the front wall of El Paso's Grand Central Hotel untenable for the loungers who gathered there each day to bask in the reflected morning sunlight from the plaza adjoining and exchange gossip. Consequently, there came a sudden cessation of conversation and a craning of masculine heads when the girl emerged from the lobby entrance. A tall girl she was, unusually tall, with shoulders wider than most, but an excellent figure withal. A range-bred girl, one of the loungers guessed, not accustomed to city ways.

"Got a good stride on her," a man observed, "like her laigs ain't used to bein' confined in sech a long skirt."

"Yeah," his companion agreed, "like a filly thet's been hobbled."

"Quite a chunk of woman — a man's woman, I'd say," from another source, and an oldster cackled, "Boys, thet's some female."

And still another lounger commented — he may have possessed the soul of a poet without knowing it — "I've seen yeller cactus blossoms jist thet same color as her hair. Seems like, with all that pale yeller hair, she'd look better 'thout that little doodad of a bonnet with all them vi'lets spilled over it."

"Don't seem like she should be wearin' no hat," the man adjacent observed. "Town clothes don't seem to be right fer her. I'd give a purty to see her on a hawss. Speakin' of hawsses . . ."

But the others weren't listening as they continued to watch the girl as, with erect shoulders and lifted chin, she steered a diagonal course across the plaza and started along San Francisco Street. A jangling sound caught her ear and she turned her head to see a mule-drawn streetcar rumbling past. She gave it only brief scrutiny. If El Paso's busy streets with its buildings, pedestrians, wagons and buggies impressed her in any way, she failed to show it. Life in the city seemed to flow over and around her without touching her in any way, as though her own immediate problems so obsessed her that all outside activity was without consequence.

Within seven or eight minutes after leaving the Grand Central, she arrived at the offices of the Texas Northern & Arizona Southern Railroad and asked to see Mr. Jay Fletcher. Mr. Fletcher, a clerk informed her, was not in at present. Would anyone else do? The girl replied that she'd like to see Mr. Gregory Quist. The clerk smiled a trifle. Mr. Quist, he informed her, rarely came to these offices. He had his own office at his hotel, where he lived. Upon further query, the clerk gave her the necessary directions for finding the Pierson Hotel. The tall girl thanked him shortly and departed.

Fifteen or twenty minutes later the girl reached the corner of St. Louis and Kansas Streets, where a recently erected brick building bore a sign proclaiming it to be the Pierson Hotel. Here there were more men lounging about, but the girl didn't seem aware of their stares as she entered, crossed to the lobby desk and inquired for Mr. Gregory Quist. The spectacled desk clerk eyed her a moment longer than was necessary, then,

"Yes, Mr. Quist is in. Whom shall I tell him is —"

24

"What's his room number?" she interrupted crisply.

Taken aback by her tone, he gave a number on the second floor, before recovering himself. "I'll send word up at once, Miss — Miss?"

"Don't bother. I know how to count," the girl said tartly, turning toward the carpeted stairway to the second floor.

A horrified look crossed the clerk's face. "But — but — wait a minute, miss. You shouldn't go up to his room —"

The girl spoke over her shoulder as she reached the first step, "Don't worry. I won't hurt him."

The clerk gasped and lost his voice as she disappeared up the stairway, then turned a sort of shocked expression on the few men around the lobby. All of them were grinning at him. One said something pertaining to "a well-turned ankle," and someone else commented on Greg Quist's attraction for pretty women.

Arriving on the second floor, the girl strode along a corridor until she'd reached a door near the rear of the building. Here she rapped on the panel. Instantly, a voice from within bade her to "Come on in."

The girl entered, closing the door behind her, and found herself in a room again as

25

large as the ordinary hotel chamber. There were the usual furnishings — dresser, bed, washstand; carpet on the floor; a couple of straight-backed chairs and a rocker; a small table held an oil lamp. There was a stand for hanging clothing. At the rear of the room, placed between two open windows, were a roll-top desk and swivel armchair. Seated at the desk, engaged in writing a letter, was Gregory Quist. At his right hand was a half-finished glass of beer, and several beer bottles, both full and empty, stood within reach.

Without glancing around at his visitor, Quist spoke over his shoulder. "Find a seat. I'll be with you when I finish this." There was a sort of musical quality to his low, resonant voice, as though the tones welled deep from his thick chest.

The girl flushed, but remained standing, as though a bit uncertain, now that she was here. Her gaze strayed through the open window at Quist's left, seeing without being conscious of seeing, the wide stretch of undulating wasteland of gray alkali soil, cactus and mesquite where it stretched in a northwesterly direction to Franklin Mountain. Nearer the hotel were unpaved streets lined with adobe structures, with here and there a frame or brick house rising above its lower neighbors. Faint sounds rose from the street immediately below.

The girl's gaze came back to Quist, writing at his desk, taking in his breadth of shoulder and shock of thick tawny hair. She couldn't see his face, but judged he was clean-shaven. This, in a country where most men grew mustaches and many wore full beards. His coat hung on a chair. A vest covered his denim shirt, open at the throat. A flat-topped fawn-colored sombrero lay on the bed, and on one bedpost hung a six-shooter in an underarm holster.

Quist stirred at his desk, put down his pen with a sigh of relief. "How I do hate writing letters," he observed, then cast a glance over his shoulder. His eyes opened wider at the girl standing just within the doorway, then, cat-like, he came to his feet, saying, "Well!" and again, "Well!" followed by, "Good Lord, why didn't you say something?"

"I don't like writing letters either," the girl said directly. "And when a person has a disagreeable task to get through, he shouldn't be interrupted." Her voice had a sort of husky quality.

They stood, taking stock of each other for an instant. Quist noted she was nearly as tall as he was, with dark brown eyes in a well-tanned face with good features — no, the features were more than good. A fine straight nose, nice lips and chin, unbelievably long black eyelashes. And, good Lord, such hair. Unaccountably, the thought of some Viking goddess entered his mind. The girl too was liking what she saw: the good space between the eyes. Unusual eyes they were, a sort of yellow. No, topaz. Topaz was the word. Or perhaps amber. They went well with the thick tawny hair, wide, thin-lipped mouth and rather bony features.

She put out her hand suddenly and as Quist took it he felt the firmness of bone and muscular fingers. Nothing weak about that hand, and yet it was feminine too. She said directly, "Mr. Quist, I'm Kate Porter. We — that is, my father and brother and I — own the Rocking-T outfit, in Clarín County, near Clarion City. I've come to ask you to help me."

Quist moved away from her then, seeking to place a chair for her near his desk and reaching for his coat. The girl stopped him: "Don't put it on, on my account. Leave it off, and I'll take mine off. I've found El Paso is rather warm this time of year." Even as she was speaking she removed the three-quarter length coat she wore, saying something in a rather disgusted tone of voice about traveling costumes, and hung it over the chair near the desk. The shirtwaist she wore looked spotlessly new, as did the rest of her attire, as though it had been just purchased for this trip.

Quist seated himself. "Well, Miss Porter —"

"It's *Mrs.* Porter," the girl said. "My father is Wyatt Thornton. My husband —"

"Of course," Quist broke in. "I've heard of the Thornton cow holdings. Right big spread." Unconsciously, he reached for his unfinished glass of beer, then stopped, smiling a trifle sheepishly. "Sorry, I haven't any refreshments for a lady up here. I could send down to the bar for a glass of sarsaparilla or a lemonade —"

The girl's short laugh interrupted. She said in her husky voice, "There's a deal of dust flying between here and Clarion City. My throat caught its full share. I happen to think there's nothing like beer to cut dust. So if you would please . . ."

Quist nodded, still hesitated. "This beer isn't iced —" he commenced.

"So much the better," the girl replied. Quist's eyes widened in appreciation. The girl went on, "And if you're worrying about my reputation, forget it. I've been talked about before." Something arrogant, defiant in her manner. "Right now, your hotel clerk downstairs is considering me no lady for coming to a man's room. Well, the way my life has been running, I've not had much time to live like a lady. . . ." Then in softer tones, "Please, Mr. Quist, may I have some of your beer?" She was in that moment, Quist considered, like a small child wistfully eyeing a stick of peppermint candy.

"Of course, Mrs. Porter." Quist rose, seeking a clean glass.

The girl's dark eyes followed his quick easy movements across the room and back again. Prying the cup-like stopper from a bottle, he poured a foaming glass of the amber fluid and handed it to the girl. She drank deeply; a long sigh welled from her breast. "That's better." She smiled. Now he was remembering it was the first time he'd seen her smile. Reaching across to set the glass on the edge of his desk, a strand of yellow hair fell across her forehead. Impatiently she raised one hand to brush it aside and in doing so knocked the small bonnet with violets askew. Still more impatiently she whipped off the hat. "Blasted silly little thing," she said tersely, tossing it atop Quist's roll-top desk. "The things women have to put up with when they go traveling." An irritable jerk of her head shook her blond hair free. Hairpins showered to the floor behind her chair, as the shining loosened strands fell to shoulder length. "Now," she stated, "we'll talk."

"It will be a pleasure," Quist said quietly, amusement showing in his topaz eyes.

Kate Porter came directly to the point. "Mr. Quist, my husband disappeared a month ago. I want you to find him, bring him back."

"I'm sorry to hear that," Quist said. "Is your husband connected with the T.N. & A.S.?"

"If, Mr. Quist," — and again a certain bitterness entered her tones — "you can prove that Lloyd Porter was ever connected with anything definitely, I'd be glad to hear it."

Quist frowned. Now he was deciding he wanted nothing to do with this business. Probably, the same old story. Husband and wife had a spat. Husband takes off. What was it they always said? Oh, yes, he took his hat and his departure. Apparently, at present at least, there was no love lost between Kate Porter and her spouse. No, Quist thought, I want no part of this deal, even if I were free to engage in such work.

He said, "Look here, Mrs. Porter, I'm afraid you've come to the wrong man. Why don't you try the Pinkerton outfit. You see, I'm a railroad operative — detective, if you like — and I work only on matters connected with the company. So —"

"That may be true, usually," Kate Porter put in. "Perhaps I can convince you — look here, we, my father and I — own quite a block of T.N. & A.S. stock. I think we're entitled —"

"The answer is still no, Mrs. Porter."

The girl bridled. "I'd expect to pay you well."

"I'm already paid well, by the company. My contract states I don't have to take on a job unless I want to. Big stockholders have tried to bring pressure before this to get my aid in their difficulties. It hasn't worked." He raised one hand to halt the girl's interruption, saying earnestly, "Actually, I can't believe your trouble is very serious. You've had some sort of love spat with your husband and he decided to clear out for a while until things blow over —"

"Who said anything about love?" Kate Porter asked scornfully.

"Perhaps I assumed too much," Quist said mildly. "But that's neither here nor there. If I left on a hunt for your husband, some serious railroad trouble might arise where I'd be needed in a hurry. I'm sorry to have to say no —"

"Suppose," the girl asked, color rising, "I

told you there'd been talk around Clarion that I had something to do with my husband's disappearance — ?"

"You mean that you'd — ?"

"Killed him," the girl said bluntly.

Quist smiled thinly. "And did you?"

"No, but I could of," the girl snapped.

Quist shrugged his broad shoulders. "I imagine most wives feel like killing their husbands now and then." He smiled. "Can't say I blame 'em either. Now, Mrs. Porter, I think this will all blow over. Pay no attention to people's talk. Some people are always ready to talk, even when there're no facts to support their gossip —"

"Look here, Mr. Quist, Jay Fletcher gave us to understand you'd help me." Quist asked a question. The girl replied, "Oh, yes, Jay Fletcher is an old friend of the family. When this trouble came up I wrote him. His reply suggested perhaps you could do something. I rode into Clarion City yesterday, intending to write him again from there. I said a while back I disliked writing letters. On the spur of the moment I bought such traveling clothes as were necessary and caught a night train to El Paso. Mr. Fletcher wasn't in, when I called at the railroad offices. I asked for you. I was directed here."

"You do things on the impulse of the moment, don't you?" Quist chuckled.

"When I want action, I want action," the girl said tartly.

"That I can appreciate," Quist nodded. "We've that much in common. But even now I can't say I'm agreeable to Jay Fletcher's idea. He knows how I feel about business outside the company. And I don't always do what Jay wants either. Sure, he's the best division superintendent on the line — could be on the board of directors, if he liked. That's just how much weight he carries, and his word goes a long way toward forming company policy. Within my contract, however, I form my own policy."

"So you refuse to help me?" the girl demanded hotly.

"I suggest you try someone else. The Pinkerton Agency —"

Kate Porter flashed abruptly up from her chair, seized her coat. Long strides carried her toward the door. "Thanks for the beer," she flung furiously over her shoulder, as she seized the knob.

"Por nada," Quist answered, rising. "For nothing. I —"

The door opened, closed with a bang. Swift footsteps hurried along the corridor, vanished. Quist raised his voice, "Hey, you forgot your bonnet —" then stopped himself. "Hair like that should never be covered anyway," he added quietly. He sank back in his chair, reaching for a bottle of beer and chuckled. "Impulsive. Hot-tempered as hell." The smile faded from his face. "A combination like that could lead to a killing."

[III]
Murder!

The girl hadn't been gone five minutes when footsteps again sounded in the hall, and there was another knock on the door. Quist half expected to see Kate Porter again, when the door opened on his invitation, disclosing instead a thin gray-haired man in a dark suit of wrinkled town clothing, with tired eyes behind rimless spectacles.

"Jay! I'm glad to see you." The two men shook hands, and Jay Fletcher, a division superintendent on the T.N. & A.S. Railroad, sank wearily into a chair. Quist offered a bottle of beer, but Fletcher shook his head, in a sort of worried, harassed way. Quist said, "You act like you had something on your mind, Jay."

"There's no doubt about that." Fletcher cleared his throat. "Greg, that was a nice bit

35

of work you did up in Utah." Quist said thanks, adding something to the effect that freight thieving was rarely hard to stop. Fletcher said he wasn't too sure about that — not all freight thieving at least. Quist asked a question.

Fletcher said, "I've got another job for you, Greg. Right in your line too. Over near Clarion City. You know the town?"

"I've been through there a couple of times. Not recently though. That reminds me, a friend of yours visited me a short spell back."

"Who was he?"

"It was a she — a Mrs. Porter."

Fletcher's jaw dropped. "Good God, I'd forgotten her letter."

"What letter?"

Fletcher explained. "Kate Thornton — that is, Porter — wrote me a week or so back. Something about her husband having disappeared. I've known her family for years. She'd heard of your work and as we both worked for the same company, she had an idea you could help her out. I answered immediately, writing for her to let me know if Porter hadn't yet returned, and that I'd talk to you when you returned from Utah. Then I forgot the matter. Other business came up. You see, her husband seems to have dropped off the face of the earth —"

"Save your breath, Jay, she told me about it. I suggested she go see the Pinkerton Agency. You see, she was about to write you, then on the spur of the moment decided to come direct to El Paso, see us both and get things rolling. But I didn't want anything to do with —"

"That's Kate, all right. Spur-of-the-moment. Very impulsive woman. Used to getting her own way, too. I don't think you should have turned her down, Greg. I'm asking that you reconsider —"

Quist said quietly, "You know how I feel about such cases, Jay. We've been through this sort of thing before. Haven't lost any arguments yet, have I?"

"Wait until you hear what I have to say. Maybe you'll change your mind, Greg. No, wait, let me talk. I know exactly what you're going to say about pressure being brought by big stockholders when they get into difficulties. This job I've got in mind will carry you over to the Devil's Drum country — Clarín County and Clarion City. While you're there, should anything arise that pertains to Lloyd Porter, you'd not be averse to helping Kate, would you?"

"No," Quist instantly replied. "But company business comes first. What is this job, anyway?"

"That's for you to figure out," Fletcher said tiredly. "You were up in Utah. All our other operatives were busy on cases. I've been riding the cars like a madman — even made a few caboose bounces — trying to learn exactly what took place. I've had other men working, asking questions and so on, too, but no regular operatives, and we require skilled minds for this puzzle —"

"Get to it, Jay. Something happened while I was up in Utah? I'm waiting to hear."

"A month ago there was a heavy rainfall over in the Clarín County section. Number Twenty-four, eastbound freight, was stalled by a landslide at Shoulder Bluff, about thirteen or fourteen miles out of Clarion City. There was the usual confusion, of course — more than usual this time — getting trains rerouted over the Rock Buttes line, and so on. Right at first, no one thought too much about the business, figuring the rain had caused the landslide, which we now think took place just a minute or so before Number Twenty-four reached that point —"

"And so freight thieves looted the freight," Quist put in.

"Let me do the talking, Greg. It has taken a month for us to hear testimony and get things partially straightened out as to what happened. We know now what happened, to some extent, but we can't figure why. In the first place, rain didn't cause the landslide. That landslide was man-made. Dynamite was used. The conductor of Twenty-four sent one of his brakemen to carry the word to Clarion City and ask for a work train. It wasn't long after the brakeman left that two mule-drawn wagons showed up with orders from Tyrus Wolcott, stating a work train was on the way, and certain freight consigned to Chicago was to be turned over to the teamsters for delivery in Clarion City."

"And of course," Quist said disgustedly, "nobody dares to violate old Tyrant Wolcott's orders. Jay, I don't think there's a meaner old bustard on any line in the country. He bullies everyone who'll let him and he's got the crews scared of their lives as well as their jobs. So, I suppose the conductor turned some valuable freight over to the teamster."

"You're right, except that it wasn't valuable. It was a shipment of fruit preserves, strawberry jam and so on."

Quist said caustically, "So old Tyrant Wolcott wouldn't be deprived of his breakfast jam, I suppose. That old —"

"Don't blame Tyrus Wolcott. He had

nothing to do with the order, we found out later. The message to the station master at Clarion City was supposedly relayed through San Julio Station, from Junctionville. You know San Julio, maybe — pretty lonely spot. Just a small shack with a bunk, chair and telegraph table. And a water tank. The San Julio operator never sent the message. Somebody had entered his station, hit him on the head and taken over the key. The poor fellow didn't even catch a glimpse of his assailant. He was in mighty bad shape for a couple of days. The company doctors had him in the hospital. But of course, the station master at Clarion City never suspected there was anything wrong. He thought the message signed Wolcott was genuine and nearly broke his neck hiring those teamsters and getting them started for Shoulder Bluff. It wasn't until San Julio Station failed to reply to messages that a train was sent from Junctionville to check into things. The crew found the operator, bound and unconscious, several yards from his shack."

"All that took pretty good timing." Quist's eyes narrowed. "Shoulder Bluff gets dynamited, causing a landslide. But to get those teamsters there, so promptly after the slide, meant that the message from San Julio had to be sent two to three hours previous to the slide. So there's at least two men to look for —"

"How do you mean?"

"Two, at least, I said. One man, some fifty miles away at San Julio, while the other was at Shoulder Bluff to start the slide. They must have had some misinformation regarding that shipment — heard it was gold bound to the Denver mint maybe. What have the teamsters got to offer on the subject?"

"Nobody's questioned them?"

"Why in hell not?" Quist snapped.

"They're dead. Their bodies were found nearly three weeks ago, only a few miles from Shoulder Bluff. Shot to death."

"A case of highjacking, eh?"

"We don't know what to think, Greg," Fletcher said wearily. "One of the teams and wagon reached Clarion City the morning after the landslide. The mules wandered home on their own. We've never found the other team."

"What about the freight?"

"Not far from where the bodies of the teamsters were found, a lot of the canned preserves was recovered. Some of the boxes as well, but I guess every box had been opened. There were wood splinters all around, they tell me. Greg, you've got to do something. The road will get a bad name if people get to thinking we can be detained and freight stolen in such fashion."

"Not to mention," Quist said dryly, "a couple of lives were lost. The road might have trouble hiring teamsters from now on too. And that key man at San Julio might have died." He stopped short, struck by a fresh idea. Fletcher asked a question. Quist explained in slow tones, "I just happened to think of something. That landslide happened one month ago. Kate Porter's husband disappeared one month ago. Do you suppose he could have stumbled onto something, or even been mixed up in the business?"

"I doubt it," Fletcher said impatiently, then he too paused, frowning. "I suppose I'd better see Kate and tell her —"

"Damn!" Quist said. "I should have asked her where she was staying. If she stopped at a hotel before starting out. Anybody as impulsive, as she appears to be, might not —"

"Likely she's staying at the Grand Central Hotel," Fletcher said. "If she's not there, ten to one she can be found at the depot, awaiting the return train home — what are you doing?"

Quist was on his feet now, stuffing clean shirts and handkerchiefs into a small leather valise. He dropped his holstered gun inside. "Me, I'm aiming to catch the 1:43 train for Clarion City. I figure I can make it with an hour to spare. With luck I can locate Kate Porter at the Grand Central and ask her to have dinner with me before we leave. I want to talk to that girl some more. And you can get a lot of talking done on a train."

Fletcher rose. "Likely that's a good idea." The thought wrinkles on his forehead deepened. "Lord, as an old friend of the family I should see her and tell her —"

Quist grinned. He was shrugging into his coat now. "Don't let that part worry you, Jay." He donned his flat-topped sombrero, pulled the belt tighter about his tan corduroy pants, flicked a soiled bandanna across the toes of his high-heeled boots. He glanced around the room, then catching sight of the violet-trimmed bonnet still resting on top of his desk, dropped it into his bag and closed it. "I'm off, Jay," he said. "No, you needn't come along with me. Catch a few minutes' rest here. I'll give Mrs. Porter your regrets that you were too busy to see her. After all, I can tell her all the things you'd have to say. Maybe more."

Fletcher forced a thin smile. "I'm not so

sure, Greg, but anyway, I'll be in your debt. Thanks for taking a mean job off my hands. You can break the news to her."

Halfway to the door, Quist stiffened, then slowly turned back. The grin was gone from his lips now. His topaz eyes narrowed as though he'd suddenly found himself caught in some sort of trap. He asked, the words slowly spaced, "Exactly what are you trying to say, Jay?"

Fletcher's eyes weren't quite meeting Quist's gaze now. "I said it would be your job to break the news to her — a job I hate the thought of. You've been moving so fast, you've not heard all my story —"

"What news?" Quist snapped. "What story?"

Fletcher swallowed hard. "Just before I arrived here, I had a telegram from the station-master at Clarion City. Among other things, he wired that Lloyd Porter was found about four hours ago. His body had just been brought into town —"

"Body?" Quist tensed.

"The body of Porter was found some miles out of town in the foothills of the Clarín Mountains on Rocking-T holdings. Porter had been shot to death. You can tell Kate about it —" Fletcher paused. "You know, sort of break the news, so she'll have

44

herself in hand by the time she reaches Clarion City . . ." Fletcher's voice fell off lamely.

Quist said irritably, "You lowdown, lousy —"

"I know, Greg." Fletcher raised one hand. "No need to go on. I'm everything you say. I don't deny it. It's a hell of a thing to ask of a friend, but I just lack the heart to tell that girl myself."

Quist drew a long breath. Abruptly, he turned, whipped open the door and stepped into the corridor. The door slammed at his back. Cursing bitterly, he strode rapidly along the hall toward the stairway that led to the lobby. "Good God, what next!" he swore. "A fine job for me, breaking such news. On top of that — strawberry jam, violets, murder! This job is taking on crazy angles even before I get thoroughly into things. Oh, Lord!"

[IV]
DOUBLECROSS

A week previous to the day Kate Porter had called on Quist at his hotel, a man sat at a table in a small *cantina* some twenty miles below the Mexican Border, idly toying with a glass of *tequila*. The man's name was

Porter and he was hiding out — or so he thought — until such time as a certain storm would have sufficient time to blow over. Ventoso, he had concluded, would be a good town in which to take cover. Calling it a town, of course, was somewhat flattering. There was just a widening of the roadway running south to points in Old Mexico, and a scattering of adobe huts, flung down helter-skelter here and there. These huts, together with a sort of general store and the *cantina* made up all the structures in Ventoso.

Ventoso wasn't even large enough to have a peace officer of any sort. The people did a small bit of farming, raised chickens and goats and contrived a rather placid easy mode of existence. It wasn't good country for farming: the soil was too rocky and there wasn't enough water. Too, the wind blew continuously down from the mountains, purple in the distance, stirring the inches-deep dust of the roadway. The man who was hiding out stated that he had come to Ventoso to shoot doves, but he'd not stirred out of the town since arriving, and no one had seen him use the double-barreled shotgun he carried on his saddle the day he dismounted before the doorway of the widowed, and ancient, Maria Bistula, and arranged to rent the spare room in her adobe for "a week or so." Since then he had slept and eaten his meals at the adobe. The rest of his days had been spent loitering in the *cantina,* at a table where he had a clear view of the entrance. Mexicans have the very good habit of minding their own business, so they didn't ask questions. Nevertheless the population of Ventoso, not more than fifty or sixty all told, couldn't help wondering who the man was waiting for. Or perhaps, whom he was hiding from.

The *Cantina del Vino Oro* — the Cantina of Golden Wine — was definitely a misnomer. The old adobe brick walls hadn't ever witnessed the pouring of any wine in man's memory. Thirsty customers drank *tequila* or *pulque.* Occasionally a bit of *mescal* or *aguardiente* made its appearance, but not often. But never any wine. Actually, it wasn't much of a *cantina,* as such places go. A blocky oblong building of adobe from which the plaster was cracking from the outer walls. A front and rear door, nearly always open, allowing free passage of wind. And dust. Always dust. There were two side windows, paneless. The inner walls had been whitewashed sometime or other, and were badly in need of another coating. The bar, of weathered pine, was rough and scarred and stained on top with many rings from wet glasses. Behind the bar was a small oblong fly-specked mirror, a shelf holding several bottles and a single box of cigars. Also there was the "makin's" for cigarettes — cornhusks and tobacco. A cigar box minus a cover constituted a sort of "change drawer" and contained a number of *pesos* and small silver change.

In one respect the Cantina of Golden Wine differed from other such establishments: around the walls were fastened at various spots, crayon and charcoal drawings of most of the town's residents — male — done on cheap newsprint paper. Diego Cubero, proprietor of the *cantina,* spent much of his time, when not serving customers, in studying and making caricatures of clients, which eventually were hung on the walls. Anyone with half an eye could tell instantly that Diego Cubero possessed no small ability as a draughtsman. Cubero was a rather stocky young Mexican with good features and the hope that some day he'd be able to dispose of his establishment and devote the rest of his life to art. But he was rapidly becoming convinced that that day was far off. Now if all his patrons were as free-spending as the Señor Porter seated across the room. Cubero, bent over a drawing at the bar, lifted his head and glanced at the other two customers at the far end of the counter. Old friends both, Mexicans, dressed in shapeless white cotton clothing and straw sombreros. One wore sandals; the other's feet were bare on the rough board floor. There wasn't any bar-rail to accommodate feet.

Cubero sighed. How many, many times he had drawn his friends. It was an old story to them; they no longer paid him or his charcoal any attention. And he had done the Señor Porter several times too, beginning last year when he had first started coming to Ventoso. Porter was an easy type to draw: regular, even features; dark-brown hair; shoulders not wide. There was a tricky-look about the eyes though, and the mouth was rather petulant. Cubero wondered how Porter had got those faint pinkish streaks across his nose and one cheek. They looked like nearly-healed slashes from a quirt. Done within the past month or so, Cubero figured. As to the rest of the man's make-up, well, clothing was clothing — gray sombrero, dark trousers tucked into knee boots, flannel shirt and necktie. The Señor Porter didn't appear to be a cattleman. Something to do with cattle perhaps, but that seemed doubtful. But he had made money; at least he spent freely. Though he bought much *tequila,* he never became real drunk. But always he seemed on the watch for some one — on this visit more than formerly — and he was never seen without the pearl-butted six-shooter at his right hip. It was very queer. . . .

Booted feet made sounds at the entrance. Diego brightened. He put down the stick of charcoal with which he'd been drawing. Ah, business with thirsty ones. And perhaps — *quién sabe?* — new models from which to work. Two men entered the *cantina,* hard rough-bitten characters they were, wearing scarred holsters. Diego's spirits sank a little. This type he knew. Border scum. But he did his best, smiling, with a *"Buenes dias, señores . . ."* And then Diego fell silent. The men had paid him no attention, but headed straight for the Señor Porter seated at the table across the room.

Porter had stiffened slightly as the two men entered, one hand reached toward his glass of *tequila;* the other, out of sight below the table also moved slightly. He didn't speak, as he watched the pair cross the floor and come to a halt across the table from him. For a moment the men just stared at each other.

Porter's lips twitched to a thin smile. He

said, "Well?"

One of the men said, "Mead had a hunch we might find you here?"

Porter's smile broadened a trifle. "Took him a long while to get his hunch, didn't it?"

"That's neither here nor there, Porter. Mead wants to see you."

"I don't think I'm interested," Porter said. "I know about what Mead Leftwick has to say, Riker." He said again, "I don't think I'm interested."

"Maybe," the other man said in ugly tones, "we can change your mind, Porter."

Porter said contemptuously, "I doubt it, Ferris. Now, you two better run along and tell Leftwick I decided to dissolve the pardnership. *Vamonos!* Get your horses and ride, boys."

Neither Riker nor Ferris replied to that for a moment. They exchanged looks then Riker said, "No use you actin' like a fool, Porter. You're outnumbered, two to one. I reckon you'd best come along with us. Mead won't like to be kept waiting —"

"You're the one's talking like a fool now," Porter snapped. "You and your two-to-one talk. I don't scare easily. You poor damn' fools! I've had you covered under the table since I first laid eyes on you. Now make your play."

Again Riker and Ferris hesitated. Their eyes went to Porter's left hand, fingers clenched around the glass of *tequila,* then in the direction of the right which was hidden from them by the table top.

Riker said, after a moment, "That's as may be, Porter, but you can't cover both of us at the same time. One of us could —"

"Ah, but that's the point," Porter laughed coldly. "You haven't the least idea which of you I'm covering. And I could get one of you. I might even have luck enough to . . ."

Even while he was talking he acted. The hand holding the glass suddenly flicked the fiery liquor toward Ferris' eyes, and at the same moment his trigger finger moved beneath the table.

The gun roared. A small bulge appeared abruptly on the scarred surface of the table, a splinter of wood sprung into view. Riker swung back, congratulating himself that Porter's shot had missed, even as his fingers clawed at his gun-butt. Porter's six-shooter came above the table, as he fired a second time. A look of surprise came over Riker's tough features, then his legs jack-knifed and he went to the floor. Powder smoke swirled through the room, then evaporated as it was swept away by the wind blowing through the doorway.

Ferris had staggered, whimpering in pain, across the room and halted against the bar, fingers dabbing at his eyes. Finally he got a dirty bandanna into action. The two Mexicans had moved as far down the bar as possible and were staring frightenedly at the dead man on the floor. Diego Cubero stood as before, thinking, *Ah, why can't these gringos keep their quarrels on their own side of the border? Trouble may come of this. The* jefe *at San Eneas will learn of this business. He will send —*"

Porter was already up from his chair, swearing at Ferris who still pawed at his eyes, cutting short Diego's gloomy cogitations.

"Now get out of here," Porter was shouting at Ferris, "before you get a dose of the same. God damn your dirty hide —" He broke off to seize Ferris by the shirt collar and hustle the whining man toward the doorway. After a few moments, rapid hoofbeats were heard leaving town. Porter came back to the bar. Diego saw that reaction had set in now. Porter's face was white; his hand trembled as he reholstered his gun. He said hoarsely, "Tequila, Diego," and spun a silver dollar on the bar.

Diego placed a bottle on the bar, followed

with a glass and saucer of salt. With a shaking hand, Porter poured the glass full and downed it at a gulp, then poured a second.

Diego ventured, "Eas a bad business, *señor,* no?"

"You saw it all," Porter's teeth chattered as he talked. "You heard those killers threaten me, didn't you, Diego? You saw Riker reach for his gun, first. I didn't want to kill him, but they would have — Diego, you could see —"

"Señor, I saw nozzeeng." Diego shrugged his shoulders and gestured toward the stick of charcoal. "I was make busy weeth the charcoal and paper, then, sodden — bang! bang! Only then deed I look. But, what ees eet we do weeth the bodee, Señor Porter?"

"Oh, yes." Porter put down his drink, and turned a half-scared glance over his shoulder at the still form on the floor. He was conscious too now of certain voices throughout the town. People were wondering at the sounds of the shooting. Still, there wouldn't be any trouble in a town this size. The two Mexicans at the far end of the bar had now changed position and started out. Porter detained them and spoke rapidly. With Diego's help he made himself understood. There was some bargaining, not much, before Porter passed over a couple of ten dollar bills and the two Mexicans picked up the body between them and carried it out the rear open door. Porter didn't look again at the body. He was still pale as he carried the bottle of *tequila* back to his seat at the table.

Porter poured another drink, and his courage began to return. After all, had Riker been caught by the U.S. authorities, the man was due for hanging. "After all," Porter told himself, "I saved the state the cost of a trial and hanging. No doubt, I should be considered a benefactor of humanity." He started to chuckle, then caught himself. Mead Leftwick had been smart, sending men to trail him down here. And now Ferris would return and report to Leftwick what had happened. That wasn't good. Definitely, Porter didn't want to have to face Leftwick. And here was Leftwick getting warm on the trail. "Blast the luck," Porter scowled, "I've got to be moving on again. Best thing I can do is get far away and stay hidden for a year or so. I can always come back and. . . ." And then his thoughts took another tangent.

Three-quarters of an hour had passed since the two Mexicans had carried out Riker's body. Neither of the Mexicans had returned to the *cantina,* nor had anyone else entered. Diego was busy with a broom and bucket of water, endeavoring to clean the floor of the dark stain where Riker had fallen. Porter still sat at the table, smoke curling from a cigarette between his fingers, a deep scowl of thought on his forehead.

A man appeared noiselessly at the open rear door and stood a moment looking within. He was a tall man of about Porter's build and coloring, dressed much the same, except that there was a sterner set to his jaw and his movements seemed more certain. Porter's back was to him, and Diego was so engrossed with his cleaning operation that he didn't see the newcomer.

Without preliminaries, the newcomer spoke from the rear doorway. "Sort of lost your head, didn't you, Lloyd?" His tones carried a slow easy drawling quality.

Porter gasped, then turned slowly in his chair, as though fearing to look. "My God!" he said, "Mead — Mead Leftwick."

"None other, Lloyd. You act surprised."

Diego Cubero had paused, broom in hand, thinking, *Por Dios! Let there be no more trouble with these gringos. The Señor Porter looks to have received a shock. Of this new man he is much afraid. And yet, the new man doesn't appear to want a fight. His hand has moved nowhere near his gun. Perhaps this meeting will be peaceful.*

Porter recovered his voice. "Why wouldn't I be surprised, Mead? Never suspected you were down here, or —"

"Or you wouldn't have acted as you did with Ferris and Riker," Leftwick completed the sentence. "That was a bad move, Lloyd."

"You don't understand, Mead. They came in and started acting rough. Riker reached for his gun —"

"Ferris told me what happened," Leftwick cut in. "Don't trouble to repeat the story. I doubt the story would agree with Ferris' anyway." Porter started a protest, but Leftwick paid no heed as he turned and spoke to Cubero. "You, Mex, bring another glass over here."

"Sí, sí, señor. Inmediatamente." In an instant, a clean glass had been placed on the table and Leftwick seated himself across from Porter. Cubero took his broom and bucket of water and retired once more behind his bar, thinking, *A new model, perhaps. But, no, I have the feeling this one would not take kindly to having his picture done.* He retired into his moody thoughts and started to wipe dust from the back bar.

Leftwick poured a drink of *tequila* and tossed it off in a single gulp. He smiled thinly at Porter half slumped across the table. "And so you thought I'd be on the other side of the border, Lloyd. You had me fooled for a spell too, before I hit on the idea you might be down here. The more I thought of it, the more reasonable the idea became. After all, we'd carried on operations through here, at one time. Ventoso's quiet, not too far from Clarion City. Lloyd, I never thought you'd do a thing like that to me. We've been business pardners too long —"

Porter coughed nervously. "You've got the wrong slant on things, Mead. If I'd known you came down here too —"

"You'd have acted differently," Leftwick smiled, though there was no smile in his hard eyes. "And because you knew you were a better man than Riker or Ferris —" He broke off. "What happened to the body? Ferris claims you killed Riker." Porter made explanations. Leftwick nodded, shrugging. "Just as well to get him buried. Not that anybody would make you trouble in Ventoso. Riker's no great loss. Both he and Ferris are dumb gunslingers — no brains. I sent Ferris back across the Rio. No use having too many witnesses around —"

"Witnesses?" Porter gulped. He looked scared.

"To our talk, of course," Leftwick said

smoothly. "The fewer people know what I'm doing, the better I like it. I didn't even want to come on into Ventoso, but your fool play made it necessary. You certain lost your head —"

"That was just it," Porter said eagerly, as though grasping at a straw. "I'll admit it. No, I don't mean as concerns Riker and Ferris. I mean the other — after the train was stopped and the goods taken from the freight — and — and all the rest" — he swallowed hard. "I got to thinking about things. Lost my nerve sort of, for a time. There's a railroad detective named Gregory Quist who works for the T.N. & A.S. He's sure to be sent down on that job. From all I've heard he's hell-on-wheels and fast with his gun. Frankly, I was scared. I thought it best to clear out for a time, then later I could look you up, when things had quieted down, and we'd go through with the job as planned. You see how it was, don't you, Mead?" His eyes were pleading, begging to be understood.

"No, I don't — not the way you tell it." Leftwick slowly shook his head. "It's not even a good act, Lloyd. Sure, you're a better man than Ferris or Riker, but you're not a better man than me. So don't lie to me, Lloyd. Let's bring it into the open. You doublecrossed me, and I don't like double-crossers."

"Except" — Porter showed a flare of spirit — "when you're the one doing the double-crossing. It was your plan to doublecross the Chicago people."

"You have a point there, I'll admit," Leftwick smiled. "But perhaps I figure they doublecrossed you and me long ago. We never did make as much money out of the deals as we deserved. The fact remains, I trusted you, and so now we come to a showdown."

Porter's jaw sagged. "Wha— what do you — mean — a showdown?"

Leftwick chuckled softly. "Scared I'm going to shoot you, Lloyd? Why, you know I'd not do anything like that. Once you're dead, I wouldn't have the least idea where you cached the stuff, so you're safe —"

"Until I tell you where it is," Porter interrupted sulkily.

"Lloyd, you're in a bad spot," Leftwick said directly. "Two teamsters were shot to death the night that train was stopped. An anonymous letter to the authorities could put them on your trail. Now, I'm a broad-minded man, and I'll concede anybody his right to make a mistake. And I can forgive such a mistake as yours — the first time it happens. Your mistake was just in being too ambitious. Like I said, you lost your head and wanted all the profits to yourself. What say we forget all that business? You and I can start in fresh, be pardners again —"

Porter swore sullenly. "Mead, I don't trust you."

"I should never have trusted you, Lloyd — not as far as I did. But now I don't have to trust you any longer, because I know you're going to do as I say. Now I've got too much on you to be afraid you'll do otherwise. So where's the stuff hidden?"

"Directions to get there would be pretty damn' difficult."

"So, Lloyd, you're coming along with me — going to take me to the spot —" He broke off, rising. "Come on, on your feet. Where's your horse?"

Reluctantly, Porter got up from his chair. "It'll take me some time to pack —"

"Hell's-bells! What have you got to pack? Where's your horse?"

"Down at the shack where I've been living. No, there's not much to pack, but I've got a good shotgun there. You see I was planning to hunt doves —"

Leftwick laughed sarcastically. "Now don't start lying again, Lloyd. Somehow I don't trust you when you start running off at the head that way. Sure, we'll get the shotgun, but don't get any ideas along with it, Lloyd. I wouldn't like that."

"I don't know what you mean, Mead?"

Leftwick smiled broadly. "Oh, yes you do. But just remember, I'm a better man than you, Lloyd, and we'll not have any trouble. Come on, stir your stumps. I want to get back across the border."

From behind his bar, Diego Cubero watched the two leave the *cantina*. The Mexican noted Porter's lagging step and uneasy manner, in contrast with Leftwick's confident bearing. For a long time after the two had departed with no good-byes to the proprietor of the *cantina,* Diego had stood staring out into the dusty, windblown roadway. "I do not think," Diego finally told himself, "that I will ever see again the Señor Porter. There was the look on his face of the man who recognizes the coming of death when he has been brushed with that buzzard's dark wing."

[V]
MISTAKEN IDENTITY?

It was about five in the afternoon when the train from El Paso, carrying Kate Porter and Gregory Quist, neared Clarion City. The ride had been accomplished in almost complete silence. Quist hadn't been able to make conversation as he'd expected to — not in view of the news he'd had to break to the girl. He'd done the best job possible under the circumstances and was considerably relieved when she showed no sign of breaking down or becoming hysterical. Not that he'd actually expected either reaction to what he told her, a short time after the train was under weigh. The girl had heard him through until he'd finished, with tightly compressed lips. When he was done, she merely murmured something that had to do with "poor Lloyd." Certainly she showed no particular grief over the news, which set Quist to speculating along other lines.

When the train pulled into Clarion City, Quist helped her dismount and glanced around the depot, the typical railroad frame building on a raised platform with a wide apron of crushed cinders around it. Farther along the platform some freight was being unloaded. There were the usual loafers on hand for the train's arrival. Quist glanced at them and saw no one who looked familiar. A few other passengers were dismounting from points along the way. Smoke plumed from the engine up ahead and swirled down around the station platform bringing with it a shower of hot cinders.

"Let's get out of this before we're smoked out," Quist suggested. "What do you intend to do first?"

"Go to the hotel and get my clothing I left there. I told them to keep the room for me. I suppose you're headed that way too." Quist said he was; the girl continued, "I left my pony at the livery, but I'd better stay in town tonight. There might — might be something for me to do. Perhaps I may be needed to identify —" She broke off as a form emerged through the smoke drifting about the platform.

"Kate!" the man called.

She responded to his greeting, calling him Gene. Then to Quist, "This is my brother, Gene Thornton — Mr. Gregory Quist."

"So you did persuade him to come back with you," young Thornton said, shaking hands. "Glad to know you, sir."

Gene Thornton looked not unlike his sister, though in a more masculine way. He was tall, with good shoulders and slim hips, with serious brown eyes. Probably twenty-two or twenty-three. He wore riding boots, faded Levi's cuffed at the ankles, blue denim shirt and vest, faded sombrero. A six-shooter was strapped at his right hip.

". . . and he wasn't inclined to help me at

first," Kate was saying, "but anyhow Mr. Quist is here, even though it is company business that brings him."

The three moved down off the platform, a man on either side of the girl, Quist carrying his satchel in his left hand. They turned from Railroad Street, along which the tracks ran and which showed mostly only the backs of buildings which fronted on Main, and turned on Austin Street. Passersby, of which there were but a few, glanced curiously at the trio; Quist noticed that the girl spoke to no one, as she strode along, matching strides with the men.

"Kate," Gene Thornton said tentatively, then hesitated. "There's something you should know — er — well — something has happened —"

"I already know, Gene," the girl replied quietly. "Mr. Fletcher had a telegram. Mr. Quist told me about it — told me in such a gentle way that I regretted losing my temper and flashing out of his office today. I think we're going to like Mr. Quist, Gene, even if I did get off on the wrong foot with him at first."

Quist felt himself flushing and changed the conversation, "Just where is the hotel in this town?"

" 'Bout half a block farther," Gene Thornton replied. "Corner of Main and Austin." He spoke to Kate again, "You see, we had no way of knowing whether you'd got the news or not —"

"Who's we?" the girl asked tersely.

"We-ell, your friends around town. We weren't even sure if you'd be coming back on this train or not. Lish Corliss had it in mind to meet you. Then when I showed up, he left."

"Very kind of Lish, I'm sure," she said shortly. Quist gathered she wanted to drop the subject, though he couldn't think why. They arrived at the hotel, and Kate got her key. She turned to Quist, cutting short some expression of sympathy from the hotel clerk, and said, "You bought my dinner today. I'd like to buy supper for you and Gene, if you'll wait until I get cleaned up. Wait for me here in the lobby."

She gave Quist no opportunity to refuse but turned and moved toward the stairway to the second floor. Quist went to the desk and found that a telegram from Jay Fletcher had reserved a room for him.

"And it's a good thing he did, Mr. Quist," the clerk was saying, as he passed across a key. "We're very crowded these days. Now if there is anything else we can do, just say the word."

"Thanks. Send up a dozen bottles of beer, right off, will you? And I don't want 'em iced."

"We'll take care of it, Mr. Quist."

Quist turned back to young Thornton. "You waiting here, Gene?"

Thornton nodded. "It won't take Kate long — or maybe it will considering the circumstances, this time."

"You're welcome to come up and have a beer with me."

"Thanks, no. I've got to slip out a minute and see — see somebody."

Quist mounted the stairway to the second floor, wondering who the "somebody" might be. He found his door number and entered his room, a large chamber on the northeast corner of the hotel, with windows on two sides to give air. There was a bed, two chairs, washstand with small mirror above it, and a dresser. A threadbare carpet covered the floor. There were shades at the windows but no curtains. Quist tossed his satchel and hat on the bed, and removed his coat. Opening the satchel, the first thing that met his eyes was a crushed bonnet with cloth violets strewn over the top.

A smile twitched Quist's lips as he picked up the bonnet. It was small, of braided brown horsehair, with a profusion of artificial violets strewn all over it. A far too feminine thing for a girl like Kate Porter, and yet, Quist mused, she could be feminine as hell if she'd only let herself go. She insists on being hard, trying to play the man's part, and without the proper equipment for such a job. A smile curved his lips at the thought, then he tossed the bonnet to a nearby small table, and delved into his valise for a clean shirt, fresh bandanna and shaving equipment. The lather had been half scraped from his jaws when a knock on the door preceded the entrance of Gene Thornton carrying a tray of beer bottles. He kicked the door shut behind him and placed the tray on the dresser. "Changed my mind," young Thornton said, "when I saw the man from the bar crossing the lobby. I took the tray off his hands."

"Open a couple of bottles, will you?" Quist said.

The beer was poured into glasses. Quist drank deeply, then returned to his shaving, the steel razor making ringing sounds as it cut through the tough day's growth of beard. When he had washed and donned the clean shirt, tied the bandanna about his throat, Quist finished the bottle. He asked abruptly, "Any idea who killed Lloyd Porter?"

Thornton hesitated, then, "Not the slightest. I could think of a lot of choice candidates for the job, though. Porter was a dirty son, if one ever lived —"

"Enemies?" Quist asked.

"He hadn't any friends around here — leastwise not the sort of folks you and I would want to call friends."

Quist laughed. "You might be surprised at some of *my* friends. Why did your sister marry Porter if he was that sort of a bustard? She seems level headed — if a bit hot-tempered." He paused, then added, "Not to mention impulsive and given to doing things on the spur of the moment — like the way she came tearing up to El Paso."

Gene Thornton scowled. "I tried to talk her out of that, but it was no good. Maybe you'd best ask her why she married Porter. It was never clear to me, especially with Lish Corliss —" He broke off. "But that's none of my business. You'd better talk to Kate."

"I intend to," Quist said. He drank some more beer. "Who's this Lish Corliss you mentioned?"

"Sheriff of Clarín County."

"What about him?"

"What about him?" Thornton repeated.

"What sort of hombre is he?"

"He's been a damn' good sheriff —"

69

"And wanted to marry your sister," Quist stated.

"I didn't say that," Thornton scowled.

"You already hinted at something of the sort. Why didn't he?"

"And that," Thornton said, "you'd better find out from Lish."

"This sheriff ever have any trouble with Lloyd Porter?"

"That's something else you can ask the sheriff, Mr. Quist."

"I'll do that too. And my name is Greg to friends. I'm hoping you and I will be friends."

"Golly —" the young man looked pleased — "I hope so too. If all this dirty business —"

"How often did you threaten Porter?" Quist snapped.

Thornton's jaw dropped, his eyes widened. "Who said I — ?"

"You've as much as admitted you didn't like the idea of Porter marrying your sister."

"That's no sign I ever threatened him."

Quist drained his beer glass. "All right, forget it for the time being. Eventually you'll feel more like talking to me." He reached once more into his bag and retrieved an underarm gun harness which he donned. Thornton eyed him curiously as he shoved a short-barreled .44 caliber Colt's six-shooter into the holster.

"That's some rig?" the young man commented with interest.

"It's right convenient at times," Quist agreed. "With this type holster, a man just has to jerk his gun straight out, instead of drawing up and out as he would with a belt holster. That's fifty percent of the motion saved right there. Saved motion means quicker draws, and often the time it takes to draw is the difference between shooting or being plugged. If there has to be any shooting, I want to be the one to shoot first. Dead men are never able to tell what happened."

"But that holster is open all the way to the bottom," Thornton frowned. "What keeps the gun from falling out?"

Quist explained. "A flat steel spring, sewed inside the leather, holds the gun in place until needed. This is a heap more comfortable to wear than a hip gun, and a heap faster to get into action."

Thornton glanced at the wide-buckled plain belt supporting Quist's trousers. "Don't you wear a ca'tridge belt?"

Quist shook his head. "Too heavy." Again he dipped into the valise and procured a handful of .44 cartridges which he dropped into his coat pocket before donning the garment. "Any man that can't do his job with what he's got in his gun and a handful extra, hasn't any business carrying a gun — not unless he's withstanding a siege or something of the sort. Then he needs more loads. But for day to day toting, a dozen or so ca'tridges are sufficient." He finished donning his coat.

"I'm beginning to get your slant, now. I heard you were pretty much of a man in a gunfight. Now I'm understanding why."

"Forget it," Quist said roughly. "Gunfighters are fools, any way you look at it — only sometimes a man has to use a gun in self-defense." Abruptly he changed the subject: "Who found Porter's body?"

"The ranger."

"What ranger — you mean Texas Ranger?"

Thornton nodded. "Yeah. Fellow named Fred Arbuckle."

"What's he doing here?" Quist asked.

"The sheriff sent for him. Sort of a precautionary measure. There's been a sort of storm boiling up hereabouts, and Lish Corliss was playing it safe, I reckon." Quist asked a question. Thornton shook his head. "I think you'd best talk to Corliss, Greg. He had his reasons for getting a ranger here. He can explain it better than I can."

"Where was the body found?"

"Over in the foothills of the Claríns. On Rocking-T holdings if you must know."

Quist smiled. "I'm not suspecting your outfit — not yet. What was the ranger man doing over there?"

"That I don't know. All's I know is that Arbuckle brought him in, slung across his saddle this morning, 'round eleven or so."

Quist's eyes narrowed. "I was under the impression the law states a dead body mustn't be touched until the sheriff or somebody in authority is informed."

"Could be," Thornton conceded. "I reckon a ranger has the necessary authority though. Besides, it wouldn't have been good to leave Porter's body out there any longer." Thornton hesitated. "The coyotes had been busy. He'd been dead for sometime. Coyotes and buzzards. He — he didn't have any face."

"Are they sure it was Porter's body? Who identified it?" Quist asked quickly. "Sure there was no mistaken identity?"

"I did. Oh, it was Potter all right. Even with his face gone, I'd know him. Recognized his clothing, his pearl handled gun, a tie Kate gave him a couple of years back. Not only that, there were papers in his pocket to prove identity. You know how it is. Often you recognize a man from just a back

73

view. I'm just glad that Kate doesn't have to undergo that business of identifying him. He wasn't pleasant to look at. Kate's got good nerves, just the same —"

"But the coyotes," Quist broke in, "— and buzzards — left enough of his face to show — ?"

"I said his face was gone," Thornton stated grimly. "It wasn't just the coyotes. Somebody had used a shotgun on him. The features were completely destroyed —"

"Just how good are you with a shotgun?" Quist interrupted again.

"I'm not so bad —" Thornton commenced, then broke off as the import of Quist's words struck him. His face went white, then crimson with anger. "Damn you, Quist! If you think —" Fists clenched, he started toward Quist.

"Hold it," Quist snapped. "All right, it was a dirty question, but I wanted to catch you offguard. My methods aren't always ethical. I learn things any way I can. If that riles you, that's too bad. But I've learned something. Either you're a damn' good actor, or you didn't kill Porter. Not with a shotgun anyway. And — I'm sorry, Gene, for acting that way."

Somewhat mollified, Thornton said irritably, "I've heard you were a right cynical

hombre and hard as nails. Now I believe it."
He forced a slight smile. "If I'd been guilty,
your methods might have worked at that.
I'll admit there've been times when I felt
like turning a gun on Porter — but I'm not
such a lousy shot that I'd have to get close
in with a scatter-gun. Matter of fact, that
sort of business would be more in his own
line. He used to hunt around here with a
shotgun — but the dirty son always used a
ten-gauge, regardless how small the game.
Oh, he brought down a lot of birds though
—"

"And likely so torn with shot there wasn't
much left to eat," Quist said understand-
ingly. "That's what I call a game-hog."

"You hit the nail on the head," Thornton
said. "And I figured him a hog in more ways
than one. Just so he could bring back more
game than anyone else, he was satisfied.
Greedy as hell." Thornton paused, "And yet
I've got to give the devil his due. There were
times when he could be right pleasant, and
put out quite a line of palaver. But after you
got to know him . . . Well, there was always
a sort of trickiness to the man — probably
what is called smart in a business way." The
young man grinned suddenly. "After some
consideration I think I'll take your kind of
ethics."

"Thanks," Quist nodded. "I reckon we'd best be getting along down to the lobby. Your sister will be waiting."

"You're right." Thornton started toward the door, then his gaze fell on the violeted-bonnet on Quist's table. He started to say something, then checked the words. Quist picked up his sombrero and followed Thornton through the doorway, closing and locking the door behind him.

[VI]
A CAUTIOUS SHERIFF

They found Kate Porter seated in the lobby of the Clarion House when they descended the stairs. Beyond the lobby a wide double-doored entrance showed the way to the hotel dining room. Quist said he hoped she hadn't been waiting long. The girl told him she'd just come down from her room. She'd left off the long traveling coat, but otherwise was dressed as Quist had seen her earlier in the day. Her shining blond hair showed it had had a thorough brushing.

Thornton said, "Kate, you should dress that way more often. It's becoming. I'd expected you'd change into riding skirt the minute you hit your room."

"I intended to, but it was too much

trouble," the girl said shortly. Her dark eyes went to Quist.

Quist said, "If you'll wait just a minute, I want to check at the desk and see if any telegrams have come for me."

"No hurry," Kate said. "It's too early for the dining room to be filled yet."

Quist crossed the lobby to the desk and complimented the clerk on getting the beer up to his room so quickly. The clerk looked pleased. "The barman was just on the way to your room, Mr. Quist, when Gene Thornton came back and said he'd take the beer to your room."

"So Gene said," Quist commented carelessly. "I'm sorry if Gene had to cut his business short on my account."

"I don't think he did," the clerk replied. "Mr. Thornton had just started out, after you went to your room, when the sheriff came in. They stood and talked near the door a minute, then the sheriff left. Gene turned back to the lobby just in time to catch the barman."

"Thanks. So long as I didn't interrupt any business," Quist said casually. The clerk asked a question. Quist said, "Oh, sure, the room's fine. Very pleasant." He nodded and turned back to Kate Porter and her brother.

Light from the setting sun still filtered

through the dining-room windows, though a man waiter was moving about the room lighting oil lamps suspended on brackets from the wall. There were only a few tables occupied. People at one table spoke to Kate and Gene, as they passed to a table in the far corner. A waiter arrived to take their order. There was little conversation until the food arrived, then Gene said something about the hotel putting out good meals. Quist surveyed his steak, fried potatoes and stewed tomatoes and conceded the food looked good. There were hot biscuits and coffee as well. Quist noticed that the girl ate very little. Later more coffee and apple pie arrived. The dining room had filled by this time. There was a buzz of conversation and sounds from cutlery and dishes. Once or twice Kate nodded absent-mindedly to diners, her manner saying plainly that she wanted no conversation or expressions of sympathy.

With the second cups of coffee, Quist and Thornton rolled cigarettes and lighted them. Kate said finally, "Gene, does Dad know?"

Gene shook his head. "Leastwise, I didn't send any word to him. He'd just feel he should get saddled up and ride in. I didn't see how that would help things any — and him not at all."

Kate turned to Quist. "Our father is a cripple." Quist expressed the usual sympathy. Kate went on, "Oh, he's not bedridden or anything of the kind. It's just that he's not up to riding very often. He does ride, now and then, but it takes a lot out of him."

Gene took up the story, "His pony went over a cutbank a few years ago, one night during a storm when he was out working with one of the herds. The herd started to run and Dad took after them. It was too dark to tell what was happening or where he was headed. Anyway, the horse broke its neck and Dad's spine caught a lot of damage — the sort of damage the doctors don't seem able to repair. So it wouldn't help any to have him make that ride from the ranch."

"I suppose there'll be an inquest," Kate said.

Gene nodded. "Doc Ingram — he's our coroner, Greg — has set it for ten tomorrow morning."

Kate bit her lip. "I wanted to get out to the ranch first thing in the morning, but —"

"Maybe it can be arranged so you won't have to show up at the inquest, Kate. After all, there's nothing you can tell. You weren't even here when — when he was brought in.

And I've already — er — identified the body
—"

"If it's necessary I be at the inquest, I'll be there," Kate said shortly. "People are mighty ready to talk sometimes, and I don't intend to have anyone saying I was afraid to show up —"

"Afraid?" Quist put in. "Why put it that way?"

"Maybe you'll realize," Kate said bitterly, "when you've been around here a day or so. Right, I wasn't here when the body was brought in. There's the chance Lloyd was killed yesterday, or the day before, for all we know now. I happened to be in this section yesterday and the day before. It may be necessary I account for my actions."

"Now, look here, Kate," Gene started, "I don't think —"

"I do," the girl said tersely, and changed the subject, with the remark that if they were through, she was going back to her room.

In the hotel lobby, Gene told her he'd see what he could learn and then return. A few minutes later, Quist and young Thornton stepped into the street. Thornton said, "Where now, Greg? Anybody in particular you'd like to meet?"

"The sheriff, for one, and that ranger who

80

found Porter's body, but first I'd just like to sashay around and look the town over, sort of settle that supper with a walk."

Gene nodded and they started out, the young man pointing out certain buildings, saloons and so on. Main Street, it appeared, had originally been named Drovers' Street, but custom had finally settled on Main. There were a number of cross streets, running north and south, the principal ones of which were known as Mesquite Street, San Antonio, Austin and Alamo Streets. Farther north and running parallel with Main were two thoroughfares given over to a residential section to a large extent, and known as Lamar and Houston Streets. South of Railroad Street, along which the tracks ran, was the town Boot Hill and a scattering of Mexican adobes surrounded by mesquite and other forms of brush. At the far east end of town were the white-washed cattle pens, at present empty but due to be filled to overflowing when beef round-up was completed, in the fall.

Only a few lights shone along Main Street by this time, but Quist spied in his walk several saloons, a brick bank, another hotel at the west end of town known as the Drovers' Rest Hotel, two good-sized general stores, now dark, a county building and various other structures of commercial enterprise. There were plank sidewalks on either side of Main and an almost unbroken line of hitchracks. The roadway was unpaved but pretty well packed down from the passing of years of wagon traffic and pounding hoofs.

A broad rectangle of light splashed across the sidewalk where the sheriff's office stood at the southwest corner of Main and Mesquite Streets. It was a blocky building of rock-and-adobe with an open doorway set to the left of a broad window. Above doorway and window a plank awning reached across the sidewalk to be supported by uprights set at the edge of the roadway, and from this awning hung a sign reading: Office of Sheriff, Clarín County. The sheriff was working over some papers on his desk, by the light of an oil lamp, when Quist and Thornton entered the office. Quist was introduced and the two men shook hands.

Elisha Corliss was younger than Quist had expected, probably in the vicinity of twenty-eight or -nine. He wasn't tall, but stockily built with not an ounce of superfluous fat on his frame. He was sandy complexioned, with steady eyes, a rather stubborn jaw and a close-cropped mustache. He wore overalls, riding boots, a woolen shirt open at the throat and a blue bandanna handkerchief knotted at his breast. A black, narrow-brimmed sombrero was shoved to the back of his head and a forty-five six-shooter was buckled at his hip.

The sheriff gestured toward a couple of straight backed chairs and Quist and Thornton sat down. Quist glanced around the office. There was a sheet-iron stove in one corner, with smoke-pipe disappearing through the ceiling. There was no fire in it at present, of course. Along the opposite wall was a cot with neatly folded blankets. A rack on a back wall held guns and hand-cuffs. Next to the rack a closed door led to jail cells at the rear of the building. There was tacked on the walls a topographical map of Clarín County, a couple of calendars from meat-packing companies and a few reward bills for "wanted" men.

The sheriff drew a cigar box from a drawer of his desk and held it open to Quist. Quist took one, Gene refused. The sheriff took one for himself and held a scratched match for Quist. The box was put back in the drawer. Blue and gray smoke swirled through the office. Occasionally men passed on the sidewalk outside or a pony loped along the roadway. The men talked triviali-ties for a time. Quist learned the sheriff was nearing his second term of office and that he'd made a good enough record so he expected to run for a third term. He had a rather deliberate manner that Quist liked, that of a man sure of himself in most things. He commented finally,

"Of course I knew you'd arrived, Mr. Quist."

"Such things usually aren't kept secret," Quist smiled, "much as I like to drop in on a job unannounced. Who told you?"

"The depot stationmaster. He'd had a telegram from one of your division superintendents, named Fletcher. It was a relief to him to know you were coming. And then the hotel clerk told it around that a room had been reserved for you. A good many people nowadays know of your reputation, Mr. Quist."

Quist uttered a deprecating laugh. "I'm afraid I'm considerably overrated. Just because I've had a lot of luck on a few cases, folks get an idea I'm infallible. I'm not, by a long shot."

Gene Thornton had been moving a bit uneasily on his chair. Now he broke in, "Lish, have you seen Doc Ingram again?"

"Not yet," the sheriff replied. "Howsomever, Gene, I don't know as it'll do any good. You know Doc — now, wait, I don't like it any better than you do, but I've got to admit Doc is within his rights." Elisha Corliss turned to Quist. "There's an inquest over Porter coming up tomorrow morning. Doc Ingram wants that Mrs. Porter testifies as to anything she might know. Gene doesn't like the idea —"

"Good God, Lish," Gene broke in, "can you blame me? That would be an ordeal for Kate. You know how a lot of folks in this town are."

"I don't blame you a-tall," the sheriff responded. "And I feel exactly as you do. But Doc figures if she is able she should testify. After all, he didn't insist on her going through that identification business. He was willing to take your word for that — for which same I was grateful. I told you how things stood when I came to the hotel this evenin'. I said I'd talk to him again, as you asked, when I saw him. I just haven't seen him yet. With no deputy here, I've got my hands full of work, reports, expense accounts and such —"

"Perhaps," Quist suggested, "come inquest time, Mrs. Porter could get an attack of the vapors or something."

Even Gene smiled. Lish Corliss grinned broadly. "You don't know Kate Porter or you'd never say that. Even if she did,

85

nobody would believe it of her — not Kate Porter. It'd be just about as ridiculous as me refusing to show up with testimony on the same grounds. I'd be laughed out of town, and while nobody will ever laugh Kate Porter out of town —"

Gene Thornton got to his feet. "I told Kate I'd be back soon. But first I'm going to see Doc Ingram, find out if he won't listen to sense."

Corliss shrugged. "Suit yourself. But if you ask me, Kate wouldn't want it that way."

Thornton said a bit testily, "You know her better than I do, I suppose?"

The sheriff colored, but replied, even-voiced, "In some ways I may, at that, Gene." He paused, "Just why are you so against Kate testifying — oh, I know, you mentioned the ordeal and all that, but knowing Kate —"

"I'm going to look for Doc Ingram," Thornton said abruptly. He got to his feet. "I'll be at the hotel tonight, Greg, in case you want to see me, or anything. Lish can tell you what's what around Clarion City as well as I can — maybe better."

Silence built up between Quist and the sheriff for a few moments after Gene Thornton had departed. Cigar smoke drifted lazily above the chimney of the oil lamp. Quist

86

finally broke the quiet. "I heard you say something about not having a deputy, Sheriff. Is he laid up?"

"I've never had a deputy here," Corliss replied. "You see, Clarín County being rather sparsely settled doesn't bring in as much taxes as some counties. I was elected to office on the platform that said I'd do without a deputy here until things got more prosperous. I've made it work through nearly two terms now —"

"Must keep you right busy — prisoners to feed and so on."

Corliss smiled. "I don't have many prisoners." The smile left his face suddenly. "Though the way things have been going of late . . ." He broke off, then, "Maybe if I don't get some prisoners right soon, there won't be any third term for me. As to running this job, well I do have some help. Clarion City has a town marshal, old Dave Eldred, and I pay him five bucks a month out of my salary to see to feeding prisoners and so on. Dave is glad for the extra money. The town don't pay much, and I don't suppose it should, considering Dave's age. I reckon you'd have to call it a sort of honorary office as much as anything. Dave helped settle this region, fought the Indians in the old days and so forth. He's due for some help in his old age — not that he's decrepit or anything of the sort. He keeps an eye on things, tells me when trouble is boiling, and generally I can nip trouble in the bud if I know in time."

"Seems like a workable arrangement," Quist nodded. "I don't suppose there is anything you can tell me about the death of those two teamsters who were killed the night the train was stalled."

"Not a damn thing more than I suspect you already know." Corliss scowled. "A dirty business that, and the town is right well stirred up. I've done what I can to uncover the killer — or killers — which seems to be exactly nothing. All I know is the station master got orders to hire two teamsters to go to a stalled train and pick up some freight. We never saw old Corny Callahan and Ringbone Pardee alive after that. And for what? For somebody to steal some jam or preserves or something. There must have been a mistake some place. Was your road shipping some gold or money through about that time?"

"Not that I know of," Quist stated truthfully. "Lish, I understand you had a Ranger sent here. Why?"

Corliss considered. "Could be I was a bit hasty, but I'd rather be safe. You see, this town was right stirred up about those teamsters. Callahan and Pardee had lived here a long time. Everybody knew 'em and they were well-liked. Of course, your railroad came in for a lot of undeserved blame for not protecting folks it hired. Like any town this size, Clarion has its riff-raff, and hotheads are always looking to stir up trouble. Like I said, if I hear of it in time, small trouble I can nip in the bud, but what's been building up isn't small. And by myself I can't scare it off. I've got my limitations."

"I see your viewpoint," Quist put in, "and so . . . ?"

"Marshal Eldred came to me one day and said he'd heard rumors that a bunch of hoodlums were going to teach the T.N. & A.S. a lesson. Y'see, your road is blamed for the deaths of those two teamsters. It was planned to set fire to the stock-pens east of town, tear up some rails and ties and raise hell in general. It was even hinted the depot would be set fire. Maybe it was just talk, but I didn't like it. On top of all this, it's known that the Thorntons, including Kate Porter, own quite a chunk of stock in your railroad, and certain unthinking people have tried to throw blame on the Thorntons too. —"

"Meaning just who?" Quist asked.

Corliss scowled. "I've a hunch it started with Judd Lombardy and his L-Bar-D outfit. They're a sort of hard bunch, and there's been bad feeling between the L-Bar-D and Thornton's Rocking-T for some time. The hands are always niff-nawing at each other. There's been some fist fights but so far no gun-play. But talk has been getting hotter and hotter between the two outfits, and I could see it would only need a spark at the right moment to have the whole thing blaze out in a range war."

"Could be," Quist conceded. "And there'd be other outfits sure to be drawn in on both sides."

"That's the way I looked at it. So there I was in a sort of fix. On one hand a range war building up. On the other, the threat of some gang rioting and destroying railroad property in my county. I needed more help than Marshal Dave Eldred could give me. Then I happened to think that my old friend Jim Craig, Captain of Rangers, Company K, was in camp at Bandera. I telegramed him about my troubles. He wired back that Sergeant Fred Arbuckle was just winding up some business at Kingboro — that's only about thirty-five miles north of here, in the next county, — and that he'd telegraph

Ranger Arbuckle to come right down here and lend me some moral support — and more if needed. Which same he did. Arbuckle arrived day before yesterday."

"I think you did right," Quist commented. "Often just the presence of a ranger has a quieting effect on a town ready to go on the prod."

The sheriff smiled wryly. "Arbuckle affected me that way too. From the moment he come in here and presented his credentials, I began to feel better. Things have already quieted down some, there's been less talk, though with Lloyd Porter's body being brought in this morning, some sort of fire may get fresh fuel."

"A ranger always inspires confidence in law-abiding men," Quist said. "And you acted right. It's better to be cautious than wrong later."

Corliss said half-apologetically, " 'Course, if I'd known you were coming, I wouldn't have yelled for help to Jim Craig —"

Quist laughed. "Buffalo chips. You pin your faith to that ranger." Abruptly, he switched conversation to another subject: "What can you tell me about Kate Porter?"

For a moment there was no reply. Quist could sense Corliss withdrawing, tightening up inside, throwing up certain barriers.

Once more the sheriff proved to be cautious. "In just what way?" he asked slowly.

"Any way and all ways you can think of," Quist replied. "I'm after information. Why did she marry Porter? Why not somebody else? Why not you, for instance?"

With an effort, Corliss held himself in check. Fiery red spots on his cheekbones burned fiercely against the angry paleness of his face. Tiny muscles bulged at the corners of his month. Finally, he spoke, "I thought, Mr. Quist, you came here to look into that theft from one of your freight trains. Is an investigation of Lloyd Porter's death included?"

Quist asked quietly, "Do you know of any reason why it shouldn't be, Sheriff?"

"That's something *I* can't say." Corliss' voice was calmer now. "As to why Kate Porter married Lloyd Porter, instead of me, or someone else, I'd suggest that you ask her about that." Abruptly, he got to his feet. "It's evening drink time for me. Let's cross the street to the Amber Cup and lift a couple. We might find Sergeant Arbuckle there too."

"That," Quist agreed, "is a right idea." He was thinking, *Corliss isn't ready yet to commit himself on Kate Porter. He's being cautious again.*

[VII]
FLIRTIN' WITH DYNAMITE

The two men left the sheriff's office, after the oil lamp had been turned low. Quist said, "You aiming to leave your door open?"

Corliss nodded. "The night air will cool it off. Get that 'dobe and rock chilled a mite and it won't be so hot in here tomorrow. Nothing to steal worth stealing. Only got one prisoner in the cells back there."

"Anybody important?" Quist asked.

Corliss shook his head. "Just one of the scum-crowd that hangs around town. He's married to a Mexican woman. Lives south of the tracks. Ranger Arbuckle was over that way the day he arrived here. Heard the woman screaming, found the man beating her up. Arrested the fellow and brought him in. The J.P. gave the dirty scut a week in the hoosegow to teach him women shouldn't be hit."

"That's one good thing about being a ranger," Quist commented. "They've authority any place in the state. Often I find myself handicapped and have to stop and get proper authority for arrests if they take place away from railroad property."

There were fewer people on the street now, and practically the only places open were saloons, lights from their windows patterning sidewalks here and there along Main. Ponies stood at hitchracks, widely-spaced, heads drooping, patient. Quist glanced up. Above, the indigo-black sky was powdered with stars. A soft breeze carried along the roadway bringing with it the faint scent of sagebrush from the open country.

They crossed the street, rounded a tierail and mounted two steps to the small porch fronting the swinging-doored entrance to the Amber Cup. A long bar ran along the right wall of the entrance, with behind it pyramided glasses, bottles and a wide mirror. A closed door was set in the rear wall. Three round tables and chairs were arranged next to the wall at the left. There was sawdust on the floor. Corliss said, "Mickey Kurtz is the only barkeep in town who'll pay money to have sawdust freighted in. Cleanest bar in town to my way of thinking."

There weren't many customers in the saloon. Five cowhands played seven-up at one of the tables. A tall man with a once-white, wide-brimmed sombrero stood by himself at the far end of the bar. Near the entrance end of the bar, three men in citizens' clothing discussed hay and feed prices over their whiskies. At the center of the long counter were four men in cowtogs, empty glasses before them. Mickey Kurtz, the bartender and proprietor, a balding, middle-aged man in a white apron, was lazily mopping with a bar-rag some drops of spilled liquor.

"There's Ranger Arbuckle at the far end," the sheriff said. "C'mon, you wanted to meet him." He nodded to the cowmen as he passed. Arbuckle shoved back his white sombrero, as they came near and smiled, "Don't speak, Sheriff. I don't think it's going to be necessary to introduce me to Greg Quist. I've heard so much about you, Mr. Quist, that I almost feel like I know you." He had very white teeth and a contagious grin.

Quist shook hands and mentioned that he'd heard Sergeant Fred Arbuckle had already had a sort of soothing effect on Clarion City.

"Nothing owing to me in particular," Arbuckle replied. "It's the rangers' reputation that does the work. Nowadays, mostly, all's necessary is for a ranger to put in an appearance, and trouble stops. But credit for that goes to the rangers of years ago, and it still has its effect on people." He had a slow rather drawly way of speaking. "Y'know, Greg Quist, if you ever get tired of being a railroad operative, the —"

"Railroad dick." Quist smiled.

"Have it your way. But if you ever want a change of jobs, I've got a strong hunch the rangers would be almighty glad to have you. You've done some great work on your cases."

Quist said thanks. Mickey Kurtz approached for orders. Both Quist and the ranger took beer. Corliss had a neat two-fingers of bourbon. Quist noted that Arbuckle wore but one gun. Many of the men in the ranger force carried two weapons. The single six-shooter said considerably for Arbuckle's ability with a gun. Otherwise he was dressed as so many other rangers of that day — the white sombrero, dark trousers tucked into knee boots, woolen shirt and bandanna. He wore an open vest over his shirt. No coat, at present.

The men drank in silence for a few minutes. Arbuckle went on, "However, I don't figure just putting in an appearance is going to do the trick this time. It looks to me like I've got my job cut out, if I'm going to find the man who massacred Lloyd Porter. Lord, what a mess!"

"You're sure it was a man?" Quist asked.

"I can't imagine any woman doing a job like that?" Arbuckle replied.

The sheriff had got slightly red in the face at Quist's words. Now, Quist continued, "What I meant — maybe there was more than one man involved."

"How you figuring, Greg?" Arbuckle frowned.

"Well, there were the two teamsters killed, and now Porter. Somehow it doesn't seem quite logical for *one* man to do all that."

"Ye-eah," the ranger said slowly. "I see what you mean." He frowned. "You got an idea that the teamsters' deaths and Porter's killing all came from one source."

"Something like that," Quist admitted. "Do you know of anything to the contrary that says I'm on the wrong track?"

"Can't say that I do," Arbuckle replied. His white teeth shone suddenly. "Y'know, this thing shapes up better than I figured. Y'see, as I saw it, the sheriff and I would be working on Porter's killing, while you would be interested only in the theft of railroad freight and uncovering the rats who killed those two teamsters. If you're right, Greg, and all this dirty work is tied together, we'll be working together. We can exchange ideas and notes and so on —" He broke off and his face fell somewhat. "But maybe working with Lish and me doesn't take your fancy. I've always heard you liked to work alone

— sort of a lone-wolf business with you."

Quist said dryly, "I've never yet seen the time when an exchange of ideas — from good men — didn't work out to everyone's advantage. Let's have another drink."

Mickey Kurtz was called up to replenish the glasses. One of the cowmen at the middle of the bar called to Corliss. "Hey, Lish, I'm just buying one. How about you hombres getting in on it?"

Corliss shook his head. "We just ordered. Thanks just the same, Judd," — and turned his back on the cowmen.

Arbuckle laughed. "Now that wasn't polite, Lish. You know Lombardy was looking for an excuse to meet Greg."

"I figure Greg will meet him soon enough," Corliss growled. "It's something he won't be able to avoid." Quist asked a question. The sheriff said, "The big hard-looking hombre is Judd Lombardy, runs the L-Bar-D outfit, that one with the black hair hanging down to his eyebrows. Two of 'em are cowhands, named Lockwood and Merker. Good hands far's I know. Never heard anything against 'em, but can't say I like 'em, either. The thin wiry-looking jasper with the beaded Indian band around the crown of his sombrero is named Gilly De-ray — and a mean customer or I miss my guess. Nor did I ever hear of him doing any work on the Lombardy outfit. Him and Lombardy just seem to sort of pal around. Maybe he's a bodyguard for all I know."

"Any reason why Lombardy should need a bodyguard?" Quist asked.

"None that I know of," Corliss replied promptly. "Deray hasn't been in these parts long. So far he's done nothing that would warrant me taking him in. But I don't like the cut of the bustard. He's got four notches cut in his gun-butt. Whether that means anything or is just bluff, I can't say. He's killed no one around here — that I know of — yet."

Quist smiled. "Meaning that you expect him to?"

"It wouldn't be any surprise," Corliss said.

Arbuckle put in, "I think Lish has the right idea. That Deray's got a cruel streak in him. Yesterday I saw him sitting out back of the Warbonnet Saloon. The skunk had caught a horned toad and cut one rear leg off, and was laughing his head off the way the poor critter was skitterin' sidewise. He was just about to slice off a front leg when I convinced him it wasn't a good idea."

"What did you do?" Corliss asked.

"Put the frog out of misery when Deray left." Arbuckle didn't explain what he'd said to Deray.

The three were midway through their second drinks when Judd Lombardy and Gilly Deray left the two cowhands and sauntered down to the end of the bar. Lombardy said, "What is this, a lawman's convention? Sheriff, ranger man and —" he paused — "the T.N. & A.S. Railroad dick, I suppose. What y'all so exclusive about?"

"Maybe we like it that way," Corliss said shortly. Arbuckle didn't speak, but Quist noticed that the ranger shifted his gun a little nearer the front. Corliss sighed, then said shortly, "This is Greg Quist — special operative for the railroad. Judd Lombardy — Gilly Deray."

Quist was engaged in rolling a brown paper cigarette and didn't see the proffered hands the two men stuck out. He looked up, nodded, and ran the edge of the brown paper along his tongue, twisted the end of the cigarette and scratched a match. Smoke spiraled slowly from his lips, while he looked the two over. Hard looking men, both. Neither had shaved for some days. A lock of hair cut a black triangle across Lombardy's forehead; the man's heavy eyebrows almost met above his nose.

Lombardy scowled and drew back his hand. Quist's gaze went to Gilly Deray, swarthy, wiry-thin; Indian-bead band about the crown of his shapeless sombrero of indiscriminate color; orange neckerchief at his throat. And the gun holster tied with rawhide thong low on right leg. Deray stared steadily at Quist. Quist considered Deray's eyes the coldest he had ever seen — pale blue with a hard marble-like shine to them. Something queer about the pupils too: it was difficult to tell when the man was looking at you. There seemed to be a perpetual unwinking stare about those eyes.

Corliss said, "I'm surprised to see you in the Amber Cup, Judd. Thought you and your outfit generally patronized the Warbonnet Saloon."

"You're right," Lombardy said shortly. "We just sort of had an idea the great" — a certain sneer in the tones — "railroad dick might come here. Wanted to see what a really big man looked like."

Quist smiled. "Could be you hombres are looking beyond your capabilities."

Lombardy blinked and brushed the black triangle of hair from his eyes. "What's that again?" he said suspiciously.

Quist said curtly, "Forget it."

Deray spoke for the first time, his voice thin and rather high-pitched. "There's some things we can't forget, Quist, the same be-

101

ing those two poor old teamsters that got killed. When's your road going to do something about that bushwacking?"

"What makes *you* so sure it was a bushwacking?" Quist asked quietly. "Just what do you know about it?"

"Me?" Deray's eyes hardened to pinpoints. "Hell, I don't know nothing about it. You insinooatin' I had anything —"

"No, I didn't think you had anything," Quist snapped. "I still don't think you have anything. And now, it's up to you to prove otherwise. It's your play, Deray."

Deray's hard gaze flitted to Quist's right leg. Not seeing a holstered gun hanging below the coat he said, "Ary man that talks that free should arm hisself."

Quist said, "Don't let that bother you, Deray. It doesn't bother me."

The ranger laughed softly. "Doesn't scare easy, does he, Deray?" His voice hardened. "Take my advice and head for your bunk, Deray. You're flirting with a bruise."

"Aw-w, cripes, ranger," Lombardy laughed harshly, "Gilly was only hoorahin' the dick a mite. No call for you to butt in. Ever see a town that didn't want to josh a newcomer, just to see what he had —"

"You saw what he had," Arbuckle said shortly, "and I don't like that kind of joshin'. For your own good I'm telling you both to get out, before Mr. Quist decides to run you out. You damn' fools don't seem to know when you're flirtin' with dynamite — and a damn' short fuse attached —"

"But, look here, Arbuckle," Lombardy started a protest, "we got rights as citizens —"

Arbuckle spoke politely, "How would you like to have your head knocked from under your hat, Lombardy? Didn't I speak plain enough for you?"

Lombardy began to back away, face working angrily. Deray said, "Come on, Judd. Let's go over to the Warbonnet. We'll see the railroad dick sometime when he's not protected by the rangers —"

"I expect to be around here a lot, Deray," Quist said quietly. "And I don't need ranger protection. Like to make a special appointment for tomorrow?"

Deray didn't reply, but headed toward the swinging doors. Lombardy was still backing away. He said hotly, "You'll hear more of this, ranger man. A citizen has rights. I'm aiming to write the governor —"

"Don't do it," Arbuckle snapped, "it might remind the governor to regret that he pardoned you."

Lombardy's jaw dropped. He swallowed

hard. Then without another word he turned and barged through the entrance doors.

Corliss laughed. "Sounds if you had something on Lombardy, Fred."

"Not a thing," Arbuckle chuckled. "That was a shot in the dark. I reckon I was just as surprised as anyone else when I see how it took hold on Lombardy. Maybe his past life might bear checking into."

Mickey Kurtz came sliding along the bar. "My thanks to you gents for the way that was handled. I'd as soon those scuts took their trade some place else. Drinks are on the Amber Cup. What are you having?"

[VIII]
DOC INGRAM'S STORY

Ten minutes later, Quist stated that he'd had enough to drink for a while and thought he'd take a walk. The sheriff asked, "Any place in particular you'd like to go, Greg?"

"I'd thought of drifting down to the undertaker's — or maybe it'd be drifting up — wherever the place is — and taking a look at Porter's body. Can't tell what might be learned."

"It's on Main, near Alamo Street. I'll take you up there. I promised Gene Thornton I'd talk to Doc Ingram again, and I've a hunch we'll find Doc still there."

"Good." Quist asked Arbuckle, "Feel like coming along, Fred?"

"Not on your tintype!" The ranger's face twisted to a grimace. "I've got a strong stomach, but don't forget I had plenty of opportunity to see that body while I was bringing it in. I've seen enough to last me a lifetime." Quist asked a question. Arbuckle answered, "Hell, it was just through luck I found Porter's body. I'd taken a ride over near Shoulder Bluff, seeing if there was any sign to be picked up after that freight thieving business. No luck of course. The sign, if any, was too cold, and of course that rain had washed out all wagon tracks. When I'd first hit town, I'd heard that Porter had disappeared just about the time of the train business, so I'd got a hunch there might be some connection —"

"It hit me that way too," Quist said.

The ranger smiled, "Somebody said once that great minds run in the same channels. I feel right flattered we think alike. Anyway, I started my horse through the foothills in the direction of the Rocking-T, figuring to ask a few questions. And then" — Arbuckle's nose wrinkled — "some buzzards flew up right near and I looked around, and there was Porter. Didn't know who he was of course."

"How far from the Rocking-T were you at the time?"

"Three or four miles, but considering I was farther west than the ranch house, I suppose, roughly, I was about fourteen or fifteen miles from town." He paused. "So I got that body loaded, and headed straight for Clarion City. I don't want that sort of job again."

"I can't blame you. Well, I'll see you later. You at the hotel?"

Arbuckle shook his head. "Ranger's pay doesn't allow for hotels, not the Clarion House, anyway, and the Drovers' Rest Hotel looked like a flea-bag to me. So I unrolled my blankets at a rooming house over on Lamar Street. In case you want to find me, just ask at Mrs. Hepsabeth Perkins' place."

"I'll do that," Quist nodded. They talked a few minutes more, then Quist and Corliss departed and started west on Main Street. The stars were brighter than ever now. Fewer ponies waited at the hitchracks, and the thump-thump of the men's boot-heels made hollow sounds on the plank sidewalks. Crossing the street at the corner of San Antonio, they paused a moment a few doors farther on, while Corliss stopped to glance into the Warbonnet Saloon. He returned, chuckling, to the sidewalk. "No sign of De-ray and Lombardy in there," he stated. "That ranger man must have made his talk stick, I reckon." They walked on.

Two doors from Alamo Street, on the south side of the thoroughfare, they came to a two-storied building, with a double-doored entrance at one side and a wide window just beyond. A dim light burned in the window, displaying some varnish-shiny furniture and red plush upholstery. Black letters painted on the pane stood out plainly: MORT CROMLECH — UNDERTAK-ING PARLORS — STYLISH FURNITURE. Corliss tried the doors, found them un-locked and the men passed into a narrow hall with a closed door to the right which apparently led into the furniture store. The hall opened into what Quist judged was the "viewing room," with folding chairs stacked against the walls, some decrepit artificial lil-ies in an ornate vase, and religious pictures on the walls. Overhead, an oil lamp turned low, was suspended from the ceiling.

Corliss crossed to another door, and the two stepped into a big barn-like room. To the right, a number of coffins rested on wooden horses. At the left wall was a sink with a pump at one end. Shelves held crocks of embalming fluid. There was a case with various shining instruments behind a glass door. Three men stood talking near the sink. One was Gene Thornton who appeared to have been putting up some sort of argument, and getting no place, with a tall spare man with thinning gray hair in citizen's clothing, though he wore riding boots. Gene nodded to Quist, and introduced him to Doctor John Ingram, the man with the gray hair. The third man was Mort Cromlech, the undertaker, who was fat-bellied and wore rimless glasses before round eyes, with his hair sticking up in straggly tufts on either side of his head. One look at Cromlech, and Quist was reminded of nothing so much as an owl.

The doctor shook hands in perfunctory fashion with Quist then turned to the sheriff. "Look here, Lish, can't you convince Gene that it's necessary for Kate to appear at the inquest tomorrow morning, if she is able? It's common sense. It'll look better all around. You know how folks are. You talk to him, Lish. I'm sick of arguing with the young whelp."

"I already told him what you said before," Corliss said helplessly. "I know how he feels — just the same —"

The undertaker broke in, appealing to Corliss too, "Doesn't it seem sensible to let me fix that corpse up so it can be viewed? I been tellin' Doc and Gene it would be more respectable. All's I ask is a photygraft to follow. With some wax and rouge and stuff I can model a face on poor Lloyd like nobody can scarce tell the difference. Mr. Quist, I ask you, don't that make sense? Folks like to line up and get a last look before the beloved goes to his final restin' place —"

"Goddamit, no, Mort!" Gene snapped. "And if you come around Kate with any such ideas, I'll tear off your right arm and beat you over the head with it. The sooner you get that — that body into a box and screw down the cover, the better for all concerned."

"Don't seem decent no how," Cromlech half sniffled. His own eyes appealed to Quist for support, but Quist was too busy closing his nostrils to the queer smells of the undertaking establishment to pay the man much attention.

Doc Ingram said testily, "Mr. Quist, I understand you've seen Mrs. Porter. What's your feeling about her testifying?"

Quist said, "Well, I can understand how Gene feels. At the same time I got the impression she was quite willing to help you in any way possible."

Gene directed a look of anger at Quist,

spun on his heel and left the building without another word. "Thank God, I don't have to argue with him any more," Ingram said testily.

"You've gone and went and made him mad," Cromlech moaned. "Now I won't never get no chance to build up that face. It would make my reputation in Clarion City too, if I coulda —"

"For God's sake shut up, Mort," Ingram snapped. "Nobody wants that face built up in wax, you — you — you damn' ghoul."

"I don't take that kindly, Doc," Cromlech half whimpered.

"I'll stay awake all night worrying about it," the doctor said caustically; then to Quist, "I understand you're here to do some detective work. You craving to have a look at that body?"

"Not craving — no," Quist smiled. "But I think I'd better."

The doctor was rolling down his shirt sleeves now. He said, "Show him the corpse, Mort."

Cromlech led the way where a long metal tank was filled with ice, containing the body. Burlap sacks filled with ice were piled on top and around the dead Lloyd Porter. By the time Quist had turned higher the wick of the oil lamp suspended overhead,

Cromlech had a couple of the ice sacks removed. Quist busied himself with the lamp, until all the sacks had been completely removed, then allowed his eyes to pass over the body. It wasn't pleasant, and he gave the discolored mask that had been a face, but a brief glance. After a minute he said, "Cover it up, Mort." And a minute later, "You got Porter's clothing around here?"

Cromlech went to a hook, took down some clothing and dropped the garments on a table. Quist went over them carefully, but could find nothing outstanding. He next examined the riding boots and found them to be of excellent workmanship. Some reddish colored mud was caked between soles and uppers; the heels were only slightly run down. The undertaker said, "If you want Porter's personal effects — you know, his papers and money and such — Lish Corliss has 'em locked up. Now, I ast you as man to man, Mister Quist, after seein' that stark naked corpse, don't you agree it would be better to use some wax and —"

"That's not my problem," Quist said shortly and crossed the room where the doctor stood cleaning up some instruments before putting them into a small black bag, while he conversed with the sheriff. The doctor glanced up, saying gruffly, "I guess you're the first one who hasn't gone green around the gills after a sight like that."

"What happened to Porter's right forefinger, Doc?" Quist asked.

Ingram looked sharply at Quist. "Well," he said softly, and again, "Well. So you noticed that, eh?"

"Couldn't very well help noticing it, the way it twisted off to one side."

"You're the first one that has noticed it, though," Ingram said. "Lish, here, didn't, until I mentioned it. Hell, I don't know what happened to it. It's broken, that's all I can tell you. Don't know how it got broken though."

"You probed out some of the pellets?" Quist asked.

Ingram nodded, delved into his black bag and produced an envelope containing a number of small shot from a shot-gun cartridge. Quist examined one of them, hefted it in his hand. "Number Two shot, I'd say," Quist guessed.

"That's what I figured," Lish Corliss put in.

"You two gentlemen should know," Ingram said. "All I know is they did a hell of a lot of damage." He put the shot away again.

Quist asked, "How long ago do you figure

Porter was killed, Doc? What I mean is —
well from the looks — well — I sort of get
an idea it didn't just happen today or
yesterday, even."

"You're correct," Ingram nodded. "The
condition of the body makes the exact time
difficult to judge, but offhand I'd say he was
killed about four days ago — say last Thurs-
day. This is Monday. I could be wrong a
half day — mebbe a full day — either way.
That's as close as I can hit it."

Quist said thanks. The doctor asked if he'd
be at the inquest the following morning.
Quist said yes, if necessary, though there
was little he could say, as he saw it. The doctor was getting into his coat now. "Well, I'm
going to have me a long drink and then go
home to bed. It's been a long day."

The three men left the undertaker's, followed by disappointed words from
Cromlech regarding the fine work he could
do with wax. On the street, the sheriff said
he'd take a last walk around town before
hitting the cot in his office, and started
toward the west end of town. Ingram and
Quist started east. Reaching the Amber
Cup, the doctor invited Quist to have a
night-cap with him, and the two men
pushed through the swinging doors and
entered the barroom. There were only two

customers at the bar now, both strangers to Quist. Mickey Kurtz sat on a stool at the far end, reading a newspaper beneath the light of one of his oil-lamps. He folded his paper and got to his feet when Ingram and Quist entered.

"H'are you, Doc? Glad to see you back again, Mr. Quist."

Quist nodded. "What happened to all your clients?"

"Fred Arbuckle allowed he was heading for the hay, shortly after you left. I guess the idea must have caught on. What you drinking?"

Ingram looked at Quist. Quist ordered a bottle of beer. "I'll take a bottle of bourbon over to a table," Ingram said. "Been on my feet too much today. They feel as though they were worn down to the hocks." Mickey put bottles and glasses on the bar, and the two men sat down at a table near the wall, Ingram heaving a long sigh as he settled to his chair. Mickey rounded the table with a pitcher of water and placed it down before the doctor. Ingram poured a tumbler two-thirds full of *Old Crow,* then filled the remainder with water. The process was a regular thing with Ingram, Quist judged as he poured beer into his own glass. The doctor lifted his glass, "Well, here's alluvial deposit in your optic."

"Mud in your eye," Quist said. They drank deeply, and again the doctor heaved a long sigh of contentment. They drank again, and this time Ingram emptied his glass and prepared another tumbler with whisky and water.

This last he left untouched for a time. Quist rolled a cigarette and Ingram borrowed the "makin's" and did likewise. A match was struck, and the doctor leaned back in his chair, blew two smoke rings and said, "Go ahead, ask 'em."

"Ask 'em?" Quist looked puzzled.

Ingram nodded. "The town doctor's supposed to know everybody's personal affairs. I figured you wanted to pick up some information. Shoot with your questions. So long as I don't have to violate any confidences, I'll tell you anything I can."

"You win, Doc. All right, what's bitten Kate Porter — what makes her so hard? Why does she insist on trying to play a man's part?"

"And why did she ever marry Porter, I suppose?" Ingram said crustily. "I suppose you've asked Gene that —"

"And he told me I'd better ask Kate — as did Lish Corliss. Lish was inclined to tell me to mind my own business, but he didn't.

He suggested I ask Kate too."

"Lish would. Maybe you'd act the same way in his boots. I'll tell you why Kate is trying to act the man's part. Because she's waging a one-man war against Clarion City for one thing — and because she's doing a man's job running the Rocking-T."

"That waging a war thing doesn't sound reasonable," Quist said.

"It's not!" Ingram snapped. "Damdest fool thing I ever heard of, but there's folks in town got their knives out for Kate. And for no good reason. That's why I want her to testify at my inquest tomorrow — so certain gossipy cats — male and female — won't get a chance to say she's afraid to testify to what she knows."

"And what does she know about Porter's death?"

"I haven't the least idea — if she knows anything. But I've got a lot of faith in Kate Porter. Look here, Quist, I'd best go back a few years when everything was running smooth on the Rocking-T and her mother was alive. Old Wyatt Thornton wanted his kids to have the best education possible, so he sent 'em off to college. Kate was the belle of Clarín County those days I tell you. She went up to the university at Austin. Gene went to Chicago —"

"Chicago?"

"There's some sort of art school there that's supposed to be extra good. Gene wanted to be an artist and paint pictures. The trouble is, he still does. Oh, he makes a good enough hand when he sets his mind to it, but he'd rather paint cows and horses than work 'em. He's got his head set on some fool notion of making a big name for himself. Thinks he has to do that on Ellen's account, I suppose."

"Ellen?" Quist asked.

"Ellen Bristol. She runs a store here. On Main, just a short way beyond the Clarion House. Sells women's fixin's — doodads, dresses, bonnets and such."

"I hadn't heard about her," Quist stated.

"You would have — sooner or later," Ingram said shortly. "She's had her own little war to wage too — only she's been fighting on the defensive. Kate Porter believes that a strong attack is the best defense."

"Could be she's right."

Ingram twisted in his chair to signal Mickey. The barkeep brought Quist a fresh bottle of beer and removed the empty one. Ingram went on: "Just when Wyatt Thornton thought he had his family running on smooth tracks, Mrs. Thornton was taken sick and died. Bad heart. That brought Kate

117

and Gene home from their schooling, of course. About the time they went back, Thornton's foreman quit. Bought a place of his own in the next county. Thornton hired another man — Chan Yount. Yount's a good man, hard worker, but he's the type that has to have someone always telling him what to do. No initiative. Give him an order and he'll carry it out to the letter, but otherwise . . ."

Ingram paused and swallowed a long draught from his glass. "As a consequence, Thornton began to supervise things himself. Horse took a tumble with him one night and Thornton's back come unglued —"

"Gene told me he was a cripple."

Ingram nodded, dropped his cigarette butt on the floor and stepped on it. "I did what I could for Wyatt, but it was a pretty hopeless job. To satisfy the family I brought in specialists. They confirmed my diagnosis. Thornton's back and legs will never be the same again. Oh, he can make to walk some, and once he's in the saddle he can ride pretty well, but the pain won't let him stand it for long. Kate and Gene had their schooling interrupted again. When they were convinced nothing much more could be done for Wyatt Thornton, Gene went back to Chicago. From that point on, Kate started to take over. It wasn't long before she was running the ranch like a veteran cowman, giving it all her time."

The doctor added more water to his glass, but no more liquor. "Got to taper off a mite," he smiled, then went on, "Things were going all right on the Rocking-T. Different men were getting pretty attentive to Kate —"

"Who?" Quist asked. "If you'll give me names now I won't have to ask later."

Ingram pursed his lips thoughtfully. "Well, now, there were several calling at the ranch Sunday nights, taking her to *bailes* and so on, church potlucks and entertainments at the schoolhouse. Lemme see, there was Jarvis Fanchon, of the Jar-F. Morley Harper who runs the Golden Wheel here — gambling house. One or two others. I reckon Lish Corliss had the inside track, though — enough so that one or two busybodies around town — you know how some women are — got to saying it was a pity Gene didn't come home from that school where he spent his time painting nekkid models, and operate the ranch, so's Kate and Lish could get married decent. That's just the way it was put."

"Some people," Quist said tersely, "never can mind their own business."

"That's the truth. Kate heard about it of course. At first she just laughed it off and suggested that certain gossips 'tend to their knitting.' And that riled 'certain gossips,' and the talk increased. Then she really put her foot in it. There was a bunch of pure blood cows to be delivered to a man in the county east of here. High grade animals. Expensive. Kate wanted to be sure they were delivered safely. She didn't want to trust them to the foreman, so she went along with the hands herself. It was an all night drive." Ingram's voice grew sarcastic. "My, can you imagine anything so terrible? A girl alone out all night with three cowhands! It ain't decent!" He resumed his normal tone of voice. "That really started the tongues to wagging. Certain old harpies said that now she'd have to marry Lish Corliss in a hurry, while she could still get a husband."

"Some nice people in Clarion City," Quist commented.

"You find some of the same breed in every town of any size. With that, Kate threw down the gauntlet and announced it far and wide she intended to live her own life as she saw fit and anybody who didn't like it could go jump in the lake, or words to that effect. Myself, I figure she was a mite rash, but then I can't blame her. I've talked to Lish. He wanted to marry her at once. Kate allowed she wasn't going to let any pack of old mewling tabby-cats force her into marriage. She and Lish quarreled, and I happen to know she refused to marry anybody else around here. It had got so she felt she had to remain single to retain her independence — at least so far's concerns suitors around here."

Ingram lighted another cigarette, puffed a minute, then, "Meanwhile somebody had written Gene an anonymous letter telling him the state of things. Gene came home in a hurry. Kate wanted him to return to school. They're both right stubborn on occasion. They ended up by quarreling too, but Gene stuck on at the ranch, doing what he could, but his heart wasn't in it. I guess he sort of turned into a sort of housekeeper at the ranch, looking after Wyatt and such, while Kate carried the man's job. Next thing that happened, Lloyd Porter dropped into town. He allowed he was looking into business opportunities. I don't know just how he met Kate, but the next thing I heard he was calling regular. I'll admit he had a pretty smooth lot of palaver. Maybe Kate was getting man-lonesome by that time."

"And I suppose the tabby-cats started

pushing out their poison again," Quist said.

"You hit the nail on the head. Gab-gab-gab, from morning to night. You'd hear all sorts of wild rumors, chief of which was that Lloyd Porter would never marry Kate, once he learned the sort of woman she was. Natural the word reached Porter and Kate both. So then the girl really took the bit in her teeth and married him. I suppose she thought she'd spite her detractors. Matter of fact, she just hurt herself. It wasn't long before people realized Porter was no good. He was looking into business opportunities all right. I think he had visions of taking over the Rocking-T. Next he tried to wangle a big job at the bank. Maybe you didn't know that Wyatt's brother, Yarnell Thornton, owns the bank. Kate put her foot down on that in a hurry —"

"No, I hadn't heard that —"

"Word got around — Porter was a right free talker on occasion — that Kate's marriage was headed for the rocks. I reckon she was a pretty unhappy girl. Gene had tried to stop her from marrying Porter. So had Wyatt. There were more quarrels. Now that Porter's dead, Gene seems closer to Kate than he has in some time. And all this time the nasty tongues were going clickety-clack, clickety-clack with vitriol in every word.

And the more the talk, the greater Kate's defiance. She went out of her way to stir up things, foolishly, of course. I remember the day she came striding along Main, smoking a cigarette — and I happen to know that she doesn't give a damn about smoking. But she was just out to show people she'd act just as she pleased and to hell with them. And all the time she was getting a little harder and more arrogant. I tried to talk some sense into her, but it didn't do any good. I knew it wasn't natural for Kate to act that way."

Ingram waited while Quist drank some beer, then continued, "Well, maybe you can get an idea how things stand. When Porter disappeared a month or so back, there were those who hinted Kate had had something to do with it. Matter of fact, the way things been going it wouldn't have surprised me any — nor could I have blamed her. Porter was a skunk, a woman-chaser from the word go; he didn't pay his gambling debts. Drank a lot too, though I can't say I ever saw him under the weather. Just made him sort of ugly. I mind the time he started some sort of argument with Kate down in front of Hawkins' Drug Store. She gave him as good as he sent and a mite more. Finally he lost his temper, and handed her a back-handed slap across the face."

"And I suppose a dozen gallant males rushed to her rescue and started more gossiping tongues to waggling."

"It caused plenty talk all right. What she did was a direct affront to gentle womanhood, not lady-like the tabby-cats smirked. But none of it was due to the 'dozen gallant males,' you mentioned. Before even one male could take a hand, Kate had hauled off and given Porter a wallop that knocked him clear over a tierail. Then followed around the rail to the street and gave him a couple of slashes across the face with a quirt she wore at her wrist."

Quist's eyebrows shot up. "Woof!" he exclaimed. "What a woman!"

Ingram nodded. "She's all of that. You must remember that Kate's a pretty husky specimen. Hard physically. As you can imagine, a crowd gathered. I was in that crowd. Kate swept us all with a glance, and two or three laughs that had started fell quiet. Then she turned back to Porter and told him, very deliberately, that if he ever laid a hand on her again, she'd put a bullet through him. At that moment, I think she meant it too. Then with nary a glance at us, she climbed into her saddle, and rode out of town, chin up, back straight as a ramrod.

It wasn't long after that, that Porter disappeared. Can you see now why I want Kate to testify at that inquest?"

"Yeah. With her under suspicion, as you might say, you feel it is better for her to put in an appearance, than stay away and have people say that she was afraid to appear because she'd killed him. At least she'll prove she's not afraid to answer questions."

"That's right." Ingram yawned. "I'm dog-weary. I've got to be getting along to bed." The two talked a few minutes longer, then the doctor rose, returned the partly empty bottle to Mickey, laid some money on the bar and accompanied Quist outside. Here they parted, Quist heading in the direction of the Clarion House.

[IX]
THE DEVIL'S DRUM

Quist had finished breakfast in the hotel dining room before eight the following morning. He stood a moment in the lobby gazing out on the street, bathed in morning sunlight. People passed on both sides of Main. Two women carrying sun-parasols and market baskets, crossed diagonally toward Hockaday's General Store, their long skirts stirring dust in the roadway. A rider walked his pony toward a hitchrack in front of the Warbonnet Saloon. Two men driving wagons pulled their horses to a halt and paused to chat a few moments. Quist drew his sombrero more firmly to his head and stepped out to the gallery of the hotel and thence down to the sidewalk where the hot sun hit him like a blast from the desert the instant he emerged from the shadow. "Going to be hot today," he told himself, as he crossed Main and turned down Austin Street headed in the direction of the T.N. & A.S. depot.

A train had just pulled out when he arrived, and a few wisps of black smoke still drifted against the cloudless turquoise sky, and the noise from the engine, far down the tracks by this time, came to his ears. On the depot platform, just starting inside, Quist saw a man wearing a stationmaster's cap. He called to him and the man paused, frowning. He was middle-aged and wore a wide watch-chain across his vest. He was in shirt sleeves. Quist introduced himself and showed his credentials. The man's name was Ott Nugent and the frown disappeared from his face when he heard Quist's name.

"Sure, Mr. Quist," he smiled, "glad to do anything I can to help. I knew you were in town, but missed seeing you get off the train yesterday. I had a telegram from Mr. Fletcher telling me to give you all possible cooperation. It's about Number Twenty-four, I suppose — that train that was delayed by the landslide — that wasn't a real land-slide —"

"That's it," Quist put in. "I'd like —"

Nugent interrupted. "I feel bad about hir-ing Pardee and Callahan for that night's work," he said slowly, shaking his head. "But I've hired Callahan before for company hauling when something became necessary. He'd always been mighty reliable. Naturally, when I needed a man I turned to him. Still and all I can't help feeling some responsibil-ity for the deaths of those two teamsters. Of course —"

"None of it can be laid to your door," Quist interposed. "As I understand it, you thought you were getting an order from old Tyrus Wolcott, and you jumped to carry out that order."

Nugent forced a wry smile. "If you'd ever had to take orders from Wolcott, Mr. Quist, you'd know how fast I jumped. Naturally, I didn't doubt the genuineness of the order for a minute when it came over the wire. It didn't seem quite right to me. Still coming — as I thought — from Wolcott, I didn't dare question it. If that order had been authentic and I'd taken time to question it, I'd probably lost my job — at best I'd have got a lay-off."

"I know what Tyrant Wolcott is, Nugent. He's got everybody along the line afraid of him. I'm going to take it up with the directors and see if he can't be toned down a mite."

"If you do, you'll have the gratitude of a lot of men working for the company. He just likes to bully anyone under him. I still don't see how whoever sent that telegram knew what was being shipped on Twenty-four that night."

"Somebody knew certain freight was being shipped and when. He — or they — tipped off somebody else in this section. Who, I don't know. Do you have a copy of the way-bill and other papers?"

"Got 'em right here," Nugent said, drawing some papers from a hip-pocket. "Thought you'd be around wanting to look at 'em, so I wanted to have 'em handy."

Quist moved over against the end of the depot and leaning against the wall, scrutinized the data on the freight shipment which had been forwarded by the Drumm & Tidwell Company, of San Francisco, and consigned to the Uhlman Wholesale Company, of Chicago. Quist scowled. "The shipment apparently consisted of Drum Brand preserves. Now what in the devil — ?" He broke off and glanced through the papers again, then, "Two-hundred-forty cans of peach preserves. Same number cans plum jam. Four-hundred-eighty cans strawberry jam. Forty-eight cans shipped in each box. Cans? I thought this kind of fodder always came in glass jars of some sort."

"That's the case, generally," Nugent said. "This Drum Brand stuff comes in cans."

"I expect so," Quist grunted, frowning. "What sort of looking cans are they?"

"Small cans. I should say" — Nugent considered — "around three inches high and three and a half across. Sort of short and squatty — shaped about like a real drum. Just an ordinary tin can, with a label pasted around it showing a picture of a red and white drum, the name of the jam, company name, and so on. Oh, yes, I remember something else. It stated on the can the gross weight was fourteen ounces. Allow an ounce or so for the can, and there'd be around thirteen ounces of jam —"

"Yeah," Quist nodded absent-mindedly, making some mental calculations. "With forty-eight cans to a box, a filled box would weigh in the neighborhood of fifty pounds. That is, box and all."

Nugent looked vague. "Yes, I suppose so. I should have kept one of the cans to show you." He paused, "You knew, didn't you, that we recovered all the cans, except the strawberry?"

"You mean just the strawberry cans are still missing?" Quist asked sharply.

"That's it. We forwarded the cans of plum and peach at once to the Chicago consignees. I suppose a claim has been entered for the missing goods — but that's out of my realm. I couldn't say for sure."

Quist swore. "So all I have to do is find four-hundred-eighty cans of strawberry jam. Some thief must have got the wrong sort of information regarding that freight shipment. What sort of train was it, anyway? Do you remember?"

"Partly." Nugent shrugged his shoulders. "It was a mixed train — box cars, flat cars and gondolas. The flats were loaded with lumber from the northwest. The box cars held the usual stuff — I remember there were a lot of cowhides. Couple of cars held machinery. Being shipped back for replacement or repairs or something, I expect. One car had a lot of furniture in it — folks moving east, probably. There were some tanks of whale-oil and a consignment of otter skins. Some dried fish. I don't remember what else. Ordinarily I wouldn't be able to give you that much information, except —"

"It doesn't matter," Quist said. "No, don't bother to dig out what that freight carried."

"The gondolas were loaded with sand," Nugent said.

"Cripes, don't they have any sand back East?"

"This is a special sort of sand — white as snow. Best for making glass. Some glass company in New York buys it. What? No I don't know exactly where it comes from. Some place along the California coast. That's all I know."

Quist shoved back his sombrero and perplexedly scratched his thatch of tawny hair. "Damned if it isn't a puzzler," he growled. Reaching for his "makin's" he rolled a cigarette and lighted it. Thoughtfully, he took a couple of inhales; smoke spiraled from his lips as he glanced along the tracks, half consciously following them where they disappeared in the vicinity of the Clarín Mountain range to the west, bright under the morning sunlight. Something else caught his eye along the top of the undulating ridges. He said, "So that's why they call this The Devil's Drum country, eh?"

Nugent followed his gaze, then nodded.

"Looks enough like a drum to be a real one, don't it — if it wasn't for the gawd-awful size of it?"

Rising from among the mountains was a huge rock formation, shaped very much like a drum, even to the wide parallel ridges at top and bottom which resembled to no small extent the hoops of a drum, even to the coloring, which was of reddish sandstone, in contrast to the rest of the rock which was of a brownish-gray cast. Running perpendicularly from top to bottom of the great formation were several strata of the same reddish-hued rock which an observer would immediately construe as the tension-rods of the drum. At one period the gigantic formation had undoubtedly possessed a rounded top, but eons of rains and winds had brought about the centuries of erosion that produced the flat surface. Possibly trees and brush grew there, but at this distance, Quist couldn't see them.

Quist gave a short laugh. "At any rate, that's no snare drum, Nugent. If that isn't the grandaddy of all bass drums, I'm a liar."

Nugent nodded. "How wide do you figure that is, across the top?"

Quist squinted toward the mountains. "Hard to say in this light. Everything appears nearer than it actually is. It's my guess that big drum is at least twenty miles from here, and probably four or five miles across the top."

"Nearer six," Nugent informed him, "and flat as a mesa up there."

"You ever make a ride to get a close-up look?"

Nugent shook his head. "Always intended to, but never seemed to get time — what with Tyrant Wolcott and other things to keep me busy. But I've talked to one or two old-timers who have, years ago. I guess nobody ever goes up there any more. Quite a climb for a horse, though I understand there's a way up, on the far side. This side looks practically perpendicular."

"I'd sure admire to hear some giant beat that drum," Quist observed. "I reckon it would make considerable boom-boom."

"You don't know how it got its name, eh?" Nugent asked. Quist shook his head. Nugent explained, "I was told the Indians in this region — Comanches or Lipan Apaches — named it ages ago. They were mighty superstitious about that big drum, because when there's a storm bringing thunder, the drum seems to take up the sound of the thunder and carry it along in big rolling reverberations." He paused, then added seriously, "The Indians couldn't figure that out, so they finally concluded an evil spirit — the devil — must be doing the drumming."

Quist laughed. "That's a lot of bosh, of course."

"I'm not so sure, Mr. Quist. One old-timer I've talked with, claims to have heard that drumming during thunderstorms."

"You ever heard it?"

The stationmaster shook his head. "I can't honestly say I have. Once or twice I sort of thought I caught a sound like a drum being rolled, but not being close, I'd hesitate to put much faith in what I heard. Could of been just the echoing of thunder. Then, again, we haven't had any real bad thunderstorms since I've been working on this division. And yet, I sort of find myself believing in it."

"Could be you're right," Quist conceded. "Well, I'd better get my mind off the Devil's Drum, and start concentrating on Drum Brand preserves. Queer how the theft of those cans with the Drum trade-mark happened to take place in this Devil's Drum country."

"It's a quincedence, all right," Nugent said gravely. "It might even make you think there was something wrong about those cans of strawberry jam."

"Exactly the way my mind runs," Quist admitted, "but I can't put my finger on it. What could be wrong about those cans?"

"It's got me beat. Well, if there's any other way I can help, just say the word, Mr. Quist."

"I'll do that. And thanks. I'd better be getting along back to Main Street. That inquest will be coming up right soon. And I've got a telegram to send first."

Nugent nodded and departed in the direction of the freight shed adjoining the depot. Quist entered the station and sent a wire to Jay Fletcher asking for all information possible regarding the consignor and consignee of the canned preserves. Then he turned his steps back toward the main thoroughfare.

The County House, where the inquest was to be held, stood on the southeast corner of Main and Mesquite Streets, a large barn-like structure of rock and adobe, with a second story built of frame construction. By this time, Main was crowded on both sides with ponies and vehicles of all horse-drawn types. People, men and women, thronged the plank sidewalks from which resin welled under the hot sun. Quite a crowd, bulging out into the roadway, had gathered before the County House. As he approached, Quist spied Sheriff Lish Corliss, Ranger Arbuckle and two or three other men he'd met.

Arbuckle saw Quist first. "Thought maybe you'd slept in, Greg," he smiled.

Quist shook his head. "I've been down to the depot, chewing the fat with Nugent about the Devil's Drum." He nodded to Corliss who stood near.

Corliss returned the greeting, then asked, "What about the Devil's Drum?"

"Nothing in particular," Quist replied. "Nugent was just telling me about superstitious Indians claiming, in the old days, it was beaten by a devil during thunderstorms. You ever heard it, Lish?"

Corliss laughed shortly. "I was over there one time, when there was a lot of thunder. Yeah, it sort of sounded like somebody rolling a drum with sticks. Not hard to understand, I guess. That big flat-topped mesa is just honeycombed with caves and tunnels. They probably pick up the noise of the thunder and set up reverberations. Don't bother to make a trip to hear it, Greg. It's tough getting a horse up there."

"I reckon so," Quist nodded. He glanced over the assembled crowd. There was a buzz of conversation all around. The heat was bringing out perspiration on red faces. "Cripes!" — Quist consulted his watch — "It's after ten now, what's holding up the

136

inquest?"

"We're waiting for Doc to bring his jury back from the undertaker's, where the jury members are supposed to be viewing the body," Arbuckle explained. "I don't envy them the job. I had the task of bringing Porter's body in. Five hours of that sort of company is enough."

"Can't say I blame you, Fred," Quist said. He glanced through the crowd again, but saw nothing of Kate Porter or her brother, Gene.

Lish Corliss gestured toward the closed double doors of the County House. "Once those doors are open, there's going to be a rush to get in — and I know damn' well that upstairs hall won't hold all this mob. I'm going to have my hands full."

"I'll help you, Lish," Arbuckle said. "You get up there ahead of the crowd. I'll stay here at the door and sort of slow 'em down. Damned if I can understand how folks who are always complaining how much work they've got to do, can always find time to come to town to attend an inquest over some murdered hombre. I call it downright morbid."

The crowd stirred. Somebody exclaimed, "Here comes Doc and his jury." Necks craned to see Ingram and the six men with him who had been chosen for duty on the coroner's jury.

Corliss took Quist's sleeve. "Come along with me, Greg, and get ahead of the crowd." Quist nodded and the two men pressed through the throng. Corliss opened one of the big double doors and motioned for Quist to precede him. "Just go straight up the stairs. Front row of chairs is reserved for witnesses —" He broke off, appealing to people who pushed toward the door. "Take it easy, folks. There's no use —"

Whatever else he may have added, was lost to Quist. Straight before him was a flight of steps to the second floor. Quist went on up with Corliss on his heels. Below they could hear Arbuckle appealing to the prospective audience to go slow. Behind them, feet thumped on the steps. A man swore and some woman informed him he was no gentleman. An instant later, Quist emerged on the upper floor where the inquest was to be held.

[X]
A Surprise Witness

The room was a large one, with open windows on either side to afford some ventilation, though not much, Quist considered, with the hot sun beating down on the roof overhead. Rows of chairs had been set out, and the instant he entered the room, Quist had spotted Kate Porter and Gene Thornton seated in the front row. He moved up and sat down next to them, receiving a pleasant enough " 'Morning," from Gene, and a serious nod from Kate. Behind him, Lish Corliss was doing what was possible to slow the rush of people and indicate chairs to them. Arbuckle was at the head of the stairs now accomplishing what he could to keep various eager ones from getting ribs crushed at the upper doorway. Voices shrilled through the room, there was an uneasy stirring until as many people as possible could get seated. It was a hopeless task: by the time the inquest started, men were jammed on the stairway and the crowd overflowed to the street.

Quist, seated next to Kate Porter in the front row which was now filled, said, "I was surprised to see you two already up here."

"Doc Ingram suggested it. We've been here over an hour. He wanted to talk to me before the inquest opened. Besides, it was better than having to push in with the crowd."

Gene Thornton scowled. "I'll be damn' glad when this is over with. I still don't like the idea of Kate having to testify."

"What's bothering you?" Quist asked.

He didn't receive an answer, for at that moment Ingram came down the aisle between chairs, followed by his jury, and the noise of conversation rose higher above the seats as various men called greetings to the jury members they recognized. The jury, dressed in its Sunday best, soberly took seats near a table at the front of the room. By this time Lish Corliss and Fred Arbuckle were also seated in the front row, though as the inquest proceeded, Corliss more than once made his way to the back of the room to quiet voices at the top of the stairway.

Doc Ingram took his seat at the table, and riffled through some papers. A clerk sat at an end of the same table, prepared to take notes on the testimony to be heard. The table held a gavel, a copy of the Bible, pens, pencils and ink. Already the air in the big room was thick with the odor of perspiration, cigarette and pipe smoke and heat. Ingram rapped on the table with his gavel and rose to his feet. The room fell silent.

After a few moments' wait, Ingram launched into a short speech, stating that he, as duly elected coroner of Clarion City, had called this inquest to determine, if possible, who had been responsible for the death of Lloyd Porter. The doctor added, a bit sharply, that the inquest was not to be construed as a trial of any one person, regardless of what testimony might be forthcoming and such baseless rumors, based on gossip, which seemed to be floating around town. No, this was not a trial, in any sense.

"However," Ingram added, "I want it distinctly understood that all witnesses will be speaking under oath. Any failure to speak truth, if discovered, will result in a charge of perjury. And the law provides very strict penalties to cover perjurers. Witnesses will please keep my warning in mind at all times. And now we'll get to business."

There were a few preliminaries, during which Ingram stated he had already done some investigating and would call to the stand to testify, certain people he thought should be heard. He described the death wound that had ended Lloyd Porter's life: ". . . a blast from a shotgun, fired fairly close to the victim. The shell had been loaded with #2 shot . . ." The doctor's medical testimony was somewhat too technical for the majority of the audience, and when some man in the seats a few rows back was heard explaining to his wife that "Doc means he had his face plumb blowed off," that appeared to fill the bill better than all the long words Ingram had been forced to employ for the sake of the record. The doctor went on,

"Due to the condition of the body I've found it difficult to establish the exact time of death, but to the best of my ability I'd say Lloyd Porter was killed on the 13th of this month. It was yesterday that Ranger Arbuckle found the body and brought it in. The 17th of the month. Therefore I'm assuming the deceased had been dead about four days when the body was found. That's as close as I can hit it, though I could be in error nearly a full day, either way, of course."

Various minor witnesses were then called, testifying as to the last time they had seen or talked to Lloyd Porter, but nothing definite was learned from their testimony. The last person apparently to see him alive, was a cowhand from the Rafter-Z named Gunnerson, who had encountered Porter ". . . oh, say just 'bout a month back. I was out lookin' for a stud-hawss that had broke outten his corral, when I spot Porter ridin' near Shoulder Bluff. Whut's that, Doc? No, he was considerable rods away, so I didn't talk to him. He waved and kept on goin'. I figgered mebbe he was out to hunt. Looked like he carried a scatter-gun. Had somethin' bulky lashed on behind his saddle — could have been a satchel, though mebbe not. I couldn't say for sure."

Quist considered the cowhand's words. It was "just 'bout a month back" that eastbound #24 had been stalled by the manmade landslide. Gunnerson was excused from further testifying, and Ranger Arbuckle called to the stand. He was sworn in on the Bible and told of finding the body in the foothills of the Clarín Mountains, repeating what Quist had already heard.

Ingram asked, "Was there any sign of Porter's horse in the vicinity?"

Arbuckle said promptly, "None. I carried the body to town lashed across my saddle, with me hanging on back of the cantle. It wasn't pleasant nowise, nor did my pony take to the idea. That dead body put him on the prod considerable. He started to buck, then took out to run. Had a job handling him. But he was headed toward town so I didn't check him none once he was straightened out. Thinking it over, I don't expect it took more than three or four hours to reach Cromlech's place, but with a grisly load of that sort, I thought we'd never get to town. Seemed like I was riding five or six hours."

"A nasty job," Ingram agreed. "Did you

see any prints or sign of any sort near the body, or find the shotgun that had been used?"

"Looked for sign. Couldn't find any. Couldn't see any gun around, either, except that pearl-handled six-shooter which was in Porter's holster."

A few more questions were asked, of minor import, then Gene Thornton was called and sworn. After asking how long Thornton had known Porter, their relations and so on, Ingram said, "You identified the body as that of Lloyd Porter, Mr. Thornton."

"I did."

"On what did you base your identification?"

Gene frowned, thoughtfully. "Oh, on a number of things. The color of Porter's hair, shape of his head, build and so forth. The clothing he wore, his boots. The boots were a rather expensive pair, most men don't buy. Then there was that pearl-butted gun in his holster. There were papers in his pocket." Gene paused.

"What sort of papers?"

"A letter addressed to him — that is, an envelope. It contained no letter, or return address. It had been posted from some place in New Mexico — Albuerque, if I remember correctly. It could have been in a woman's handwriting, though I'm not sure. There were a couple of receipted bills from firms in town, here. I recognized a pocket-knife Porter carried."

"And you feel sure of your identification?"

"I'm positive. Other men who saw the body at Cromlech's agreed with me it was Porter's body."

"Mr. Thornton, do you happen to remember where you were on," — Ingram hesitated — "we-ell, let's say on the 13th of this month — or on the days before and after the 13th?"

Thornton flushed. "On the 12th I was in Clarion City. Rode in to get the mail. Stayed all day. On the 14th I was at the ranch all day. On the 13th I was painting."

"Where?"

"On a bend of Clarín Creek — Rio Clarín some folks call it."

"Why did you pick that particular spot?"

Thornton's face reddened. "Look here, Doc, that's some few miles from the place where Porter was found by Arbuckle —"

Ingram cut in sharply, "I'm not insinuating anything. I'm just trying to learn why you happened to go there that day."

Thornton swallowed hard and said, "I'm sorry. As a matter of fact I hadn't intended to go there, that is, not to paint, leastwise. Sowbelly — Sowbelly Handson — he's our cook on the Rocking-T — mentioned it would be nice to have a change of food on the table, so I took my shotgun —"

Thornton paused as a buzz of conversation rose through the room. Ingram picked up the gavel and rapped for silence. When the hall had quieted, Thornton continued, "I took my shotgun thinking I might find a few prairie hens for cookie's pot. Didn't happen to see any, by the time I came to Clarín Creek. There's an old cottonwood there with one bough stretching out across the water and the reflections were so fine I —" He broke off. "Anyway, you don't care about that. I always carry some paper and paints with me, when I go out, so I stopped and made a number of sketches. Before I realized it, the sun had started to drop and I came home."

"Without getting any game?"

"I didn't even fire my gun," Thornton said emphatically.

Ingram smiled to relieve the tension. "I think possibly your mind was more on painting than getting prairie chickens."

"That's possible," Thornton said soberly.

A minute later he was allowed to be reseated. Kate Porter's name was called. She

146

rose and took her oath on the Bible. Conversation again rose through the room; there was a good deal of chattering among the women, and Quist distinctly heard a couple of derogatory remarks from a pair of old crows seated three rows back. There was considerable pious sniffing. Kate had changed her clothing of the night before, and now wore riding boots, a divided riding skirt and a mannish gray flannel shirt with blue bandanna tied at the throat. A worn spot across the right hip of her skirt showed where a gun-belt and holster usually rested. Her mass of blond hair was tucked beneath a flat-crowned black sombrero, which looked as though it had seen plenty of wear.

The mutterings and whisperings increased through the room. Ingram was rapping sharply on the table with his gavel. Gradually the noise subsided, while the girl stood straight, defiant, challenging, looking out over the rows of faces, her steady brown eyes almost contemptuous, imperious. Quist thought, *Lord, what a handsome woman. And with plenty courage, too. But stubborn as hell.*

With the room finally silent, waiting eagerly for Kate's testimony, the doctor started his preliminary questioning. Kate answered clearly and with sharp incisiveness each question. Somewhat impatiently, she finally broke in, "It may save time, Doctor Ingram, if I tell you now I also was out with my shotgun on the day of the 13th. I'd heard cookie's remark about a change of diet for our table too. I, also, decided to see if I couldn't bag a few prairie chickens, so I saddled up, took my gun —"

Various gasps were raised in the room, again voices were set buzzing. A man behind Quist muttered to his companion, "Probably the two of 'em ganged up on Porter . . ." Ingram pounded furiously with his gavel. Two of the jurors looked definitely enraged and the looks they directed toward Kate were ominous. Quist said to himself, "Dammit! She'll be putting a loop around her own throat with her arrogant manner."

Gradually, the noise died away. Kate continued steadily as if there'd been no interruption, "I didn't know of course that my brother had set out for the same purpose as I. As a matter of fact, I didn't know until he testified, where he had gone that day. I saw him ride in that night and he said something about painting. That was all I knew." Again her eyes swept the audience as though to say, "Make of this what you will and to hell with it."

Ingram said, "Thank you very much for volunteering this information, Mrs. Porter.

It has saved time. And I'm sure no one will be foolish enough to assume anything from your testimony beyond the fact that you're doing all possible to expedite this inquiry." He paused, eyes suddenly hard, as they gazed steadily at various individuals about the room. Then he smiled suddenly and turned back to Kate, "I hope you had better luck than your brother, Mrs. Porter."

"I brought back seven birds," the girl stated.

"And where did you do this shooting?"

"Within a few miles from the ranch house." She added, "I was nowhere near the foothills of the mountains where — where my husband's body was found."

"Did you see your brother that day?"

Kate hesitated, then said "No — that is, I saw him right after breakfast and when he rode in late that afternoon, but not during the hours between."

"How long were you away from the ranch house?"

"Several hours."

"It took some time to scare up those birds, I imagine."

"Not so long, actually," Kate said, "but I was in no hurry to return. I — I had certain problems to think out. When I'm at the ranch there are always things coming up to be attended to."

Ingram said, "I quite understand. Mrs. Porter, when did you last see your husband?"

"It was just a month ago yesterday — I'm not sure of the exact date. Anyway, it was the morning of the day that freight train was stalled. I remember it because I was in Clarion City the next morning, and I heard people talking about it."

"That sets the date closely enough," Ingram stated. "Did your husband tell you where he was going that morning?"

Kate shook her head, then conscious of the clerk writing nearby said, "No. However, when he saddled up near the corral, he told one of the hands he was riding to town. It was quite early, and I was rather surprised to hear of him leaving at that hour."

"You hadn't talked to him before he left?"

"No. We each had our own rooms at the ranch. He hadn't waited for breakfast." Kate's mouth hardened a trifle. "I don't think it is any secret around here, that my husband and I saw very little of each other, nor was I aware of his different business ventures."

"What exactly did Lloyd Porter do?" Ingram asked.

"I haven't the least idea," Kate said tersely.

"He talked vaguely of business here and there. Sometimes he said he dealt in cattle. Sometimes mining. He spoke once of buying up a bunch of horses and reselling them. Oh, he hinted at a number of deals, but never anything definite."

"Did he often leave for long periods of time?"

"Quite frequently, but he was never gone as long as this last time. A week was generally the longest. Sometimes when he returned he'd say he'd been to Chicago, or out in California some place. I'll say this, he always had money from these deals. I wasn't particularly interested, but more than once he's insisted on showing me big rolls of greenbacks or small sacks of gold coins."

Ingram nodded, "And this last time you were worried over his long absence?"

A small frown appeared between Kate's eyes. "Let's say I was somewhat concerned," she stated tartly. "People in town were doing a lot of talking. I didn't like what they were saying —"

Ingram broke in hastily, "I understand that —"

"Doc!" — a man at the back could no longer contain himself — "Why don't you ask her about that time on Main when she slashed him with her quirt and threatened to shoot him — ?"

The room broke into an uproar. Swearing angrily under his breath, Lish Corliss was already hurrying down the aisle, even before Ingram's sharp, "Sheriff, eject that man!" cut through the noise. There was some short disturbance near the doorway before the disturber was put out and there came a rush to occupy his vacated seat by those crowding about the stairway. Corliss returned, face flushed. Order was quickly restored. Ingram said in cutting accents, "One more interruption from a fool of that sort — or fools — and we'll continue this inquest behind closed doors. In justice to Mrs. Porter I want to say that that individual who caused the interruption was once jailed for six months for stealing Rocking-T cows. Doubtless he holds a grudge. I'll brook no more of that sort of thing."

His hot gaze swept the audience. Within a few minutes he again turned to Kate. "And when your husband had been gone a month, I understand you decided to have a search made for him."

Kate said, "That is right." She continued, telling about her trip to El Paso to see Quist, and of her hearing of her husband's death while in El Paso. A few minutes later Kate's testimony was concluded and she resumed her seat.

Quist was next called to testify. After giving his name and occupation he confirmed Kate's visit to his office, under the doctor's questioning. Ingram continued, "And you agreed to come here and instigate a search for Lloyd Porter, Mr. Quist?"

"On the contrary," Quist replied. "Other business — for my company — brings me here. I was unable to accept Mrs. Porter's offer of a job."

"Did you feel that she was sincere in her request?" Ingram asked.

"Very much so," Quist stated definitely. "In fact she appeared very," — he hesitated and glanced at Kate whose cheeks had crimsoned — "disappointed," Quist concluded, "when I had to refuse to help her."

His words had a favorable effect on the jury, in view of Quist's reputation as a detective.

"At any rate," Ingram smiled, "no one can accuse Mrs. Porter of not trying to get the best man for the job. It is my feeling that she deserves considerable credit for her efforts."

A commotion occurred at the head of the stairway just as Quist had concluded. Someone at the back of the room called, "Hey, Doc, here's a man wants to testify." A man came pushing through the crowd and started up the aisle. He was a hard-looking character in cow-togs. A scarred holster hung at his hip and he didn't look as though he'd shaved for a week or so. All told, an unprepossessing-looking character. Two or three cowhands in the audience spoke to him as he headed toward Ingram's table, but he didn't reply.

"Gawd," the man ejaculated as he reached the front of the room, "if it hadn't been for Marshal Eldred back there" — jerking one thumb over his shoulder — "I never would have got in here."

"You've got some pertinent information you wish to place before this inquiry?" Ingram asked, eyes sizing up the man.

"I ain't reckonin' to be impert'nent, Doc." The man gave a surly laugh. Ingram flushed. "I'll make it clearer," he stated curtly. "Have you any information regarding the death of Lloyd Porter?"

"Yeah, I got information 'bout Porter —"

Ingram swung to the clerk. "Swear this man."

The man took the oath. Ingram had him repeat his name for the benefit of the audience. The man said, "Name's Luke Ferris."

"Occupation?" Ingram asked.

"I work for Judd Lombardy — punch

154

cows for the L-Bar-D — on and off. You can ask Judd. Plenty folks 'round here know me."

"Are you working for Lombardy at present?"

"I reckon so."

"Why haven't you come forward with your information before?"

"I been out of town for a spell. Sort of a leave of absence. You can ask Judd —"

"I'm not doubting your word, Mr. Ferris. Where have you been?"

"Away — visitin' my dear old mother in Albuquerque."

"New Mexico?"

Ferris owlishly looked over the audience, then back to Ingram. "I don't know of no other Albuquerque. I just got in a mite back. Lotta miles between here and —"

"I'm aware of the distance between here and New Mexico," Ingram said icily.

"Then, Doc, you'd oughter know how long a train takes to get here," the man guffawed.

Ingram looked somewhat exasperated. Ranger Arbuckle spoke sharply from his seat, "You mind your tongue, Ferris, and answer the coroner's questions, without trying to be funny." Ingram shot a quick look of thanks to Arbuckle when Ferris immediately sobered.

Ingram went on, "So your address has been in another state for a while past. May I ask that address?" Ferris hesitated. Ingram said curtly, "Come, come! You say you've been visiting your mother. What is her address in Albuquerque?"

Again the hesitation. "Uh — uh — One-Twenty-Three — er — er — Ventoso —"

Impatiently, Ingram asked, "Well, Ventoso what? Street? Avenue? Road?"

Ferris swallowed hard, then noticing Arbuckle's frown, gulped, "That's it — One-Two-Three Ventoso Street. Anyway, that don't matter. My address now is at the L-Bar-D Ranch."

Ingram drew a long sigh. "Well, I'm glad we got that settled anyhow. All right, Mr. Ferris, what do you know of Lloyd Porter, or his death?"

The man straightened a little, seeming more confident now. "Can't say I know much about him, Doc, 'cept what's generally knowed hereabouts. I just heard when I got off'n the train this mornin', that folks was claimin' he was dead. Well, facts must be sort of 'xaggerated, 'cause I was talkin' to Lloyd Porter just yesterday, in Albuquerque."

There ensued a stunned silence, then,

"What?" Ingram fairly yelled.

Again an uproar filled the big room. Men stood up from their chairs, necks craned for a better view. No one could hear what Ingram or Ferris were saying now. Suddenly, Quist heard Ingram exclaim, "I'll be goddamed!" then he started an apology as he rapped furiously with his gavel. Quiet once more settled over the room.

[XI]
SCRAMBLED FACTS

Ingram looked considerably bewildered now, as he resumed questioning. "You're absolutely certain, Mr. Ferris, that the man you talked to was Lloyd Porter?"

"Certain sure," Ferris replied. "I guess I know Porter, talked to him plenty times when he visited the L-Bar-D."

Ingram tried in various ways to make the man change his story, but it was no good. He could shake Ferris' testimony not at all. Finally, "May I ask, Mr. Ferris, exactly what you and — and this man you claim was Lloyd Porter —"

"Dammit, I know Porter when I see him —"

"Apparently," Ingram said weakly. "Do you remember what you talked about?"

"We-ell," — again the hesitation — "to tell the truth we didn't *habla* but a few minutes. I asked him how things was in Clarion City. You see, I was down by the depot trying to raise the price of my ticket back here — I was sort of on my uppers after not workin' for a spell — when Porter come up to the ticket window. I spotted him immediate. At the same time I remembered he owed me ten bucks from a poker game we had 'bout three months ago at the L-Bar-D, so I braced him for the money —" Ferris paused.

"And did you get it?" Ingram prompted.

"Sure, Lloyd Porter was always good pay. It was just that he'd forgot, I reckon."

"And where did he go after you got the money?"

"I ain't got no idea, Doc. I went to my mother's place to get my grip and say goodbye. Then when I got here I heard about Porter havin' been brought in dead yesterday. I knowed the facts was scrambled some place, so I come here soon's I could make it."

"And you are absolutely sure it was Porter," Ingram persisted dubiously.

"Ain't I told you?" Ferris demanded in aggrieved tones. "Ain't I told you more'n once? You callin' me a liar?"

158

Ingram drew a deep breath. "No." And added, "Not yet, any way. Thank you for your testimony, Mr. Ferris. You are excused." He turned to the jury. "Considering the testimony we've had, I see no reason for longer continuing this inquiry. It is now up to you gentlemen to come to some sort of verdict, regarding either Lloyd Porter's murder, or the murder of some man unknown. You may begin your deliberations as soon as this room is cleared." Then to the audience, "This inquest is closed. Please clear the room as quickly as possible."

One of the jurors spoke, "Hey, Doc," he complained, "how's for getting our dinners first? I'm starved fit to eat the Lord's Supper. We can do our deliberatin' later."

"In view of the facts we've had," Ingram said grimly, "food is of small importance. If you get at your deliberating now, you'll get through quicker. So start in, gentlemen."

Below, on the street, as the audience thronged past talking excitedly, Quist waited for Corliss and Arbuckle to emerge. He nodded to Kate and Gene Thornton as the two came through the wide doorway. Kate looked for a moment as though she were about to stop, but Gene spoke to the girl and they moved on in the direction of the hotel. Corliss and Arbuckle appeared on the heels of the last stragglers. With them was a little old man whom Corliss introduced as Town Marshal Dave Eldred. Eldred was rather scrawny with wide sun-bleached mustaches and watery blue eyes. One of the last of the old-timers, Quist thought, and a good man in his prime, but nowdays elected to office through gratitude for good deeds accomplished in the past.

"Glad to meet ye, Mr. Quist," Eldred spoke, shaking hands. "Whut ye think of the preceedin's?"

Quist shook his head. "Damned if I know what to think."

"Same here," from Eldred. "Ferris shore called the turn when he said the facts wuz scrambled. Ferris swears he talked to Porter yesterday. Musta been nigh the same time this ranger brought in the body that wuz 'dentified by young Gene Thornton as Porter. Who's a man to believe?"

Arbuckle said, "Me, I'd be most inclined to swing along with Thornton. At the same time, Ferris took his oath. You can't overlook that point. But it's a cinch somebody's mistaken."

"What about Ferris?" Quist asked. "He claims to be known around here."

"That part's right," Corliss said. "He's been working on and off for Lombardy for

a year or so now. I've seen him around town
—"

"He's a no-good, if you ask me," Marshal
Eldred put in. "No, I can't say nothin'
definite 'bout him. Jest feel it in muh bones."

"Well, I feel it in my bones I'd better get
some dinner," Corliss laughed. "My belly's
beginning to think my throat's cut. How
about you, Greg — Fred? There's a Chink's
restaurant just beyond San Antonio Street
that serves a mighty tender steak."

"Sounds like a good idea," Quist said,
"but I want to step down to the railroad
depot a few minutes first —"

"That reminds me," Arbuckle cut in, "I
want to send a telegram to Captain Craig at
Bandera. I'll go along with you —"

"Bandera ranger headquarters now?"
Quist asked.

"For Company K," Arbuckle nodded.
"We've been in camp there about six
months now. For a time there was some
wire-cutting trouble outside of San Antonio,
so the whole company was shifted to Bandera which was conveniently near. We
haven't been moved yet, even though the
trouble is ended. But I want to keep Jim
Craig posted on developments here."

"You hombres," Corliss suggested, "drift
on down to the depot. I'm almighty thirsty

so I'll wait for you in the Amber Cup. Meet me there."

The other two nodded and started off, turning the corner at Mesquite Street where it led to Railroad Street. Arbuckle said, as they strode along, "Well, if Ferris' testimony didn't do anything else, it got Mrs. Porter off the hook. I was watching those jurors close, and I figured they was set to return some sort of indictment against her. Then Ferris' spiel really threw them off the track."

Quist said dryly, "You sound sort of relieved, Fred."

"Jeepers!" Arbuckle exclaimed. "Certainly you can't blame me. A woman as beautiful as Mrs. Porter — well, no man in his right senses wants to see her convicted of murder. I just wish —" He hesitated.

Quist grinned. "Come on, out with it."

"Well, I just wish she wasn't married. I'd admire a heap to go calling on a woman of her caliber — and with honorable intentions."

"You sound like you've been hard hit."

"I'm beginning to suspect it myself. If only she wasn't married I might —"

"Maybe she isn't," Quist said.

"I thought that way too — until Ferris showed up with his talk of seeing Porter yesterday. From all I can learn around town,

162

Lloyd Porter was really a skunk."

"So I hear."

They turned into Railroad Street, passing heaps of rubbish at the rear of buildings fronting on Main, and within a few minutes reached the station. Quist found a telegraph blank at a desk against one wall and quickly scribbled out a message directed to a T.N. & A.S. operative in New Mexico, then took it to the ticket window and passed it in to be sent. He glanced at Arbuckle, stub of pencil in right hand, frowning over the pad of telegraph blanks as though uncertain what to say.

Quist said, "I'll wait for you out on the platform, Fred."

"Right. I'll be with you in a couple of minutes."

As Quist stepped outside, he could hear the *clickety-click-click* of the telegraph key forwarding his message. Over the course of years' employ with the T.N. & A.S. he had picked up considerable knowledge of the Morse code, which from time to time was of value to him. While unable to send, Quist could listen in and interpret messages being sent, and had fallen into the habit of unconsciously listening whenever he was in the vicinity of a telegrapher.

His eyes roved along the platform and saw

Stationmaster Nugent busy with way-bills and checking some freight. Nugent saw him and called that he'd be with him in a minute. Through the open windows of the station, the telegraph instrument crackled and snapped. Quist could pick up the message: "*. . . Craig, Company K, Bandera . . .*" The next few words were too fast for Quist, then he caught some more: "*. . . and developments here too complicated . . . for wire . . . Will keep you posted . . . Will write . . .*" And the signature: . . . "*Fred Arbuckle, Sergeant. . . .*"

Quist chuckled. "Damned if I'm not getting to be a regular eavesdropper."

At that moment Nugent approached. "Anything I can do for you, Mr. Quist?"

"Maybe. Did you happen to see who got off eastbound #18 when it stopped this morning?"

Nugent nodded. "I saw several people. Few folks I know in town. A whisky drummer that makes regular stops here. Salesman for building materials. You expect anybody in particular?"

"Do you happen to know a cowhand by the name of Ferris, works for the L-Bar-D?"

Nugent shoved his cap to the back of his head and frowned. "Ye-es, think I do," he said slowly. "Seen him around town on occasion. If it's him you mean, he didn't get off #18 — at least I didn't see him. I didn't see any cowfolks get off, for that matter. You can generally spot 'em."

Arbuckle came up at that time. Quist said, "I'm trying to get a line on Ferris. I gathered that he meant he had arrived on #18 — that's the eastbound passenger that arrives here at ten-thirty each morning. The stationmaster says he didn't see him get off."

Arbuckle's eyebrows raised. "Could be Mister Ferris is telling lies."

Quist nodded. Nugent said, "Of course, he might have ridden in the caboose. That stops down the track farther. In that case I might not see him get off."

Quist said, "Or he may have bummed his ride. Rode the rods, or beat the fare some other way. He mentioned being short of cash, and to me he didn't appear to be the sort of hombre who'd pay money for a ticket if it could be avoided."

"It's possible," Arbuckle said dubiously.

Quist shrugged. "Well, I'll give the bustard the benefit of the doubt, until I learn something more definite. Thanks, Nugent."

He and Arbuckle pursued their way back to Main Street and thence into the Amber Cup where they found Corliss and several other men discussing the inquest. Corliss said, "Have one on me?"

Mickey Kurtz took Quist's order for beer. Arbuckle asked for a "touch" of *Old Crow.* They had just been served when Doc Ingram entered and joined them at the bar. "Thought I might find you here, Lish," he said, and to the bartender, "Nothing right now, Mickey."

"Your jury reach a finding yet?" Corliss asked.

Ingram nodded. "They just finished deliberating. The verdict is to the effect that Lloyd Porter or someone unknown — they couldn't decide which — met his death as the result of an inflicted gunshot, fired by someone unknown — if all that makes sense." The doctor swore, and continued, "Also the sheriff of this county is directed to immediately take steps to apprehend the murderer."

Corliss groaned. "And now they hand me a puzzle to solve," he said bitterly.

"Hell's-bells!" Ingram said, "It might have been worse. Juror #3 held out for some sort of a verdict of suicide. Claimed Porter might have shot himself — presumably with a shotgun. I had to remind him that no shotgun was found, but he was stubborn as a hawg on ice for a spell."

"Juror #3," Corliss scowled, "that's Jiggs Tanner. I'd figure him as the smartest man in the lot too. I guess they're all nitwits."

"You rounded 'em up for me," Ingram reminded the sheriff.

"Hereafter," Corliss said sourly, "I'll pick nobody but personal friends for your juries, Doc — people who won't hand me puzzles to figure out."

"Gosh, Lish," Ingram asked, "what else can you expect?"

"Damned if I know," the sheriff conceded. "I reckon they did the only thing possible." And to Arbuckle and Quist, "Let's go eat. No man can think without proper nourishment in his bread-basket."

The three men left with Ingram, carrying his black bag, close behind. The doctor declined an invitation to accompany them on the plea that he had to make the calls he had missed that morning. "And if we don't have another inquest for months," Ingram said acidly, "it will be too soon. They take up too much of my time."

The Chinese restaurant was a small place just west of San Antonio Street, on the south side of Main. The three men entered and three-quarters of an hour later emerged feeling better prepared to meet the rest of the day: the Chinese cook's steaks had lived up to Corliss' praise "so tender they could be cut with a fork."

On the street once more, they paused at the edge of the sidewalk to roll and light cigarettes. Quist said, "Well, Lish, you've had your orders from the coroner's jury. Just when do you aim to start apprehending that criminal?"

"The minute you or Fred tell me where to start," Corliss stated dolefully. "You two have had more experience with this sort of thing than I have. I just don't seem to have an idea of my own —" He broke off, a frown creasing his forehead, and pointed along the street. "Here comes Dave Eldred, galloping like a stampeded steer. Now I wonder what in hell has gone wrong." He started toward the approaching marshal, Quist and Arbuckle following closely on his heels.

Old Eldred came puffing to a stop. "Bin — lookin' — for ye — Lish —" he panted, then paused to catch his breath. The oldster's lungs were working like a worn-out bellows.

"What's up, Dave?" the sheriff asked sharply.

" 'Nother — 'nother body — has been found," Eldred jerked out. "Gilly Deray — jist brung — it in — on a wagon. Doc's down to Cromlech's Undertakin' — Parlors.

168

Said to fetch — you — t'oncet."

Quist asked quickly, "Who's the dead man?"

Eldred shook his head. His breath was coming easier now. "Ain't got the least — idee. Stranger 'round here. I ain't never seen him before. Somebody plugged him in the back and — and Doc is swearin' to beat all git-out. Says he wishes somebody — would bring in a fresh body for once —"

"Goddamit," Corliss swore fluently. "This means another inquest I reckon. Don't wonder Doc's riled."

The men were walking swiftly toward Crumlech's place now. Arbuckle asked, "Dave, where did Deray find this body?"

"On L-Bar-D holdin's — so Deray claims. Couple of miles north of the ranch house, just a short way off the trail that runs north to Kingboro and joins the L-Bar-D road into Clarion City."

Quist scowled. "I'm blasted if I like the way the L-Bar-D keeps coming into things around here. Porter was known to be friendly to the L-Bar-D. Went there to play poker. Ferris — an L-Bar-D man — claims to have talked to Porter yesterday. Lish, you said there was bad feeling between the L-Bar-D and the Rocking-T. And now De-ray, an L-Bar-D man discovers a dead body on L-Bar-D property — and Deray's word I wouldn't trust any farther than I could throw a brick house. I've got a hunch there's some sort of explosion due right soon, and it wouldn't surprise me a-tall if it centered right on L-Bar-D holdings!"

[XII]
POWDERSMOKE

A crowd had gathered about the undertaker's by the time they arrived. The three men pushed on through, entered the building and made their way to Cromlech's back room. Cromlech had thrown wide his rear doors to admit air. Quist's eyes ran quickly over the caskets on wooden horses at one side, and beyond near the open doorway the glassed-in hearse with the plumes at each corner. Near the center of the room, Doc Ingram, Cromlech, Deray and Luke Ferris stood talking near a table on which the dead man lay with a canvas sheet covering the body. Another crowd just beyond the rear doorway stood peering inside and talking excitedly.

Ingram looked up and nodded as the men entered, and growled to Corliss, "Lish, you'd best start rounding up another jury for an inquest. This is your chance. You said you were going to get only personal friends this time."

Deray nodded to Quist and Arbuckle. Ferris didn't say anything. Quist asked, "How long's he been dead, Doc?"

"I'm not sure yet," Ingram snapped.

"Won't the *rigor mortis* — ?"

"Hell's fire!" Ingram said testily. "*Rigor mortis* has come and gone sometime since."

"Condition of the body bad?" Quist asked.

Ingram's nose wrinkled and he jerked his head in the direction of the body. "Do you have to ask?" Then, "Well he's in better condition than Porter was, anyway. On my preliminary examination I'd say he had been shot a couple of days after Porter."

Arbuckle said, "Dave Eldred said the fellow had been plugged in the back."

"That's right," Ingram nodded. "My guess is it was done with a forty-five, though I can't say for sure until I probe out the slug. Where is Dave, anyway? I intended to send him to my house to get some instruments I'll need."

"I left Dave out front," Corliss explained, "to disperse that crowd that gathered."

"Looks like most of 'em came around to the rear," — Ingram gestured toward the grouped faces looking curiously in at the wide doorway. "Get rid of that bunch, will

171

you, Lish? They're just blocking off a lot of air."

"And you've no idea who the man is, eh?" Quist asked.

Ingram shook his head. "Nobody's come up with an answer yet. You take a look, Quist."

Quist, followed by Corliss and Arbuckle, moved closer to the long table, and drew away the canvas sheet. Cromlech offered, "Tall feller, light hair, 'round thirty-five, I'd say. We just got the clothing off him. Now I got to get some ice —"

Quist cut in, drawing back the sheet. "I never saw him before."

"Nor I," from Arbuckle. "Naturally I'm not well acquainted hereabouts, so —"

"He's a stranger to me," Corliss frowned. He left the table and went to the doorway at the rear, telling the crowd to "scatter and be quick about it." Reluctantly the assembled men began to move off.

Quist started to say something to Deray about the L-Bar-D, then paused. "I'll be back shortly," he said to Arbuckle and Corliss. Without waiting to explain he turned and hurried from the front of the building.

Deray scowled, "Now what in hell got into the railroad dick? He acted as if he was ready to start an argument with me."

"Maybe he was, Deray," Arbuckle said quietly. "Just remember, if he does, he's likely got a good reason — and he's a bad man to argue with. I'll be interested to see what he has to say."

Leaving Cromlech's place, Quist cut diagonally across the street toward the Clarion House and entered the lobby. At the desk he asked the clerk for the number of Kate Porter's room. ". . . or Gene Thornton's room," he added. "It doesn't make any difference."

"I'm sorry, Mr. Quist, they've both checked out."

"You mean they've gone to the Rocking-T?"

"I believe I heard them say something to that effect. I know I saw Mr. Thornton when he brought the horses from the livery stable. Mrs. Porter waited in the lobby until he'd tied them at the hitchrack out in front. I heard Mr. Thornton tell her that there was no need to stay in town any longer, now that the coroner's jury had delivered its verdict."

Quist nodded. "It doesn't matter. I'll see them out at the ranch when I get time. Thanks."

Turning, he left the hotel and walked slowly back toward the undertaker's. Two or

three men nodded to him. Quist returned
their greetings in absent-minded fashion. In
front of Cromlech's place he saw Deray and
Ferris just about to climb to the seat of a
wagon waiting at the tierail. "Just a minute,
Deray," Quist called, and quickened his
step.

The two men moved back, leaning against
the hitchrack. "What's on your mind, railroad dick?" Deray asked insolently.

"Where you heading?"

"Back to the L-Bar-D, if it's any of your
business. Doc and Lish Corliss both said it
would be all right. Ferris wants to get back
to the ranch and get to work again. He's
nigh broke. It'll save him hirin' a bronc at
the livery."

"And he's sure of getting a job with Lombardy, I suppose."

"Sure. Why not? The boss always takes
care of his boys."

"That I can well imagine," Quist said
caustically. "Probably covers up for you
whatever happens."

"Now, you look here —" Ferris started.

Quist snapped, "Shut up, Ferris. I'm talking to Deray."

Ferris "shut up," and looked appealingly
toward Deray. Deray's pale blue, marble-
hard eyes stared steadily at Quist. His

swarthy features tightened. "I don't like what you said — about covering up," he stated harshly. "What you meaning?"

"Put any meaning you like on it," Quist said evenly. "I want to ask you a few questions."

Deray said, "You've got no authority to question me, Quist."

"I've got a hell of a lot more authority than you think. And if I need more, I'll get it from Lish Corliss or Ranger Arbuckle. Whose word carries the most weight with them — yours or mine, Deray?"

Deray considered, then shrugged his shoulders. "All right, have it your way. What's your questions?"

"That body you brought in — who killed that man?"

"I ain't got any idea."

"How'd you happen to find the body?"

Again, Deray shrugged. "Just luck — maybe bad luck — you might say."

"I'm not saying it. I'm waiting for you to tell." Quist's steady gaze bored against Deray's eyes. That was the word. Against. Hard eyes. No fathoming what lay behind them. It was even difficult to see the pupils, and at no moment was Quist absolutely certain the man was looking at him. It was, Quist admitted to himself, rather frustrating.

A harsh laugh twisted Deray's lips. "Let's put it this way, Quist. I was ridin' north, this morning, from the ranch. Had a houn'-dawg with me. We were followin' the trail that runs north. Looking ahead I see a flock of buzzards circling low. So I figgers there must be a cow down at that spot and I moved in to investigate. The buzzards took off when I got there, and I couldn't see a damn' thing. But the houn'-dawg kept a sniffin' and whinin' in some thick brush. Well, there was the body, covered with rock. Satisfied?"

Quist shook his head. "Who put the body there?"

"How the hell you expect me to know? There it was, that's all. Somebody had dug a shallow grave, rolled the corpse in, and piled loose rock a-top of it. So then I come back to the ranch and got a wagon —"

"You expect me to believe that yarn?" Quist asked quietly.

Deray's features worked angrily. His words took on an aggrieved tone. "Why in hell not?"

"I don't think there'd be a whole flock of buzzards hovering over a grave that was piled with rock and was underneath thick brush. Generally buzzards go for anything dead out in the open — now, wait!" —

sharply — "I don't doubt the body was as you say you found it — but I don't think the buzzards led you to the spot."

"You calling me a liar?" Deray demanded.

"I haven't yet, but it's not a bad idea," Quist said scornfully.

"By God, Quist! You act like you wanted trouble," Deray flared and one hand moved down toward his holster.

Quist's left hand flicked to his coat lapel, his right hand flashed to his shoulder holster. Here he paused, saying, even-voiced, "Yes, I do, Deray. Do you feel like taking part of it?"

Deray hesitated, eyes more opaque than ever. Quist cast a swift glance at Ferris who had shrunk back against the tierail, face white. There were horses and wagons on either side of the three men and no one happened to be passing at the time, so the scene went unnoticed. Slowly, Deray's right hand moved well out from his holster. Reluctantly he muttered, almost to himself, "Yeah — but not now. The time's not ripe. So you use a hideout gun —"

Quist's short contemptuous laugh cut in on the words. "Let me know when the time is right, Deray, now that we both know where we stand. Meanwhile, what's the trouble between your outfit and the

Rocking-T?"

Deray hesitated. "Who said there was any trouble? Porter used to come visiting, friendly-like —"

"I don't consider Porter as a real part of the Rocking-T. Corliss has mentioned there's bad blood between the two outfits."

"All right, so there is, but it started before I went on the L-Bar-D payroll. You'd better ask Judd Lombardy about it. All's I know, old man Thornton wants to hawg all the range in these parts — him and his daughter. Porter was willing to give Judd a break, but old Thornton and Kate they said no. They act so high and mighty like they was —"

"All right, I've heard enough," Quist said shortly. "You can get going now."

"You think I got to wait for your permission to leave?" Deray demanded hotly.

"I note you stayed until I got through questioning you," Quist jeered, and turned away.

Goaded by his anger and the taunt in Quist's tones, Deray threw discretion to the winds, reaching for his six-shooter with one hand while with the other he seized Ferris and swept the unsuspecting man in front of him as a barrier.

But the maneuver with Ferris occupied

Deray to an extent that slowed his draw, and before he quite realized what had happened Quist had whirled completely around and sent a shot winging from his .44 Colt gun. Powder-smoke swirled in the air.

Ferris emitted a wild yelp of pain and slumped down, twisting loose from Deray's grip, and partly jerking Deray off balance. The man cursed, but his gun wasn't yet out of holster, when Quist spoke:

"Get it out and go to work if you think you've got a chance, Deray," Quist said, tones icy-cold, .44 level on Deray's body.

Deray's mouth sagged open. Slowly he shook his head and held his hands level with his chest. "No," he said, and again, "No — I've had enough, Quist," the words coming hard.

"Suckered into it, weren't you?" Quist said contemptuously. "Thought when I turned away, you had me just where —"

Excited yells along the street drowned the words. Men came running and gathered at the hitchrack. Ferris was prone on the earth, moaning. Arbuckle and Lish Corliss came plunging from the undertaker's doorway, followed by Doc Ingram. Quickly they made their way around the hitchrack to reach Quist's side.

"What in the devil's happened, Greg?"

Corliss exclaimed.

"I had a little discussion with Deray, and he objected to what I had to say. When I turned away to leave, he didn't figure on me making a circle so's I could face him again and draw at the same time. What I didn't figure on the bustard doing was jerking Ferris in front of him to shield himself from my fire. At the same time he was so busy with Ferris he couldn't get his own iron out. And it was too late to hold my fire —"

"A doctor," Ferris groaned, "get me to a doctor."

"I don't think he's bad hurt," Quist said. "When I saw what was happening I shifted aim at the last instant. And then" — Quist laughed shortly — "Deray just lacked guts to get on with what he'd started." Deray cleared his throat but he remained silent.

Quist added various details while Ingram bent over Ferris. In a minute, the doctor rose and said disgustedly, "I don't figure Ferris is damaged much. Get him into Cromlech's and I'll see if I can't glue him together again."

Deray had been standing without saying a word, though he still kept his hands high. Corliss started toward him, "I reckon you'll be better off in a cell, Deray —"

"Let him go," Quist said. "I'm making no charges."

"But, Greg," Arbuckle protested, "you say he was going to plug you in the back. He'd best be in jail."

Quist shook his head. "Let him go," he said again. "I don't want him cooped up. He's talked bad medicine. I've won this hand. I want to see if he has the guts to try again."

Corliss looked dubious. "We-ell, if you say so." He turned to Deray. "Get going, mister. Climb up on that wagon and get back to the L-Bar-D as fast as that team will haul your dirty back-shooting carcass."

"And the next time you show your face in town —" Arbuckle threatened, but the words weren't finished. Ferris had started to groan again. Deray without another word climbed to the driver's seat, backed the horses and headed them at a fast gait out of town. Quist plugged the empty shell from his gun cylinder, inserted a fresh cartridge from the handful in his pocket, and shoved the gun back in its holster. Arbuckle eyed him curiously.

"You sure must have got that underarm gun into action fast," the ranger said.

"Not so fast, considering," Quist replied. "I half expected Deray to act as he did the minute I turned my back —"

"For God's sake," Ingram interposed, "will you men get Ferris into Cromlech's so I can stop that sheep-bleating of his? Lucky Eldred got back with my instruments. Looks like I'll have another slug to remove now."

The crowd was dispersed and Ferris led to the back room of Cromlech's place. Ferris' wound proved to be slight: Quist's bullet had lodged just under the skin below the left ribs, and the man was more frightened than hurt. To escape the sound of his yelling while Ingram extracted the slug from Ferris' side, Quist, Arbuckle and Corliss once more made their way to the street and stood smoking at the hitchrack.

Quist said, "Didn't learn anything more about that man's identity, did you?"

"A little," Corliss said. "Fred and I went through his clothing. We figure he was somebody named Mead Leftwick — but I don't think anybody around here knows him."

"How'd you get the name?" Quist asked.

Arbuckle said, "The butt of his six-shooter, that was still in the holster, had initials stamped M.L. There were two old receipted bills in his coat pocket from hotels — one from the Menger Hotel in San Antonio and the other from the Driskill

Hotel in Austin — made out to one Mead Leftwick. Also three letters were found in the pockets of the clothing, one each to Mead Leftwick addressed to the Menger Hotel, the Driskill Hotel and the Hotel Palace in Denver."

Quist said dryly, "Sounds like the dead hombre's name must be Mead Leftwick. Letters give you any information?"

Corliss shook his head. "Not much. One each addressed to Leftwick at the Hotels Menger and Driskill stated simply that 'shipment has been received. Your check being forwarded today.' Both letters were signed by Uhlmann Wholesale Company, Chicago, Illinois."

"No particular name signed?" Quist asked, frowning. Corliss shook his head. Quist said, "How about the third letter?"

"That was signed," Arbuckle said, "Drumm & Tidwell Company, San Francisco, and merely stated, 'Shipment goes forward on the thirteenth of this month, as per request.' That was dated five months back, Greg. The other letters were dated two and three months ago. What do you make of it?"

Quist frowned. "Hell's-bells on a tomcat! I don't make anything of it, Lish. It's a puzzle to me. Drumm & Tidwell is the company that shipped the preserves I'm trying to run down. Uhlmann Wholesale was the consignee. I'll see what I can do about checking on those two companies, to see what connection they have — or had — with some hombre named Leftwick. Meanwhile, why don't you shoot a telegram to those hotels — Menger, Driskill and Palace — and learn if they can tell you anything about Mead Leftwick? You may get some sort of lead in that direction."

"I'll do that," the sheriff said. "We'll see what can be turned up."

The three men stood talking and speculating some minutes longer on the sidewalk before Cromlech's Undertaking Parlors. Ferris came walking slowly from the entrance of the building, his face very white. He slipped past Quist and the other two without saying a word, holding his side and with an agonized expression on his features. The three men followed him with their eyes and saw him enter the Warbonnet Saloon, a few doors beyond Main Street.

Arbuckle grinned. "Well, Ferris isn't hurt so bad that it destroyed his taste for liquor, I reckon."

"That type," Quist smiled, "is damn' hard to discourage where a taste for liquor is concerned. Come to think of it, if I'd been plugged with a .44 and had the slug extracted, I'd welcome a couple of fingers of whisky myself."

"Who wouldn't?" Corliss chuckled.

Doc Ingram, followed by Mort Cromlech, appeared from the doorway of the undertaking establishment. Ingram said, "Ferris wasn't bad hurt. He yelled like a stuck pig while I was probing out your slug, Greg, but that just showed he was a mite yellow. I bandaged him up, and he'll feel as good as new, come mornin'. That .44 bullet scarcely got under his skin."

"What about that dead man Deray brought in?" Quist asked.

Ingram frowned. "Nobody seems to know who he is. I've arranged with Mort to have his body on view through tomorrow morning, to see if anybody hereabouts knows him. Lish, will you pass the word around town that I'd like to have folks take a look at this unknown hombre, and see if we can learn anything about him."

"I'll do that," Corliss said. "Y'know, I keep thinking about that hombre being plugged in the back, and then I think about Deray waiting until Greg's back was turned before going for his gun."

"You figuring Deray shot this Leftwick hombre?" Arbuckle asked.

185

"I'm damned if I know," the sheriff confessed. "But it's something to think about."

Arbuckle said, "Yeah — maybe." He didn't seem entirely convinced.

Quist said, "Suppose nobody appears who can tell us anything about Leftwick, Doc?"

"We'll hold an inquest tomorrow afternoon," Ingram said. "Get any testimony that's possible, then bury the man at county expense. I don't know what else we can do, do you, Greg?"

"Damned if I know what to say," Quist replied slowly. "I just hate to have that fellow put under earth until we get more chance to learn something about him." He turned to Arbuckle and Corliss. "What about Leftwick's clothing? Cow country stuff?"

"Cow country, probably," Corliss replied, "but not cowman. In the first place, Leftwick's hands didn't show the calluses a puncher acquires in his work. At the same time, worn places in the pants showed he'd done plenty of riding." Quist asked a question. Corliss said, "Nothing unusual about the togs. Dark gray woolen pants, flannel shirt, necktie, instead of a bandanna. You see dozens of similar sombreros every day. One thing did sort of bother me. Cromlech swears that when he undressed the body, the pant-legs were outside the boots. And yet the lower part of the pant-legs were unfaded, as though Leftwick had been accustomed to tucking them into his boot-tops — knee-length boots, incidentally. Make anything of that, Greg?"

Quist shrugged. "Not at the moment. Maybe the guy was used to tucking his pants in his boots, but the last time he dressed he was in a hurry, and just let 'em hang." He turned to Ingram, "Look here, Doc, can you postpone the inquest on Leftwick for a spell?"

"Why?" Ingram wanted to know.

"I'm not sure," Quist admitted. "I'm just working on a hunch. Maybe if we stall off the inquest, something will turn up to give us some facts to go on."

"How long would you want the inquest postponed?" Ingram asked.

"I'm not sure about that, either," Quist stated. "I'm just asking that you keep that body on tap until I say go ahead with the burial."

"Hey, Mr. Quist," Mort Cromlech protested, "don't you realize holding that body will cost money? Ice don't come cheap in this country."

Impatiently, Quist said, "You'll get your money — and I don't care if it costs enough to cover the whole town with ice —"

"It'll be expensive," Ingram cut in. "I'm not sure the county will approve a cost of that sort —"

Quist half snarled, "Nobody's asking your county to approve anything, Doc. Charge the cost to the T.N. & A.S. I'll be responsible for my company paying."

"Well, if you insist —" Ingram began dubiously.

"I do insist," Quist snapped.

Arbuckle asked, "Greg, what do you know that we don't?"

"I'm not sure I know a blasted thing," Quist said morosely. "Dammit, didn't I just tell you I was working on a hunch? And I learned long ago not to disregard hunches. I can't say why, but I just feel I'm working in the right direction. Sure, maybe it sounds foolish to you, but I'm so sick of problems cropping up that can't be explained, that I'm ready to try something else — something foolish."

Arbuckle smiled. "Seems I've heard it said that when Greg Quist acts foolish — he's acting foolish like a fox."

Quist glared at the ranger, but didn't make any reply.

[XIII]
SUSPECTS

Quist spent the remainder of the afternoon strolling around, visiting barrooms here and there, listening to conversations in the hope of picking up information that might prove valuable, but he had to admit when, just before supper time, he dropped into the Amber Cup for a beer, he knew little more than he had known before. Men had talked quite freely when questioned, but Quist had gained nothing definite on which to act. A couple of times Ellen Bristol's name had entered the conversation, connected with not only Porter and Gene Thornton, but Damaret Gilmore, owner of the Diamond-G, as well. One man claimed to have overheard a quarrel between Porter and Gene some five weeks previously, in which the girl's name had played a part. Quist remembered now that Doc Ingram had commented that Gene "wanted to make good," on Ellen's account. Quist mused, "It might pay to get acquainted with that girl and ask a few questions."

By the time he'd finished his beer and stepped out to the street, the sun was low behind the tumbled ridges of the Clarín Mountains, the Devil's Drum being silhouetted sharply against the reddening sky. Stores along Main Street were being closed for the day. When Quist had gone to his hotel room, shaved and changed his shirt and again descended to the lobby, the dining room looked quite full. He noticed a girl standing in the lobby as he passed through, but beyond taking note of the fact she was of slight build and extremely pretty, he thought nothing of the matter, judging she was waiting for someone.

There was a buzz of conversation in the dining room and the sounds of cutlery and dishes. The door leading to the kitchen seemed almost continually in motion as waiters passed through. Quist glanced over the room and saw but one table unoccupied, and that in a far corner. He sat down and within a few minutes his order for ham and fried potatoes had been taken. The waiter had scarcely left when, glancing around, Quist saw the girl he'd noticed in the lobby, just entering. She looked uncertainly about, seeking a table; with the exception of Quist's all the tables were filled. The girl started toward him, then paused. Quist, sensing what was in her mind, immediately rose and indicated a place across from his own. She approached immediately.

"Do you mind if I sit at your table?"

"On the contrary," Quist replied, "I'd be honored." He drew out a chair for her, then reseated himself. He added something about the dining room being crowded, which was interrupted by the waiter arriving for her order. A few minutes later he said, "May I introduce myself? I'm Gregory Quist."

The girl smiled. "I doubt there's anyone in Clarion City doesn't know Mr. Quist. Just your coming here created something of a stir. You're quite famous." Quist protested that in polite tones. The girl went on, "I'm Ellen Bristol. I have a ladies' goods shop here."

Quist nodded. "I believe we have mutual friends — Gene Thornton and Mrs. Porter." Ellen Bristol made some appropriate remark. The girl was definitely pretty, somewhere in the vicinity of Gene's age, though probably a year or two older. She had very dark hair, almost ravenwing black, parted in the center and drawn to a big knot at her nape. Her eyes were a deep blue, well spaced, her face oval, the lips full and red. There was a touch of lace at the throat and wrists on the dress she wore. Not tall and with small bones.

Conversation lagged. Food arrived and they commenced to eat. Quist noticed the girl appeared slightly nervous. Once or twice she had appeared about to say something, then changed her mind. Quist washed down a chunk of ham with a swallow of coffee, and said quietly, "Miss Bristol, what's on your mind? You were waiting in the lobby when I passed through. You undoubtedly knew the dining room was filling up and yet you waited until I was seated, before coming in." He smiled suddenly and the girl read the laughter in his topaz eyes and knew he'd not been fooled. "And so there you were, a poor helpless woman, and only one table left at which you might find a seat. You did want to talk to me about something, didn't you?"

Ellen Bristol bit her lip. "It was a pretty cheap trick, wasn't it, Mr. Quist?"

"Let's call it a maneuver that didn't fool anyone — I'm afraid not even some of the people in this dining room. Conversation at various spots sort of picked up when you decided to come to my table."

The girl gave a slight shrug, chewed a moment at a morsel of food. "Conversation where I'm concerned has picked up before. I try to ignore it, not —"

"Fight as Kate Porter does?" Quist put in. "Well, I'm not sure which provides the best defense. But you did want to talk to me, didn't you?"

The girl said directly, "I wanted to talk to you as soon as Kate told me she was going to try to bring you here."

"Mrs. Porter told you — ?"

"We're quite good friends. I sold her her traveling outfit, just before she left to see you in El Paso." Ellen Bristol smiled. "I don't think she cared much for it. Kate feels more at home in range togs than anything else, I guess" — she paused — "anyway, that's what she says nowdays."

"She's carrying a 'range-togs' job, I hear," Quist said, smiling, "though I seem to remember a very feminine bonnet covered with violets." Ellen Bristol smiled, and Quist concluded, "Anyway, we were to talk about you, not Mrs. Porter. Exactly what is it you want to tell me?"

"I wanted to ask you to do all possible to find Lloyd Porter's murderer, Mr. Quist." The girl explained, "I think the sooner that is cleared up, the happier Kate will be. Things will straighten themselves out, and Gene — well, Gene will be more happy." Her last words came with a rush, "I love Gene terribly, Mr. Quist, and the sooner we can be married —" She seemed very earnest.

"Doc Ingram gave me to understand

something like that was in the wind," Quist said. "But is there any reason why Gene can't marry you now, Miss Bristol?"

Apparently, there were a number of reasons. Gene wanted to make a name as an artist. He didn't want to get married while Kate was in trouble. There seemed to be talk, since the inquest, that Lloyd Porter wasn't the man found dead and that increased the difficulties. There'd been trouble about Porter too . . . Quist broke in on the girl's talk: "What sort of trouble did you have with Porter?"

Ellen hesitated, then, "If I don't tell you, you'll hear it around town. The fact is, Lloyd Porter visited my shop much oftener than I cared to see him. It caused a great deal of talk, but I couldn't seem to get rid of him. There was trouble —"

"You mean, Gene threatened to kill him if he didn't stay away from you." It was a statement rather than a question.

The girl gasped, "I didn't say that at all —"

"You said more than you intended to say, Miss Bristol. I can tell from your manner that I made a good guess. All right, if it makes you uncomfortable, we'll drop the subject, so far as Gene's threats are concerned. But I can't see why Porter couldn't

194

be stopped from bothering you. A word to Sheriff Corliss, or Marshal Eldred —"

"That would just have made more talk around town — it might have brought things into more prominence."

"What things?" Quist asked. "Apparently, you feared Porter. Why?"

The girl bent silently over her food. Quist swallowed a couple more mouthfuls while he waited. Finally she lifted her head. "I think I've said enough, Mr. Quist. I seem to be involving others. Just please remember that I've never fired a shotgun in my life."

"Great Christopher!" Quist exclaimed. "I've not suspected you. Whatever gave you the idea — ?"

The girl said again, "I think I've said enough, Mr. Quist. For the present." Nervously, her fingers plucked at the cloth on the table. "But please do one thing for me. If you hear of — of anything — concerning me, will you please first give me a chance to explain, before taking any action?"

"Of course," Quist promised, smiling. "Now forget your troubles for a while. We'll talk no more about Porter. I'm afraid this conversation has spoiled your dinner. Tell me about yourself . . ."

The girl's manner changed and she talked of early school days in San Antonio, of experience in dressmaking and millinery. "There seemed to be better opportunities in a small town," she said. "Clarion City seemed progressive, so I came here to open my shop . . ." By the time supper was concluded and Quist was lighting a cigar, the girl seemed gay and cheerful, though Quist could tell she had something on her mind. He accompanied her out to the lobby, asking if he could pay for her supper. When she refused with thanks, he didn't press the offer.

When she had left the hotel, he stood on the gallery mulling over what he had heard. It was dark along Main Street now; only a few lights shone here and there. The end of his cigar glowed and died in the darkness. "Dammit," he growled at last, "she was holding something back. What was it? Something she was afraid I might uncover. Else, why ask me to give her a chance to explain before taking action?" He added a trifle bitterly, "I wish to hell pretty women would stay out of my job."

He left the hotel gallery and strode down to the depot to see if any telegrams had arrived for him. None had, but he took the opportunity while there to send a wire to the T.N. & A.S. operative in San Antonio. That done, he walked around town a while and eventually wound up at Lish Corliss' office, only to find that the sheriff wasn't there. Turning back, he passed the Chinese restaurant and saw Fred Arbuckle through the window, seated within. "Looks like Fred goes for those steaks," Quist chuckled, and walked on. Eventually he ended up at the Amber Cup Saloon where he requested a bottle of beer "not too cold."

There were only a few customers in the saloon as yet. Mickey Kurtz made him acquainted with two of them, Damaret Gilmore, lean, thin-faced, with high cheek-bones, and owner of the Diamond-G Ranch; and the burly Jarvis Fanchon, who ran the Jar-F outfit. Both were in their early thirties. Gilmore had the sort of reddish complexion that usually accompanies a hot temper. Fanchon had the features of a man who is always on the defensive and always fears to get the worst of a bargain. Quist put him down as a grudge-holder, having heard Fanchon made various derogatory remarks about local people.

The two men had been apparently discussing some sort of mutual cattle deal, or trade, so Quist, after shaking hands with them, moved his bottle of beer farther along the bar. When that was empty he ordered a second bottle. Arbuckle showed up after a time and joined him in a drink. Arbuckle said,

"I cornered Luke Ferris down the street a spell back, and —"

"Able to get around, is he?" Quist said.

"Hell, he was lucky. Your slug just furrowed in under the skin. No worse a wound than you and I have had many a time in just ordinary work. 'Course, he belly-aches a lot and swears he'll get even with you. I pointed out to the damn' fool it was Deray's fault for shoving him in front of your gun —"

"You said something about cornering him," Quist reminded.

"Oh, yeah. You know we were wondering just how he got here from Albuquerque. Well, I persuaded him to 'fess up. He never bought a ticket for that train. What he did was sneak on that train and ride between the coaches."

"Bummed a ride, eh?" Quist laughed. "The law provides penalties for cheating a railroad of its due fare. If he starts to get tough with me I'll threaten him with prosecution."

Arbuckle grinned. "Yeah — I can imagine you bothering your head over small scum like Ferris." He sobered. "But damned if I could shake the scut's story that he talked to Porter yesterday." Kurtz came along the bar and turned higher one of the oil-lamps swinging overhead. Arbuckle watched the bartender, then straightened from his lounging position on the bar. "Well, I've got to get along to my room and write a letter to Captain Craig about developments here. Hate letter-writing worse'n poison, too — but there's too much to put in a telegram." He and Quist chatted a few minutes longer, then the ranger took his departure.

Ten minutes passed. Judd Lombardy entered, followed by a man Quist was to learn later was named Tank Janney, foreman of the L-Bar-D. Lombardy tried to appear friendly as he introduced Janney to Quist. All of Lombardy's men appeared turned from the same mold, a matrix that turned out heavy-featured hard-eyed individuals with unshaven jaws and scarred gunholsters. Lombardy asked Quist to have a drink, but Quist refused, indicating his unemptied bottle of beer. Kurtz served Janney and Lombardy. They downed their drinks at a gulp and Lombardy said, "I was hoping to find you in here, Quist."

"Some particular reason?" Quist asked politely.

Lombardy nodded. "I wanted to apologize

on Gilly Deray's behalf for what happened today."

"No apology necessary," Quist said. "It wasn't any trouble for me. Maybe it cleared the air some and showed Deray how far he can go."

"He knows all right," Lombardy agreed. "Trouble with Gilly, he just tried to mount a bronc on the wrong side and the critter throwed him. He realizes it too. He admitted frank that he was in the wrong. Only excuse he has, is he lost his temper."

"I reckon," Quist nodded. "A temper's a bad thing to have, but a good thing to keep."

Janney put in with a coarse laugh, "Gilly will keep his temper from now on I reckon, after the hide-strippin' Judd give him."

"That's right," Lombardy nodded. "I give Gilly plenty hell. 'Course, maybe you give him some provocation, Quist."

"In what way?" Quist demanded.

"We-ell" — Lombardy seemed more uncertain now — "you sort of doubted his story about finding that dead hombre, and he was talkin' Gawd's truth, too. Then you mentioned the trouble between me and the Rocking-T outfit, like maybe somebody in my outfit was responsible for Porter's death — if he is dead. Ferris swears he talked to —"

"I didn't say that at all, but maybe it's an idea, Lombardy. How do I know *you* didn't kill Porter?"

Lombardy's eyes bugged out. "You crazy, Quist?" he exclaimed. "Why should I kill Porter — ?"

"I haven't found out — yet."

"Oh, now, look here, Quist — well, hell, yes, I've had some trouble over grazing privileges with the Thornton folks, but it wa'n't no killing matter. Besides, Porter and me were friends. He used to visit regular and play poker —"

"Men have been killed in poker games before this," Quist pointed out. "How do I know — ?"

Lombardy swore an oath that carried through the room, causing others at the bar to turn from their drinks. "Goddamit, Quist!" He half shouted, "You're just trying to make trouble for me and my crew. I could name three or four men who had more reason to kill Porter than I ever had — not that I ever had —"

"I doubt it," Quist said insultingly. "I'd be surprised if you could name even one hombre who'd be li'ble to kill Porter —"

"I'll show you, by God!" Lombardy snarled, voice rising higher than he realized. "One?" He laughed nastily. "Ask Morley

Harper, of the Golden Wheel, about the time Porter hit him over the head with a whisky bottle. Find out if Harper has an alibi —"

"I never even heard of this Harper —"

"I'll name names you have heard of then," Lombardy raged. "Ask Jarv Fanchon what he was fighting with Porter about, down on the corner of Austin and Main, the day before Porter disappeared. Ask —"

From farther down the bar, Fanchon snapped, "What's that you said, Lombardy?"

"— ask anybody that seen that fight if I'm not speaking truth," Lombardy raged, carried beyond reason by his anger. "Hell! Why don't you question the sheriff? Everybody in town knows he threatened to kill Porter." His eyes blazed at Quist. "Tell me I can't even name one name. And there's Damaret Gilmore. Ask folks about the fight he had with Porter over Ellen Bristol —" Lombardy paused for breath. "And Kate Porter's own brother said he'd kill Porter if —"

That was as far as Lombardy got. There came a rush of footsteps along the bar as Damaret Gilmore closed in, seized Lombardy by the shirt and swung him around. "You'll keep her name out of this, you foulmouthed skunk!" Gilmore roared as his right fist landed hard on Lombardy's nose.

Lombardy sat down hard, blood running from mouth and nostrils, then heaved himself up from haunches, right hand clawing at his gun-butt. Gilmore backed off, also reaching to holster.

"Hold it!" Quist said sharply. As though by magic the .44 had appeared in his right fist. "You, Lombardy — Gilmore! Keep your paws off those guns —"

"An' keep 'em off fast," Mickey Kurtz growled, coming up from behind his bar with a sawed-off double-barreled shotgun, which he swung menacingly toward the two would-be combatants. "I don't want no trouble in my place, you hear?"

Lombardy and Gilmore glared at each other, but slowly relaxed, and resumed their places at the bar, Lombardy muttering something about getting even before long. Jarvis Fanchon's face worked angrily as he opened his mouth to say something to Lombardy, then he thought better of it, and lined up beside Gilmore.

"That's better," Quist said. "Maybe this was partly my fault. I goaded Lombardy into saying things he might not have said in a cooler frame of mind, but that's no sign there's going to be any killing here, on my account. Mickey, you can put that scatter-gun away. The boys have simmered down considerable, I figure."

"Just the same, Mr. Quist, I'm obliged to you for acting quick like you did," the bartender said.

Quist smiled thinly. "I had a reason. There're certain things to be learned before I leave this town, and I never yet heard of a dead man doing any testifying, did you, Mickey?" He turned to the others. "All right, certain names have been named. I hope everyone of them can prove an alibi when the time comes for a showdown —"

"Hell, Quist, you ain't suspecting me!" Gilmore looked aghast. Fanchon voiced a similar remark.

"I'm suspecting everybody and anybody until they're proved innocent," Quist snapped. "Now think it over, you hombres. I'll be glad to hear your alibis when you find a good one." He turned back to Lombardy. "In view of what's just happened, maybe it would be a good idea if you and your foreman did your drinking some place else for the evening —"

Lombardy flared up. "You ordering me and Tank out of here?"

"Not at all," Quist said mildly. "I was just making a peaceful suggestion." He looked steadily at Lombardy.

Lombardy's gaze dropped after a minute. "Could be you're right, Quist. C'mon, Tank, let's drift across to the Warbonnet."

Quist watched the two men leave. Gilmore edged along the bar. "Look here, Quist, I've just been talking it over with Jarv. On the day Doc Ingram figured Porter was killed, Jarv Fanchon was at my ranch. We've been working on a trade —"

"So you alibi each other, eh?" Quist smiled. "That's fine."

Fanchon bristled. "You act like you don't believe us."

"I didn't say that, but think it over, hombres." He paused, then, "Lombardy mentioned somebody named Morley Harper. Who's he?"

"Owns the Golden Wheel — gambling house," Gilmore said sulkily. "On the corner of Alamo, right across from the Mex restaurant. He's not in town, at present. Up in Denver."

"You know of any trouble he had with Porter?" Quist asked.

Gilmore hesitated. "You'd better ask Harper about that. There's already been too much name-spilling here tonight."

"But not enough facts made public," Quist said coldly. "You and Fanchon think it over, and when you decide to tell me of your troubles with Porter, I'll be glad to listen." Gilmore growled something unintelligible and swung back to the bar. Fanchon glared angrily at Quist a moment, then followed suit. Quist laughed softly. "Sorry if I've disrupted your evening, gentlemen, but remember confession is good for the soul." He nodded pleasantly and with an *"Adiós,"* to the bartender, sauntered out to the street and headed in the direction of the depot.

He chuckled with some elation as he strode along. "Get a man mad and he'll really spill over," he mused. "Lord! Plenty of suspects. First, Lish Corliss, then Jarv Fanchon and Gilmore. Maybe I'd better rule out Gene Thornton — maybe. And some hombre named Morley Harper. All scrapping with Porter sometime or other. Until I know more, the little Ellen Bristol will bear watching perhaps . . . Hmmmm. . . ."

At the depot he found a telegram from Jay Fletcher awaiting him. It read:

BOTH UHLMANN WHOLESALE AND DRUMM & TIDWELL SMALL COMPANIES. LATTER REFUSES COMPANY CLAIM SETTLEMENT FOR LOSS OF JAM. DEMANDS EXORBITANT SUM OR THREATENS SUIT. SUGGEST YOU EXPE-

Quist read the telegram through a second time and felt his ire rising. Angrily, he crumpled the paper and stuck it into one coat pocket, as he left the lighted depot. "Expedite search strawberry jam!" he snorted, striding out to the deserted station platform. "Damn that Jay Fletcher! What in hell does he think I am, some grocery man's clerk? All that fuss over a few cans of preserves."

Abruptly, the humor of the situation rose above his anger and he burst into a howl of laughter. He was still grinning widely by the time he reached his hotel room. Here he lighted the oil lamp and started to remove his coat. His gaze strayed to the table where lay a small brown bonnet covered with cloth violets. Slowly, the grin died from his face. "Maybe," he told himself, "my time for laughing hasn't come yet."

[XIV]
A Pair of Clues

The hotel dining room wasn't yet open when Quist stepped through the lobby the following morning, and the night clerk was still on duty. The man said something about

Quist being an early riser. Quist agreed and kept going through to the street. There weren't many people abroad yet. None of the stores were open; hitchracks were deserted. Quist found a small all night restraurant and grabbed a hasty breakfast, then headed for the White Star Livery where he had arranged the previous afternoon to hire a horse and saddle. Here a sleepy-eyed liveryman waited, yawning, while Quist saddled his mount, a rangy, clean-limbed buckskin animal.

Heading west on Main, Quist walked the horse to the edge of town, where a plank bridge crossed Clarín Creek — it was only a few yards wide at this point, though the banks were high and steep — before spurring the buckskin into an easy lope across the open range of waving mesquite, sagebrush and prickly pear; grama grass appeared here and there, though in insufficient quantity to provide good grazing. The horse moved steadily ahead, and at the end of a half hour, Quist was satisfied that he had a good mount under him.

His course was roughly paralleling the T.N. & A.S. right-of-way, the tracks of which ran to his left until they'd disappeared beyond Shoulder Bluff, which still lay nine or ten miles ahead. Shoulder Bluff marked the southernmost end of the Clarín Mountains, now touched with gold along their upper ridges. South of the big craggy bluff, the range flattened out to a wide spread of catclaw, creosote bush and gray sandy soil. Toward the northwest, lifting high against the turquoise sky, was The Devil's Drum, it's stratified rounded face detailed clearly in the bright morning sun, appearing closer than it actually was. The sun was warming on Quist's back now, after the chill of early morning.

His forehead was creased with thought as he rode. "I don't know," he speculated dubiously. "Maybe I'm just wasting time coming out here. Ten to one there won't be a damn' thing to see worth while. But when a man gets a hunch, it's been my experience he'd best act accordingly." He chuckled, "Anyway, I'll be able to tell Jay Fletcher I visited the 'scene of the crime,' and he won't be able to claim I'm neglecting my duty."

Occasionally, great outcroppings of tall sandstone were passed, rising above the range plant growths. The terrain lifted gradually. Once Quist stopped to rest the horse, while he rolled and smoked a cigarette. He again mounted and pushed on. Abruptly the railroad tracks to his left began to hum, announcing an approaching train.

Within a few minutes a passenger train, eastbound, rushed past, the fireman lifting one gloved hand to wave when he saw Quist. Quist raised one arm in reply, thinking, "Well, #16 wasn't delayed by any landslide, anyway," just before a cloud of black smoke rushed down to envelop him. The roar of the train faded at his rear, and the smoke dissipated in the clear air; cinders ceased showering down.

Three-quarters of an hour later, Quist had reached the point in the tracks where they curved widely to round Shoulder Bluff. He guided the pony up the slight incline of the right-of-way and the animal carefully picked its path across the ties and gleaming rails. A few yards beyond the tracks Quist turned the buckskin and pulled to a halt while he looked around. As he had half suspected, there was little to see.

High above him rose Shoulder Bluff, the signs of a dynamite explosion still visible in the cracked surfaces of sandstone and sandy earth. On either side of the right-of-way was considerable debris showing how the work-train had disposed of tons of earth and great split rocks that the tracks might once more be cleared for passage of trains.

"I'll bet that work crew slaved like hell to get the line cleared," Quist mused. "It must have been a hell of a job." Here and there plant growth was crushed flat by great chunks of sandstone. Gravel was piled high at spots. "It was a man-made landslide all right."

He sat his saddle, surveying the scene, in his imagination seeing the point at which the locomotive had come to a panting halt. His gaze ranged along the tracks, counting a space where each freight car had stood waiting. "If I remember rightly," Quist pondered, "that report Nugent showed me stated that the car that was opened was the fifth one from the rear, not counting the caboose."

Acting on the impulse of the moment, he dismounted and dropped his reins on the earth. Then he started walking along the tracks, scrutinizing the ground on either side. Now there was no debris from the landslide to bar his path. Nothing but sandy gravelly soil and low sparse plant growth. What he was looking for, Quist had not the least idea. As he put it to himself, he was still following his hunch. After a month's time, there'd be no footprints certainly, and whoever had placed the dynamite would have had no occasion to come to track level. That job had been done half way up the bluff itself.

Abruptly, a few feet from the left-hand track, Quist spied a splinter of raw pine wood. It looked fairly new and was only a few inches long by a half wide. It looked like something that might have been broken from a packing box of some sort. Quist remembered now something else in the report he had read: Conductor Fraley of train #24 had stated that when the boxes of preserves were being unloaded, teamster Pardee had dropped one box to the earth and it had burst open. Time had been lost while the contents of the box were retrieved and repacked.

And then something about three yards farther on caught Quist's eyes. For a moment he just stared, then said softly, "I reckon those cans weren't repacked very carefully. Just tossed in careless like I reckon. And teamster Pardee missed a couple."

He took three quick strides, stooped and picked up a couple of tin cans, lying almost side by side. Tops and bottoms of the cans were rusted, but the labels, though faded by days of blistering sun, were almost intact. Quist read the label on one can: Drum Brand Strawberry Jam (though the red of the drum was a washed-out pink by this time); Contents 14 oz. gross; Drumm &

Tidwell Co., San Francisco, California. There was further smaller lettering having to do with "finest fruit procurable" and sugar content.

Quist gazed at the cans he held. He shoved back his sombrero and scratched his head. "I suppose I might figure this is some sort of clue — two clues — but just how they help, I'm dam'd if I know." Suddenly he chuckled, "I've got a notion to send a telegram to Jay Fletcher, saying, 'Dear Jay. Search expedited. Two cans being forwarded.' Wow! Jay really would fly off the handle."

Finally he slipped a can in each coat pocket, strode back to the buckskin and mounted.

It was nearing noon when Quist first sighted the Rocking-T Ranch buildings, surrounded by stately old live-oaks. There was the ranch house proper, a low rambling building of rock-and-adobe structure, fronted with a wide gallery and overhanging roof. Fifty yards back of the house were barns, corrals, a blacksmith shop and combination bunk-house and cook shack. Quist heard the steady clank-clank of a windmill as the vanes turned steadily in the warm breeze. "A darn nice looking spread," he com-

213

mented mentally, as he drew near.

There was no one in sight near the house, so Quist guided his pony down toward the bunkhouse. A couple of men in range togs sat on a bench near the bunkhouse door, both slightly under middle-age, and both grizzled bronzed specimens of the cowman of that day. One of them spoke to Quist and Quist gave his name, as he dismounted. The man proved to be Chan Yount, foreman of the outfit; the other was named Olcott and was one of the hands. Sowbelly Handson, the ranch cook, an individual with a thick middle, long mustaches and a red nose, put in an appearance from his cookhouse and got into the conversation, while Quist and Yount were shaking hands.

"Won't be many in to eat today, Mr. Quist," Handson invited, "but we'll have some chow on the table inside the hour. You're welcome to stay."

"Thanks," Quist nodded. "I'll be able to use some food."

Yount spoke to the hand, "Gus, you take care of Mr. Quist's bronc. Put 'im in that corral with the other saddlers, when he's been watered." Olcott moved away with Quist's horse.

Quist said, "I was hoping to see Mrs. Porter or Gene."

"Miz Porter," Yount said, "ain't to home. Wyatt — that's her paw — I reckon you knowed he was crippled up some — he was feelin' pretty good this mornin', and he allowed to do some ridin'. Miz Porter rode with him like she always does. Gene, he's 'round some place. Last time I see him he was headed 'tother side of that barn yonderly. Had his paintin' tackle with him, so like's not he makin' some picters. Gene's right good at it too. Go stir 'im up. Tell him chow time's nigh. Once he gits to paintin', time don't mean nothin' to him and he forgets to eat."

Quist nodded and headed " 'tother side of that barn yonderly." Rounding a corner of the big rock-and-adobe structure, Quist spied Gene seated on the earth a short distance away, bent over a board on which was stretched a sheet of watercolor paper. Near at hand was Gene's palette and box of colors, and a jar of water which had been turned to a dirty grayish color. Gene's brush was moving steadily across the paper, and from time to time he dipped into his box of paints and jar of water.

It wasn't until Quist was almost on top of him that Gene glanced up. A sort of faraway look faded from his eyes, and he smiled briefly. "Good to see you, Greg. Be with

215

you in a minute, I want to get this finished. . . ." His voice trailed off as he once more concentrated on the paper before him. Quist moved around behind Gene and squatted down nearby where he could watch. Now he saw what Gene was depicting: One corner of the barn, with an old gray saddled cowpony standing tethered to a hitch rail extending from the barn. Back of the horse, standing in full sunlight, was a huge old oak tree for a background. The whole made a nice triangular composition — barn at one side, lower down the pony and leafy oak boughs reaching to the upper corner.

The painting was nearly completed. A few penciled spaces remained white paper. Patches and lines of white paper spotted variously made highlights. Gene was working swiftly now, brush flowing color here and there, touching in other color while the first was still wet.

Gene spoke without raising his head. "How do you like my model?"

Quist chuckled, "Looks to me like that old pony would make a better model than a work horse."

"Right. Too old for work any more . . ." He continued talking while he painted. "I have to work fast in this sun. Color dries almost as soon as I put it down. And then, ten to one, once I get this picture inside, the colors won't be near so bright as they look now." His brush, a round one and rather big, Quist thought, considering some of the finer lines being painted, moved to the barn. As though by magic, rectangles of gray rock appeared in the wall. The horse was already finished, as was the oak tree. A broken window in the barn caught a bit of reflected light, with beyond the jagged edge the darkness of the interior. Small rocks and earth color, straggly grass commenced to appear in the foreground. "Damn foregrounds," Gene muttered, then, "How's it look to you, Greg?"

"We-ell, can't say I know anything about art, but it looks damn' good. Just an old cowhorse patiently waiting for its rider to show up."

Gene's brush moved with darker color now. Black shaddows, details, accents appeared. "Jeepers!" Quist exclaimed, "Those shadows really bring out the light, don't they? Now I can see the sun just blazing down. That looks pretty wonderful to me. Don't wonder you want to paint."

Gene shook his head, stuck his brush in water and gave it a couple of sharp flicks. "It's finished, but it's far from wonderful,

Greg. I can't draw yet —"

"T'hell you can't!"

"All right, let's say I've got a lot to learn about drawing. Look at that pony's lower jaw. Too thick by far," — indicating with the wooden end of the paint brush. "My line's too thick, too much shadow. Ever see any of this man Remington's pictures in *Harper's Weekly*?" Quist nodded. Gene said, "There's a man who can handle horses. There's a hombre up in Montana, named Charley Russell, who's damn' good too." Gene emptied his water jar and started gathering up his equipment. "But for sheer line drawing that can't be beat, I'll take a Mex from down in Ventoso. Why, he can express more —"

"Ventoso?" Quist said quickly.

"Yeah. What's up?" The two men got to their feet, Gene carrying his equipment.

"I happened to think that it was on Ventoso Street that Ferris had been visiting in Albuquerque — so he claimed."

"Oh, yes he did. I remember. That's a coincidence. The Ventoso I mean is down in Mexico, about thirty-five miles due south of Clarion City. This Mex, as I understand it, is trying to save enough money to go to art school. Lord, he's clever. No, I don't know him. He did a sketch of Porter one time —"

"What was Porter doing in Ventoso?" Quist asked.

Gene's face darkened. He shrugged. "That's something I don't know. Something to do with his business deals — which he never explained to any of us. This Mexican, name of Cubero, had done the sketch while Porter was in his *cantina* and gave it to Porter. Porter brought it back and gave it to me. Seems the Mexican just sits in his place all day, sketching anybody that comes in."

"I've been wondering if you had a photograph of Porter at the house. I'd like to see what the hombre looks like."

"There's a photo of him in his old room. I'll show it to you and the sketch too, after we've had chow. You going to Porter's funeral tomorrow, Greg?" Quist said he didn't think so. Gene said moodily, "Kate says she's going, so I reckon I'll have to accompany her." He untethered his "model" and led it back to the corral while they talked.

At dinner, Quist met a couple more Rocking-T hands. Kate and her father hadn't returned from their ride yet. Dinner concluded, Gene led the way to the house. While Quist waited in the main room, a large airy chamber with Indian rugs on the floor and a huge rock fireplace, Gene went to an inner room. He reappeared in a few minutes, bearing the photograph and sketch. Quist studied the photo and saw a man with even regular features and a rather petulant mouth. Not bad looking though.

"Now look at this sketch," Gene urged, holding up the paper with its charcoal lines. "See how the Mexican caught Porter's likeness, even if it is a caricature? And the few lines he needed to do it! I've never seen anything like it, and I saw a lot of fine stuff in Chicago. Look at this long curve — What that man can express with a single line! The way the line thickens and diminishes gives him the modeling. And this line here, from forehead to chin, with the nose and mouth between. It's just a sort of 'squiggle' actually, but it tells the whole story. Can you see it?"

"Jeepers! I couldn't miss it," Quist exclaimed. "The Mexican has got everything with just lines, that shows in the photograph, only he's brought out a certain weakness you don't see at first, in the photo. How in the devil can a man do that?"

"The Mexican is a genius. I've always been intending to ride down to Ventoso and talk to him, but never got around to it." Gene placed the sketch and photograph on a table. "Drop down and take a load off your boots, Greg," he said, seating himself.

Quist settled to a comfortable chair. "I'd thought to see your sister, but maybe you'll do just as well. Wanted to talk to you, anyway. What gauge shotguns do you and Mrs. Porter use generally?"

Gene's eyes narrowed. "You're remembering that Kate and I were out with shotguns the day Porter was killed — if it was Porter."

"I'm riding along with the idea it was," Quist said. "I think Ferris lied."

"Lord, I hope so," Gene said darkly. Then, "That's a hell of a thing to say about a brother-in-law, I suppose, but that louse —"

"I was asking about shotguns," Quist cut in dryly.

Gene nodded, smiling wryly, "So you're still wondering if Kate or I had anything to do with the job."

"And I'm still asking about shotguns. Come down off your high horse. I've made no accusations. I'm just trying to eliminate certain factors."

Gene drew a long sigh. "Kate uses a 16-gauge, shells loaded with #7 shot. I use a #12-gauge. Usually I shoot shells loaded with #5 or #6 shot. I can see what you're aiming at, Greg. Let me remind you that Doc Ingram testified that the shot that tore Porter's face loose, was much larger — a

#2. I've been thinking things over. Porter always loaded with #2. Do you suppose there's a chance he was killed with his own shotgun?"

"It's possible," Quist said. "I was sort of playing with that idea myself. When you identified him, did you notice whether his six-shooter had been fired?"

"I checked on that, first thing. The cylinder carried five cartridges, with the hammer resting on an empty shell. The barrel was clean. To get back to Kate's and my loads a minute. You want me to show you our shells?"

Quist smiled. "I'm willing to take your word for it. If either of you had loaded shells with #2 shot, you'd not admit it to me now, anyway. So I'm giving you both the benefit of the doubt — at present."

"Thanks for nothing," Gene said tersely.

"Look, you damn' young idiot," Quist snapped. "Don't be so blasted suspicious. If you'd use your noodle, you'd realize I'm trying to help you and your sister — clear you of guilt."

"I know, Greg," Gene said apologetically. "It's just that things have been so damn' muddled, I — I — well, I guess like you said, I don't use my head. I'm sorry. You got any more questions?"

"Yes. What's been the trouble between your outfit and Lombardy's L-Bar-D — ?"

"That reminds me," Gene said, "one of our hands was in town and he brought back a report that you'd tangled with Gilly De-ray —"

"It didn't amount to much," Quist said, and gave brief details. "Then, last night, I sort of goaded Lombardy into talking too much. He talked plenty. One of the things I've picked up around town is there's bad feeling between the Rocking-T and the Lombardy crowd."

"I think we're in the right there," Gene said. "The L-Bar-D hasn't too much graz-ing in bad seasons, and sometimes their wa-terholes run low. Lombardy tried to chisel in on our holdings, a couple of years back when we had a near drought. There was just enough water for our herds, so we turned back Lombardy's cows. Lombardy swore he'd get even some day. Since then, our hands have had orders to always turn back L-Bar-D cows when they stray over our way. It's made hard feelings between the two crews, too, of course. But I guess Lombardy got discouraged. He sold most of his herd to Jarv Fanchon." Gene frowned. "He never did reduce his crew though, and those L-Bar-D hands always seem well heeled."

"Maybe Lombardy is running some other sort of game. Meanwhile, I'd like to know why you and Porter quarreled over Ellen Bristol —"

Gene's face flamed. "Now, look here, Quist —"

Quist said sharply, "Cut it, Gene. I've talked to Ellen. She's worried. Now use sense. If you won't tell me, somebody else will." He related briefly his talk with Ellen Bristol.

"All right," Gene sullenly surrendered. "Ellen and I expect to get married. Porter was smitten with her, and took to hanging around her shop too often. I was already sore over the way he was treating Kate. Also, Ellen acted like she was afraid of Porter. I told him off on Main Street, one day. Several people heard me tell Porter if he didn't stay away from Ellen I'd use a gun on him. Now make of that what you will. I was mad and lost my temper." Quist merely nodded. Gene went on:

"Then, later Damaret Gilmore got into the argument. Gilmore had sparked Kate, until she married Porter, then he switched over to Ellen. He didn't like Porter hanging around Ellen either, and he made certain threats. Maybe Gilmore killed him — if Porter has been killed. I just know I didn't.

I've the inside track with Ellen now, but I imagine Gilmore is still hopeful."

"Thanks for clearing up a few matters," Quist said. The two men conversed a while longer, then Quist rose and stated he'd have to be getting back to town. Gene glanced curiously at his bulging pockets, saying, "Greg, looks like you're getting sort of 'hippy.'"

Quist laughed. "I was over near Shoulder Bluff before I came here. Found two cans of those missing preserves. I'm aiming to send 'em to our division superintendent with a sarcastic message." They left the house and walked down to the corral to get Quist's horse.

As Quist was about to leave, Kate and her father rode in. Wyatt Thornton had been a big man in his prime, but now his frame was wasted through long illness. He and Kate greeted Quist cordially, after the elder Thornton had been assisted down from the saddle. Quist said, "I went to the hotel yesterday to inquire as to the trouble you and Lombardy's spread had had, but you'd already left. However, Gene has explained it." They discussed that subject a few minutes. Quist mentioned the dead man, Leftwick, being found and brought to town.

Thornton said in his old man's voice,

"Seems to be an allfired lot of skulduggery taking over this country in past years."

Quist asked if they knew or had ever heard of Leftwick. All three shook their heads. Quist started to mount. The elder Thornton invited him to stay for supper. Quist refused with thanks, saying he had to get back to town. In that case, Kate said, perhaps Quist could deliver a message to Lish Corliss. Quist said he'd be glad to and asked what the message was. Kate explained: "Dad and I found my husb— Lloyd Porter's horse, today, over in the foothills. It should be reported to the sheriff —"

"The devil you did!" Quist exclaimed.

Kate nodded. "The horse had stepped into a gopher hole and snapped a front leg. Someone had put a bullet in its head."

"You're sure it was Porter's horse?" Quist asked.

"I'm certain," Kate said firmly. "Both Dad and I recognized the saddle too. The carcass was only about half a mile from where that ranger found the body. I'll have to send a couple of the boys out to bury the horse tomorrow."

"You didn't see any sign of Porter's shotgun, did you?"

Kate shook her head. Old Thornton said, "Nary a sign. Maybe it ain't Christian-like,

226

but whoever used that scattergun on Porter did a good job. Was I a jury, I'd never convict him."

Neither Kate nor Gene said anything. A few minutes later, Quist rode away from the ranch after promising to come again soon.

[XV]
BLACKMAIL

It was late afternoon when Quist reached Clarion City. Crossing the plank bridge over Clarín Creek, he turned the buckskin right to reach Railroad Street and made his way to the T.N. & A.S. depot where he found two telegrams awaiting him. He read them through, then remounted and headed the pony for the livery stable. To the livery man he gave explicit instructions regarding the care of the horse: "And give him a good rubdown and a feed of oats. I'll be needing him again tonight, maybe, and I want him in prime condition."

There were the usual pedestrians along Main Street as Quist headed toward the sheriff's office. Here he found both Lish Corliss and Fred Arbuckle who hailed him with questions as to where he'd been all day. Corliss added, "I heard at the livery that you'd saddled up and headed out."

"I've been out to the Rocking-T. Saw Gene and Kate. Kate asked me to give you a message, Lish."

"Lucky Lish," Arbuckle grinned. "I wish some beautiful lady —"

"Kate did?" Corliss interrupted, face brightening.

Quist explained, "She and her father were out riding today. They ran across Porter's horse. It had been killed after breaking a leg in a fall." He turned to Arbuckle, "It was only about a half a mile from where you found Porter's body, I understand."

"T'hell you say," Arbuckle said. "That just goes to show I should have circled wider in my search for sign. But I was damn' anxious to get that body to town —"

"Finding that horse reminds me of something else," Corliss said. He looked somewhat disappointed that Kate's message hadn't been of different import. "You know one of the teams and wagons those teamsters drove that night, never was found. Well, the team and wagon was turned in today. Feller living south of the tracks claims he found the mules and wagon right near his place one morning, 'bout three weeks back. Well, he had some hauling to do, toting his in-laws to Junctionville, so he just kept the wagon until he got back. Then, so he says, he got to thinking he'd best turn it in to the sheriff's office."

"Do you believe him?" Quist asked.

Corliss nodded. "Jeff Fargol — never does work much. Seems to visit between here and Junctionville most of the time. But he's honest. I reckon those fool mules just strayed into his neighborhood."

Quist dismissed the subject. "I had an answer to our investigator in Albuquerque regarding that address that Ferris gave. One-Twenty-Three Ventoso turns out to be a Hay & Feed store. And they never had any dear old lady named Ferris there."

"Proving Ferris lied." Arbuckle frowned. "Next time I see him in town —"

"I'd just as soon you let it ride, Fred," Quist said. "Let the scut think he's got us all fooled. Maybe he'll hang himself yet."

"You're probably right," Arbuckle agreed reluctantly. "Just the same I wish I'd known about that today. Lish and I were out looking at the place where Deray claims he found that Leftwick body."

"Uncover anything?" Quist asked.

Both men shook their heads. "Oh, it looked like there had been a grave there — the earth and tumbled rock and so on," Corliss added, "but we couldn't find anything to shake Deray's word. He's in town now and I talked to him again a spell before you got here. He insists he found that body just as he told it."

"So we'll have to let that lay as is, until we learn different," Quist said. "I mentioned the finding of Leftwick's body to Mrs. Porter and her father and brother. They know of no one by that name. Lish, you were going to check with those hotels —"

"Got replies this afternoon," Corliss answered, "from the Denver Palace, the Menger in San Antonio and the Driskill in Austin. All have records of a Mead Leftwick staying at their place, at various times, but they could tell me nothing else about him."

"And that doesn't help any," Quist grunted. He turned toward the door. "Well I'm going to get along to the hotel and clean up, then get some supper."

"How's for a drink at the Amber Cup first?" Arbuckle invited.

Quist hesitated, then refused reluctantly. "I've got a couple of other things to do first. I'll take you up on it another time, Fred."

He nodded good-bye to the two, then strode along Main Street until he'd reached Ellen Bristol's store, which was on the north side of Main just beyond Austin Street. He stepped within and heard a bell tinkle overhead as he opened the door. The shop was empty and Quist had a chance to glance around. There was a worn carpet on the floor and a couple of chairs. Against one wall was a long mirror and several closed cabinets with drawers. A table held a number of women's hats, and there were two small glass showcases holding ribbons, pins, artificial flowers, and sewing materials. At the rear was a curtained doorway beyond which, Quist judged, Ellen Bristol had living quarters. The curtain was drawn aside and Ellen entered. "Oh, it's you, Mr. Quist. I was out back, emptying some rubbish. I thought I heard the bell —"

Quist grinned. "No, I didn't come in to buy a bonnet — especially one with violets on it. Last night you refused to let me buy your supper. I wonder if you'd change your mind tonight?"

The girl came farther into the room, hesitated, "Well, er —"

Quist said, "You asked me if I learned anything concerning you, to give you a chance to explain."

The girl's color heightened, her blue eyes were round and wide. "What — what — ?"

"What about supper?" The girl nodded nervously. Quist went on, "Shall I come here for you in, say, a half hour — ?"

"Suppose I meet you in the hotel lobby,"

Ellen suggested. She smiled bravely. "And no matter what you have to talk about, please remember that I told you I'd never fired a shotgun in my life."

"I've not forgotten it," Quist smiled, doffed his sombrero and left.

But a moment later, strolling back toward the hotel he mused, "Though many a woman has persuaded a man to use a gun on her behalf."

Twenty-five minutes later when he descended from his room to the lobby there was an intense frown on his forehead. Ellen hadn't arrived yet, so he stepped to the desk and asked the clerk to send a message to Doctor Ingram asking him to come to the hotel as soon as possible. The clerk looked alarmed. "Are you sick, Mr. Quist?"

"Not yet, anyway," Quist smiled. "Don't worry. It's just a matter of business."

The clerk promised to send the message at once. At that moment Ellen entered the lobby and Quist escorted her into the dining room. It was early and they had no trouble in getting the same corner table they'd dined at the previous night. Despite Ellen's questioning, Quist refused to satisfy her curiosity until the food was eaten and they were finishing their coffee. He finally confessed that he hadn't wanted to spoil her dinner with serious talk. Finally he could put it off no longer. Drawing from his pocket one of the telegrams he'd received that day, he passed it across the table to her.

Nervously, Ellen read the wire. For an instant all the color left her face. Then she faced Quist directly. "Didn't take you long to learn about it, did it?" she said bravely.

"It wasn't difficult," Quist confessed. "You told me last night you'd been raised in San Antonio. I sent a telegram to our company investigator there. We have ways of getting information faster than the average person. I don't imagine your case proved difficult."

The girl passed back the telegram and sat twisting her handkerchief between her fingers. "Have — have you told Gene — ?"

Quist shook his head. "And I can see from your manner, you've never told him either. So now I'll leave that job to you. Miss Bristol, how long were you married to Lloyd Porter?"

"I left him after a month. I was only seventeen at the time."

"Why did you leave him?"

"We didn't get along. I was young enough to want romance. It had meant instead that I went to work to provide food. I gave him money at first. He lost it gambling. Other women interested him. The instant I received an annulment I left San Antonio and came here to make a new start. I'd hoped never to see him again. I became acquainted with Gene. I was — was afraid if I told him —"

"You were very foolish," Quist stated. "You should have told Kate too."

"I didn't know Kate too well at the time. I didn't know how she'd receive such news. Oh, I know now I was very wrong. I considered telling her before they were married, but I kept putting it off. And then suddenly they got married — and it was too late. You see, Lloyd Porter threatened me from the first that if I told I'd been married to him, he'd ruin my reputation in town —"

"But he couldn't have done that."

"I was afraid he could. He was quite popular when he first came here. I wasn't yet known too well. He swore if I said anything, he'd — he'd swear he knew me in San Antonio when I was — was living a fast life. And those days I think his word carried more weight than mine. And I didn't know how Gene would react to such a story. And so I kept my mouth closed and Lloyd Porter would drop in here every so often to get the money —"

"What money?" Quist said quickly.

"That was part of the bargain for keeping my mouth closed. Every so often he'd lose money at poker or some other way, and he'd come to me for some . . ." Ellen fell silent.

Quist felt his ire rising, but held his voice quiet, "So Porter was a blackmailer as well. Nice hombre. Miss Bristol, I understand you kept company with Damaret Gilmore at one time." The girl inclined her head. Quist continued, "Did you ever tell him of your marriage?"

"No," Ellen replied, "but I've sometimes thought he might have heard of it. He has relatives in San Antonio and visits there occasionally. However, he never said anything about it, so I don't know."

Quist questioned her regarding Porter's business activities, but she appeared to know nothing of them. Finally the supper was concluded and they rose from the table. As he accompanied the girl from the lobby he said, "I'm sending a messenger to Gene tonight, saying you want to see him the first thing in the morning. Then, when he gets here, you tell him what you've told me —"

The girl shook her head. "No, *I* will send that message to Gene. It's about time I started showing some initiative. And I'm so glad that — that you — well, I don't know how to thank you —"

Her thanks were cut short by the appearance of Doctor Ingram in the lobby. He looked somewhat relieved at seeing Quist in good health. "I thought — I —"

Quist chuckled. "No, nobody's shot me — yet, Doc." He procured his room key from the desk and handed it to the doctor. "I'll be back in five minutes or less, Doc. Go on up. I've got something to show you."

Ellen insisted she could return to her shop alone, but Quist insisted on escorting her. It was nearly dark on the street now. Lights shone along the way. Quist unlocked her door for her, accompanied her inside and lighted an oil lamp. Then, cutting short further thanks, he said goodnight, and turned back toward the hotel.

"Women," he grunted as he strode along, "if they don't —" He broke off, "Anyway, her mind is a lot easier tonight than it has been in a long time."

The doctor had the lamp lighted by the time Quist entered his room. He chuckled as Quist closed the door. "What's wrong with you, Greg, you got female complaint, or something?" — gesturing toward the bonnet trimmed with violets on the table.

Quist's color reddened. "No, that's — that's —" He grinned sheepishly. "Look, cut out the ribbing. I wanted to see you about something serious —"

"Then tell her not to forget her hat next time," Ingram said dryly.

Quist laughed, "I could wish that —" He broke off. "Blast it, let's forget that bonnet. Sit down and listen." He went on, "You've heard about those missing cans of jams. Today I was out to Shoulder Bluff and I found two cans labeled strawberry that had been lost from the shipment. There's been a hell of a lot of fuss made over that missing jam. The consignor is threatening to sue my company for a damn' sight more than the stuff is worth — I thought. Before going down to supper tonight, I got to wondering what made this particular jam so precious. So I got out my knife and opened a can. Damnedest strawberry jam I ever saw. I've got my own suspicions, but I'd like you as a doctor with more experience along such lines, to confirm what I'm thinking."

He rose from his chair, went to the dresser and returned with the opened can. Ingram took it, pushed back the raggedly-cut tin top and inspected the contents by the light of the lamp. The can contained a dark brown tarry substance of about the consistency of moist adobe mud. Ingram grunted and sniffed at the can's contents. Next he took a tiny particle on one fingernail and tasted it. After a moment he lifted his eyes and stared at Quist. Quist waited, tense.

Ingram said, "While I'm better acquainted with its derivatives, morphine, laudanum and so on, than I am with the product in this raw state, I'm ready to swear this can contains opium. Lord, Greg —"

"Opium," Quist nodded triumphantly. "I thought so; wasn't sure. Saw some once before, but it was darker in color."

"This is probably more refined. Opium's a great pain killer. In the hands of the right people, it's a blessing in disguise. But of late years the wrong people have been trafficking in it. And that has led to a lot of crime. Some men, y'know, will do anything for money."

Quist indicated the can. "I reckon that particular 'Drum Brand Strawberry Jam,' is the real Devil's Drum in this section, eh, Doc?"

"If it gets into the wrong hands. As a doctor I've learned our government is considerably alarmed over the increasing number of drug addicts. Washington hasn't yet legislated proper laws to combat the use of opium by crooks, but it's working steadily on the proposition, endeavoring to turn its import into only the proper channels. But smuggling continues despite the best work of the Customs officials. The stuff was being brought up through Mexico. Less than two years ago, one smuggling ring was broken up, and with the help of Mexican officials, less than fifty miles south of here, but the ringleaders weren't caught. Now apparently they're getting the stuff through again. I happen to know government agents are watching out for shipments from California at present, as the stuff is landed on the West Coast from the Orient and —"

"And so, to evade agents at the California line, the opium is being shipped as jam," Quist put in. "Doc, what's this stuff worth?"

Ingram frowned. "I'm not sure exactly, but I'd say anyway it would sell between ten and twelve dollars an ounce. Roughly, this can holds about one-hundred-forty dollars worth of opium, for certain people. The price may run lower or higher — but not much lower."

Quist made mental calculations. He gave a sharp whistle. "Cripes! There were four-hundred-eighty cans labeled strawberry. That runs to around seventy thousand dollars. Somebody was playing for damn' high stakes, knew the shipment was coming through and highjacked it. And he didn't let a little killing stand in his way —"

"Didn't I hear there were cans labeled

plum and peach as well as strawberry?" Ingram asked.

Quist nodded. "Every one of the plum and peach cans were recovered, so I'm figuring they contained just what the label said. It's my hunch they were just sent along to make the shipment look good — but the highjacker had to get all the cans from that freight train to make sure he got all the strawberry."

Ingram nodded. "Looks that way. Do you think Lloyd Porter or that man named Leftwick had anything to do with this opium business?"

"I'm thinking more that way every minute." Quist nodded. "Doc, you keep these cans for me until they're needed for evidence, will you? I've got to be away for a day or so, and they might be safer in your hands if anybody learned that I'd found them."

Ten minutes later, Quist said good-bye to the doctor and headed toward the White Star Livery. As he strode along the darkened street, lighted here and there by a few lamps in windows, he spied Gilly Deray on the opposite side of Main, just emerging from the Warbonnet Saloon. Upon seeing Quist, Deray paused on the saloon porch, then stepped back into shadow. Quist hadn't missed the movement, but he had no time now to stop and talk to Deray. He continued on to the livery, saddled up the buckskin and mounted.

Turning down San Antonio Street, he headed for the railroad station and dismounted. Here he sent a telegram to Jay Fletcher which read:

SUGGEST YOU EXPEDITE ARREST OF CONSIGNOR AND CONSIGNEE ON CHARGE SMUGGLING NARCOTICS. HAVE PROOF. SECURE AID FEDERAL AUTHORITIES.

As he remounted his pony, Quist muttered savagely, "And put that in your pipe and smoke it, Mister Jay Fletcher. I'll teach you to wire me to expedite search for strawberry jam. All right, it got expedited. We'll see how you like it."

Then he turned his horse and rode due south across the T.N. & A.S. tracks. Three-quarters of an hour later he had reached the Rio Grande and though the river was nearly a hundred yards wide at that point, he located a flat and shallow place to ford, and climbed the opposite bank into Mexico. He kept going until a light in a small Mexican farmhouse suggested a place to get something to eat and bed down for the rest of the night.

[XVI]
ROARING GUNS

The way to Ventoso was easy to follow as it led between low rocky hills, dotted with sahuaro and barrel-cactus. The sun broiled down, and there was a continual siroccolike wind bringing fine particles of dust to sting eyes and clog nose and throat. Quist had drawn his bandanna up across the lower part of his face to avoid the dust. Far ahead he could see the rugged grayish-purple peaks of distant mountains, looking as though they had been cut flatly from cardboard and stuck up against the cloudless sky. A few buzzards soared and wheeled and dipped against the wide blue expanse.

As he rode, Quist's thoughts dwelt on the events of the past days. He thought of Kate Porter, and then his cogitations shifted to Ellen Bristol. She had acted foolishly, that was certain, and yet he couldn't help feeling sorry for the girl. He wondered if Damaret Gilmore knew of her marriage to Porter. "A man as hot-tempered as Gilmore," Quist mused, "would be capable of killing Porter, if he had heard of that marriage. He might be fool enough to think that getting rid of Porter would install him in Ellen's good graces, and he could gain the inside track against Gene. But I reckon Ellen's choice is Gene, no matter what she may have thought of Gilmore at one time or another. For that matter, Lish Corliss made threats. He, too, could profit from Porter's death . . ." He pushed steadily ahead, not forcing the buckskin to any great speed in this heat.

Ventoso, when he arrived, looked like dozens of other small Mexican hamlets he had seen. Small scattered adobe houses, nearly all of which had a few flowers growing about; two or three patched corrals, holding a pony or a mule. Goats grazing in front yards. Chickens picking in the roadway. A few ragged or entirely naked children playing in the dust. A yelping dog or two. At the second house he came to, a courteous Mexican saw that he got water for his horse, and protested in hurt tones when Quist tried to pay him, even though water in Ventoso wasn't plentiful. A good people, Mexicans, Quist considered, as he rode toward the center of town.

The Cantina of Golden Wine was located without difficulty. Quist left his horse in the shade of one wall and entered. There were three of the local inhabitants at the bar drinking *pulque,* men in loose white garments and huge straw sombreros, dawdling away an hour while their women folk were at home preparing the *tortillas, chili* and *frijoles.* All of the men nodded pleasantly as Quist came in. Quist returned the greetings and made his way to the scarred pine bar, his spurs making jangling sounds as he crossed the rough floor. The stocky young proprietor put down his charcoal and paper and surveyed Quist with interest. "*Buenos dias, señor.* I can be of the service, no?"

"You sure can," Quist said. "I'll take a beer."

An expression of regret crossed Diego Cubero's round face. "Of the *cerveza* I no got, *señor.*" Then hopefully, *"Pulque?"* Quist made a grimace. Cubero said, "You no like the *pulque?"*

Quist quoted in Spanish:

"I have heard of the pulque,
"With its flavor benign,
"Which the Aztec gods quaff
"When they have no fine wine."

He added, "But I'm no Aztec god. You have, perhaps, *tequila?"*

The old Mexican verse, the use of the native tongue, Quist's denial of godlike existence, brought laughter from the customers and proprietor, and an air of friendliness invaded the small *cantina.* The customers moved a little closer as Cubero set out a saucer containing salt and a slice of withered lemon, and then poured *tequila* into a small glass. Quist put a pinch of salt on his tongue, downed the fiery *tequila,* and then drew the slice of lemon between his teeth. He took out his tobacco and papers and rolled a cigarette. While he smoked he gazed around the walls at the drawings hung there. Already Cubero had moved farther along the bar and was busy with charcoal and paper on this fresh model. Beyond the coolness of the interior the roadway was a white glare under the broiling sun.

Cubero glanced up once at Quist, "You do not object, señor?"

"Not if it affords you pleasure," Quist replied.

A few minutes later, Cubero passed the paper with Quist's likeness along the bar. Quist looked at his picture and marveled at what the man accomplished with few lines. "It is very good," Quist complimented him. "I should like to pay for this, señor."

Cubero beamed. "I shall be honored if you accept it as a gift."

Quist made the usual protests before accepting with thanks. He said, "I have a friend in Clarion City who says Diego Cubero is a very great artist. He plans to come and visit with you in the future. He had much praise for your work." Enthusiastic words of agreement came from the three customers. Cubero's wide mouth was a smiling pattern of even white teeth. "It is in connection with this I have come to see you."

The customers were quick to take a hint. Ah, this was a matter of business between their good Diego and the *gringo* — a very pleasant *gringo* for all that — and it could result in many *pesos* for Diego. Smiling and with many pleasant nods, the customers departed, leaving the *cantina* to Quist and Cubero. Cubero requested the name of Quist's friend. Quist mentioned Gene Thornton and his work with water color. Cubero said thoughtfully, "I do not think I know the Señor Thornton."

"Once you gave one of your so fine sketches to a man named Porter. He gave it to Thornton."

At the mention of Porter's name, Cubero's eyes became veiled, the smile vanished from his round brown features. Upon questioning he reluctantly admitted that Porter had visited the Cantina of Golden Wine.

Quist placed all his cards on the table, telling of his connection with the T.N. & A.S. and of his need for information. "There was a matter of thieving from a freight train," Quist stated. "I think Porter was involved and others from near Clarion City."

It took considerable persuasion before Cubero consented to tell what he knew. Yes, Porter and others had been in the habit of coming to Ventoso from time to time. But that was nearly two years ago, except — Cubero paused. Quist asked further questions. No, Cubero didn't know why they came. They stayed a day or two, and then in the night someone would arrive from the south with pack-horses which were turned over to Porter and the men with him to drive toward the north.

"And the pack-horses were loaded with what?" Quist asked.

"That I can not say with a certainty," Cubero replied cautiously.

"Could it have been narcotics?" Quist pursued.

Cubero studied Quist with a long stare. "I have sometimes thought so," he admitted. "But it is not wise for us to meddle with *gringos'* affairs, Señor Quist. Your pardon for the word *gringo*. All are not as you. Then came a day when agents from your government came here. And they waited long, but no more pack-horses with loaded sacks arrived. Nor have any come through since that time, and the Señor Porter and his companions came no more, until —" He paused, "Not too far back, the Señor Porter arrived here, stating he would hunt for the dove. He carried a fine shotgun, but spent all his time in my poor *cantina.* I thought he watched for one to come with much uneasiness, and he had the look of hoping that one would not come . . ."

Cubero continued, telling of the arrival of men named Riker and Ferris, and of Porter's killing of Riker, and the later arrival of one named Mead Leftwick. "It was very plain," Cubero continued, "that the Señor Porter feared greatly the man named Leftwick, and when Leftwick persuaded him to leave here, I could see a look of death on the Señor Porter's face. And that is all I know," he finished simply.

Quist thanked Cubero and said, "Could you from memory make a picture of Porter?"

Cubero smiled. "That would be of the most ease." He seized a sheet of paper and charcoal, and within a few minutes spun the paper to Quist. Quist glanced at it and saw it was much like the sketch Gene had shown him. Quist complimented the Mexican on the work, saying, "You have a fine memory. Could you do the same for this man Leftwick and others who formerly came here with Porter?"

Cubero was smiling again. Here, in the Señor Quist was a man who appreciated art. Again he seized his charcoal and sent it rapidly darting over sheet after sheet, sometimes pausing to smear a line with one thumb or finger to represent shading. It seemed no time before Quist had a dozen or more sketches of Porter's accomplices. Cubero had scribbled names to the papers, in such cases as he knew them. It was easy for Quist to recognize Lombardy, Gilly Deray, Ferris and two or three other L-Bar-D punchers. Cubero completed a final sketch. "Here is the one known as Mead Leftwick."

Quist studied the drawing intently. Cubero said, "Him, too, you have seen?"

Quist said grimly, "I've seen him." He drew out his wallet after rolling the drawings together, and placed some money on the scarred bar. Cubero protested payment, but Quist said, "You have done me a very great service. It is my understanding that you hope to attend a school of art."

"Sí, Señor Quist. Someday — it is only a matter of money — I shall go to Mexico

City. What I do now is nothing. There I will learn much, the painting with water color and oils. Someday, too, I hope to paint murals on great walls. But the saving of money requires much time —"

"I promise you it will not be too long. In the matter of the freight thieving I mentioned, my company offers a reward of five hundred dollars. Perhaps I can persuade the company to make it more. I will recommend you to receive that reward. So, you see, Mexico City is nearer than you thought of."

Cubero's features were a study in all that is wonderful. He couldn't find his tongue to speak his joy. And then another voice spoke:

"Only fools plan ahead, hombres."

Quist spun around facing the open doorway. Gilly Deray stood there, leveled forty-five six-shooter bearing on Quist. How long the man had been standing there, Quist didn't know, but apparently long enough to learn what Quist had been doing.

"Raise 'em high, Quist," Deray ordered. Quist raised them. Deray continued, "You had your innings in Clarion City. Now it's my turn and I'm going to make it count. You're headed for a long journey — and the Mex too. He's too goddam free with his drawings. I'll fix him so he'll make no more of them sketches —"

"I suppose," — Quist spoke easily — stalling for time — "you trailed me here, Deray."

"You suppose correct, Quist. We've had enough of you around. It was plumb easy to pick up your sign. I saw you when you rode out of town last night. Me, I'm curious. I wondered what you were up to. I found out." His eyes grew even more hard, becoming almost opaque, his voice flattened tonelessly. "You won't be going back, Quist." He added, "And don't try to reach that hideout gun of yours. You couldn't make it in time. Just get reconciled to the fact you're not going back."

Cubero finally found his voice. With all the dignity he could summon to his quavering tones he said, "Señor Deray, it is that I order you *inmediatamente* to make the depart of my *cantina*."

"Shut your greasy face, Mex," Deray rasped. For just a brief instant the man's gaze shifted to Cubero, and it was the chance Quist was waiting for.

Abruptly, Quist threw his body to one side, hearing the roar of Deray's thundering forty-five as he moved, feeling the breeze of Deray's bullet as it passed dangerously close. His ear caught the savage thud of the heavy slug as it spatflattened against a rock in the adobe wall, even as his own six-shooter was jerked into action.

Twice the .44 Colt's jumped in Quist's right fist, smoke and white flame mushrooming from the short barrel, the twin explosions coming so closely together they seemed almost one.

Deray was spun half around by the impact of Quist's fire, as the man endeavored to lift his forty-five for a second try. From a crouching position near the floor, Quist thumbed a third shot.

Fighting to stay erect, Deray was smashed back against the doorjamb. He coughed convulsively and lost his gun. For a moment he seemed to hang poised there in the doorway, then slowly his legs buckled beneath him and he slid down, his body sprawled half in, half out of the entrance.

Powdersmoke drifted, was caught up by the draft of wind, and vanished in air. Suddenly, from somewhere out on the street, a woman screamed. Followed an excited chattering of Mexican voices along the glare-hot roadway. A trembling voice called to Cubero.

Quist straightened cautiously from his crouching position, gun in hand, crossed the floor and kicked Deray's gun out of reach. It was a needless maneuver: Deray was already dead, his shirt front stained darkly with slowly spreading moisture. Quist plugged out his empty shells, inserted fresh loads in his weapon and spoke to Cubero:

"Go quiet your people, Diego. They are concerned for your welfare. Tell them no trouble will come to you because of this business."

Eyes wide, Cubero nodded. His knees were still shaking a little as he made his way to the street.

[XVII]
A DEFINITE THREAT

There were details to be taken care of in Ventoso that day. So that no trouble might attach to Cubero, due to the killing, Quist went with him in a wagon to visit the *jefe* at San Eneas, seven miles farther south. Deray's body traveled with them. The *jefe*, a man friendly to *gringos*, listened quietly to the story. There were certain papers to be signed, the address of Quist's railroad company taken. No, the *jefe* told them, there would be no trouble, and, yes, burial for the dead man would be seen to at once. It was evening by the time they returned to Ventoso. That night, Quist slept at the home of the ancient Maria Bistula, and the following morning made an early start for Clarion City.

It was shortly after noontime when he pulled his pony to a halt at the T.N. & A.S. depot. A telegram from Jay Fletcher awaited him. Quist read it, and said to himself, "For once Jay didn't argue. Apparently, he's getting action." He paused long enough to send a couple of wires, then left the station and stepped out to the platform. On the platform he saw Stationmaster Nugent. Nugent said, "Did you see Duval Sloan, Mr. Quist?"

"Who?" Quist asked, frowning.

"Sloan — Duval Sloan. The telegrapher at San Julio Station — you know, the feller that got knocked on the head, the night that fake message came through, signed Tyrus Wolcott, and we thought it had been relayed by Sloan —"

"Sure, I remember, now." Quist's brow cleared. "What about him?"

"He was looking for you. Took a couple of days off to come up here to see you."

"About what?" Quist asked.

"I don't know. Wouldn't tell me. He appeared right nervous. Every so often he'd come slinking in here to ask for you, like he was afraid of being caught at it. I hear he inquired at the hotel, too." Quist asked a

254

question. Nugent said, "I don't know where he is now. He came once this morning asking for you. Haven't seen him since. Could be he returned to San Julio on #18. But nobody knew where you were."

"I've been out of town. What's this Duval Sloan like?"

"A whiz at a telegraph key. Otherwise sort of timid. The kind that scares easy. Whines a lot about railroad working conditions."

"Well, if he shows up again, tell him I'm back." Quist remounted and rode the buckskin to the livery stable. That done he went to his hotel, washed up and descended to the street again. The hotel clerk mentioned that a man named Sloan had been looking for him. Quist nodded and left to find some dinner. An hour later he entered the sheriff's office.

Lish said, "Where in hell you been, Greg? We've been sort of worried. You weren't here for Porter's funeral, either."

"Who was at the funeral?" Quist asked. "And who's the *we* that did the worrying?"

"The L-Bar-D crew showed up for the funeral. Kate rode out with Gene, but didn't speak to anybody. Fred and I went just to look things over. And there was the usual number of curious people. It was Fred and I were bothered when we didn't see you around. You took off 'thout a word. Fred got to thinking about your brush with Gilly Deray and thought maybe Deray had been up to some skulduggery. Said he had half a notion to ride to the L-Bar-D and question Deray some —"

"Did he?"

Corliss shook his head. "No, he's around town someplace."

"Well, Deray's not bothering me any," Quist said. It wasn't until later that Corliss remembered that Quist hadn't explained where he'd been the previous day. Quist now changed the subject, "I want some information, Lish."

"About what?"

"About two men — Jarvis Fanchon and Morley Harper — I understand Harper's out of town at present."

Corliss nodded. "He runs the Golden Wheel Gambling House. Morley's up in Denver right now. Went there to buy himself a new roulette table. But what about them?"

"At one time, both Fanchon and Harper were calling on Kate Porter — Thornton, that is."

Corliss' face reddened at the girl's name. "I don't figure it was anything serious," the sheriff said. "Sure, they took her around some to dances and such, but a lot of us —

a lot of fellows did."

"Couple of nights ago in the Amber Cup, I sort of taunted Lombardy into making some talk. To get me off his shoulders, he tried to shift my viewpoint to Fanchon and Harper — said they'd both had fights with Porter. Lombardy hinted maybe they killed him. Do you know anything about it?"

Corliss smiled. "As to Fanchon, I doubt it had anything to do with Mrs. Porter. Fanchon is eternally on the defensive. You know he brands his cattle with a Jar-F. A design shaped like a jar with a letter F inside. Well, some of his cows were branded with a running iron, and the cowhand who made the jar design, couldn't draw for beans. Consequently, the jar on a lot of cows came out looking more like a spittoon — or something else. Well, Porter had a sort of nasty tongue. He got to jeering at Fanchon and calling the brand the Spittoon-F. Fanchon thought he was being belittled and, having no sense of humor, it made him mad everytime Porter said it. Then one day Porter suggested next time Fanchon was branding, he'd better put a handle on the jar. With that, Fanchon went higher'n a kite and he hauled off and knocked Porter out to the gutter. Porter didn't attempt to fight back."

"And that's all there was to it?" Quist

asked, smiling.

"So far's I know, Greg." Quist asked about Harper. The sheriff said, "I can explain that too. I don't know's you'd say it was a fight. Harper got the worst of it, in a way. Now Morley Harper is a pretty good hombre. A square gambler if there is such a thing. Well, Porter was shooting craps in there one day, and a new man Harper had put to work inserted a pair of crooked dice into the game, and Porter lost a pile of money." Corliss paused, "It likely wouldn't have made any difference if the dice were crooked or not. Porter always lost when he gambled."

"There's men like that," Quist nodded. "No gambler's luck."

"That was Porter. Anyway he discovered the dice were loaded, and he complained to Harper. Harper investigated, saw that Porter was right for once, and returned the money. Then he kicked the crooked craps shooter out of the Golden Wheel. You'd have thought that would have satisfied Porter, but no. Thinking he had something on Harper, he tried to make a deal, said deal being that Harper was to sell him a half interest in the Golden Wheel on payments, to be made from house winnings. Otherwise, Porter threatened to tell it all over town that Harper ran crooked games. Naturally, Harper refused to be blackmailed in such fashion and he said no. The two men got to arguing. Harper ordered Porter out of his place. When Harper's back was turned for a minute, Porter picked a bottle from the bar and struck Harper over the head. Could have hurt Morley bad, except that it was a glancing blow. Then he pitched Porter into the street. Morley came here and told me about the ruckus right after. I wanted him to prefer charges against Porter, but Harper preferred to let the matter drop. And so far as I know, Greg, that's all there is to that scrap. If anything else happened I don't know about it."

Quist considered. "Well, that don't sound like Harper had done any threatening to kill. Gradually I'm running all these threats to earth. You don't know of anybody else who threatened Porter, do you?"

"Nary a man, Greg —"

"Except one," Quist interrupted. Corliss frowned. Quist continued, "Lombardy claims you threatened to kill Porter."

Corliss just stared at Quist a moment, some of the color left his face. "That's a lie —" he commenced, then, his shoulders slumped and he said, "All right, it's true, but that's a long time back. I was pretty sore at the time, and I said things I shouldn't

259

have. Porter was here in the office, and Lombardy happened to be passing. He heard what I said."

"Tell me about it," Quist said.

"I guess you know Kate and I were to be married one time. Then we quarreled. Before things could be patched up, Porter had come to town and the next thing I knew they'd got married. Porter knew about Kate and me and one day he came in here and start kidding in a nasty way about Kate picking the best man. It made me see red for a minute, and I told Porter if he wasn't good to Kate, or if he mistreated her in any way, I'd kill him. Lombardy spread the story all over town, of course. Kate heard about it, and sent word to me that she didn't require my protection. I guess she was still mad at me. Anyway, that put things beyond the patching point. But hell, Greg, that was a long spell back —"

Quist said. "Sure, and a man can hold a grudge for a long time too. The fact remains, Porter did mistreat her, and the question is what did you do about it? You admit you made a definite threat."

"I didn't do a damn thing," Corliss said miserably. "I wish to hell now that I had."

"You've got an alibi for the day Porter was killed — ?"

"Now, look here, Greg, there's no absolutely certainty that Porter is dead. Ferris swore that he talked to him in Albuquerque —"

"Do you believe Ferris? Would you take his word for anything?" Quist snapped.

Corliss drew a long sigh. "You win, Greg. No, I wouldn't believe Ferris if he swore on a stack of Bibles Hereford-high. But as for me — hell I've been in town every day, except once or twice."

"That once or twice — what days were those?"

"I don't remember right now, but, hell, Greg" — perspiration was starting on Corliss' forehead — "I wouldn't kill Porter."

"Maybe you can dig up some sort of alibi," Quist said quietly. "I'm making no accusation, Lish, but I do like to eliminate suspects. I'll be glad if you can help me."

Corliss didn't reply. Quist turned and left the sheriff's office.

An hour later, Quist found Gene Thornton in the Amber Cup. The instant Gene spied Quist he called to Mickey Kurtz. "Take Greg's order, Mickey. This one is on me."

Quist joined him at the bar and ordered a beer. There were a few other men in the place, quietly drinking. The noise of pedestrians and passing horses floated dimly into the barroom. Quist downed half a glass of beer and said, "Thank God Mickey doesn't keep his beer too cold." He turned smiling to Gene. "Ten to one I can tell you where you've been today."

"As well as yesterday," Gene admitted. "Jeepers, Greg, we owe you a lot for getting things straightened out."

"Things aren't straightened out yet by a long shot," Greg said, "but I'm glad your affairs are smoothing out. Ellen should have told you long ago."

Gene nodded seriously. "Yeah. She realizes it now. But she was so afraid it would make a difference between her and me. Well, hell, yes, I was surprised of course to even learn she'd known Porter, let alone being married to the skunk — but that's all dried grass on last year's range now. I can tell you, Greg, Ellen's a lot easier in her mind. So am I for that matter, now I understand why Porter visited her so much. We can't thank you enough —"

"You've already thanked me more than enough," Quist interrupted. "Let's forget it —"

"I can't forget it —"

"Then," — Quist was beginning to feel embarrassed at the profuse gratitude of young Thornton — "I'll give you something

else to think about. I've got a roll of drawings up in my room. When I get through
with 'em, you can have 'em —"

"Yeah? Who did them?"

"Diego Cubero. I —"

"T'hell you say." Gene sounded delighted.
"Are they good — no, I don't have to ask
that. I know they are. That man's stuff is
wonderful. One of these days I'm aiming to
ride down to Ventoso and see if I can't give
Cubero a helping hand —"

"What's this about Ventoso?" a new voice
asked. Quist and Gene turned from the bar
to see Fred Arbuckle behind them. " 'Bout
time you put in an appearance, Greg." Arbuckle laughed. "You just seemed to dis-
appear off the face of the earth. Don't tell
me you've been down to Ventoso."

"Actually, I went to San Eneas," Quist
said. "Had a lead from my company." He
smiled wryly. "You know, that damn strawberry jam that's missing. Anyway, to get
back to Ventoso, Gene knows an artist down
there, that he says is damn' good. So I
stopped in to see his place. He runs a *cantina*. I don't know anything about art, but
this Cubero hombre made a good sketch of
me."

"Don't know anything about art, myself,"
Arbuckle said, "but hearing you mention

263

Ventoso reminds me of something. There was a lot of smuggled dope came through there a year or so back. The Federal authorities busted things up though. They had some rangers working with them too."

"Did you work on the job?" Quist asked.

Arbuckle shook his head. "No, the rangers were from Company C. I just happened to hear about it. Your lead in San Eneas turn up anything, Greg?"

"Nothing I'd talk about now," Quist said. He glanced meaningly at Gene, who was lifting his glass. Arbuckle gave an imperceptible nod to show he understood. Quist had another beer. Arbuckle ordered a whisky. The three stood talking idly a few moments, then Gene stated he had business elsewhere and left.

Arbuckle laughed when the swinging doors closed behind Gene. "I'll bet I could tell you what his business is too. Yesterday and today I've seen him going in and out of Ellen Bristol's place. I'd say he's hit hard. I'd also say he'd raise hell with her business if he hangs around her shop too much. But she's a damn nice looking girl and I can't say I blame him. Wish I knew him better. He might invite me out to the Rocking-T where I could see his sister."

"Hell's-bells!" Quist said, "Why don't you

just go visiting?"

Arbuckle laughed shyly. "I don't know, Greg. Somehow, where women are concerned — especially a woman like Mrs. Porter — well I just go tongue-tied. And then, marriage to a ranger isn't the best sort of life for a woman. She never knows when her husband may get shot to death. It's like your own job for instance. You're always running risks."

"Just the same," Quist said, eyeing the foam on his glass speculatively, "sometimes I think it would be good to have a regular home to settle down in."

"I guess you're right. For that matter I've been thinking lately I ought to get back to Bandera. There doesn't seem any threat of the trouble now that Lish feared. As for other things, I don't know's there's anything left to clean up that you and Lish can't handle." He downed the remainder of his whisky. "Lish and I were sort of concerned when we didn't see you yesterday. I got to thinking about your little fuss with Deray and thought maybe he'd been up to some helling. Haven't seen him in town, but I sure aimed to question him plenty — oh, yes, there's some jasper named Dural Sloan looking for you too."

"So I heard. Did you hear what he

wanted?"

Arbuckle shook his head. "He asked at the sheriff's office if Lish knew where you could be found. I happened to be there at the time. Somehow, I didn't like the guy's looks. Acted like he had some grudge on his mind. Had a gun stuck in his pants' waistband, too, though he didn't look like a hombre that was accustomed to handling a gun. Sometimes, though, that type is the most dangerous. I intended to keep an eye on him, but he seems to have slipped out of sight."

Quist said, "He works for the railroad. Stationmaster Nugent had an idea he might have returned to his job in San Julio. Probably didn't amount to anything. I don't know him personally, anyway, so if he had a grudge against someone, it couldn't have been me."

The two men talked a while longer, then left the saloon and parted, taking different directions along Main Street.

[XVIII]
A Narrow Squeak

The remainder of the day and that evening passed without incident. Quist remembering that Doc Ingram had told him the local bank was owned by Wyatt Thornton's brother, decided to look up the banker and see if he could throw any light on Porter's activities. He found Yarnell Thornton at his home on Lamar Street and was cordially invited in. The banker's wife placed cigars and a bottle of whisky and glasses on a table and left the two men to their discussion.

But there was little Yarnell Thornton could tell Quist about Porter. "I felt the girl was making a mistake when she married him so suddenly," the banker said. "I knew it for certain when Porter came to me with his ideas for expanding the bank. If I'd listened to him and taken him in with me, I'd likely have found myself outside looking in before long. Oh, I'll admit he had ideas, all right, but they weren't based on sound banking theories. Too much gambling to them — and as we came to know Porter better, we learned he was a mighty poor gambler. As fast as he got any money, it disappeared over the card tables or some other way. I happen to know the hands at the L-Bar-D came to look on Porter as a steady source of poker income."

"I wouldn't be surprised from what I've heard," Quist nodded.

"Well, Kate, heard about him trying to work into my bank and she put a stop to it.

Told him he'd mooched enough on her own people without trying to make money off of me. By that time, Kate knew the scoundrel. He hadn't been able to fool her for a long time. She's done a good job with the Rocking-T, but just the same I wish she wasn't so hard and defiant when anyone criticizes her. I've tried to talk to her, but she's a willful arrogant woman, if she is of my own blood, and unless she finds some man who'll show her what's what, I'm afraid she'll be an unhappy woman all her life."

"About the way I'd sized her up," Quist said. "She's too beautiful a woman to go through life that way."

"You're right. Kate is beautiful. Maybe running the ranch the way she has tends to make her hard. It was a good thing for Wyatt, my brother, that she did take hold though. I think if he hadn't been an invalid, he might have taken things into his own hands and killed Porter himself. I've seen him just that mad at times."

"He seems able to ride on occasion," Quist pointed out.

The banker nodded. "Yes, but it takes it out of him. Not good for him at all. But he won't admit to feeling pain. A mighty stubborn man, Wyatt is. Probably that's where Kate gets her headstrong ways."

No, there was little Yarnell Thornton could tell Quist that he didn't already know. After a time he thanked the banker for a pleasant visit and took his departure. Later he dropped into the Amber Cup, thinking to find Arbuckle or Lish Corliss there, but neither man was in sight. He had a couple of drinks, and then decided to seek an early bed at the hotel and try to catch up on some of the scanty sleep he'd had on the trip to Ventoso.

It wasn't more than ten-thirty when he stepped out on Main, but few lights shone along the street. Here and there a pony or a wagon stood at the hitchrack before saloons. Diagonally across the street, lights shone from the Warbonnet Saloon and considerable loud talking, profanity and clinking of glasses floated above the swinging doors. Judging from the number of broncs waiting patiently at the tierail, Quist guessed there were a number of L-Bar-D men drinking there. The Warbonnet seemed to be the regular Lombardy crew hangout.

As he reached San Antonio Street, Quist decided to walk down to the depot and see if there were any further messages from Jay Fletcher. There wasn't a light shining along San Antonio, and as he turned on Railroad Street it seemed even darker, with the moon not yet above the horizon. The lights from the station shone dimly through the gloom ahead. He was about half the distance to the station when it happened:

Behind him, there came the detonation of a six-shooter, and almost at once two more explosions, spaced evenly close together. Even before the noise of the shots reached his ear, Quist had caught the whine of a slug through the air, close by. At the same moment he heard a cry of agony, then someone yelled, "Greg! Look out!"

Quist whirled, .44 already in hand, and moved toward the back of the nearest building, flattening his form against the wall, gun held at ready. He peered through the thick darkness and could see a moving form just this side of San Antonio Street. Then the voice again — Arbuckle's tones: "It's all right, Greg. I got the backshooting son!"

Gun still in hand, Quist made his way back. There was a man sprawled face-down on the earth, and kneeling close by was Fred Arbuckle.

"Didn't ping you did he, Greg?" Arbuckle asked anxiously.

"The slug came close enough to hear it," Quist replied. "Who — ?"

"It was a damn' narrow squeak," Arbuckle said. "I thought I —"

Excited yells sounded on Main Street. The rear door of the Warbonnet Saloon, dark until now, flew open and several men appeared.

In the light from the open door Quist sized up the still form on the earth and the six-shooter on the ground just beyond the out-stretched fingers of one extended arm, as though the gun had fallen from the man's grasp as he went down. The crowd gathered closer, partially cutting off the light. Quist put away his own gun, scratched a match and then picked up the six-shooter on the earth, which he stuck into the waistband of his trousers. The match flickered out after a moment.

Somebody said in sneering tones, "The railroad dick must have shot the poor buzzard in the back." Quist recognized Lombardy's voice, but before he could reply, Arbuckle said sharply, "That's enough out of you, Lombardy. I was the one that shot this hombre. He was trailing Quist. Tried to shoot him."

Lombardy slunk to the rear of the crowd, and Arbuckle continued, "This is that hombre I was telling you about, Greg — Duval Sloan. The feller who was looking for you. Happens I was headed for the Amber Cup, thinking I might find you there. I was a half a block off when I saw you just leaving. I was just about to give you a hail, when I see this scut sneak out of the shadow and start to follow you. I was curious to see what he was up to, so I trailed him in turn."

"I'm damned if I know why he'd want to take a crack at me," Quist said. "I never saw him before." He frowned thoughtfully.

"That's whatever," Arbuckle continued. "I followed you both down San 'Tonio Street, and saw you make the turn into Railroad. It was too dark to see good, so I closed in quiet. I was almost too late, but I caught the glint of this hombre's gun as he leveled it. I couldn't stop his shot, but I reckon my two shots reached him in time to spoil his aim."

"I'm much obliged, Fred," Quist nodded, and again knelt at the side of the man. The man moved slightly and muttered something. Quist said, "He's still alive! Somebody go get Doc Ingram. Hurry up!"

A man in the crowd volunteered to go, and Arbuckle said sharply, "Jump to it, then." He added as the man left, "Though I doubt Doc can do much good. My slugs got this hombre plumb in the back, under the left shoulder."

"If Doc can bring him around," Quist said, "I may learn why the man wanted to gun me."

Somebody yelled something from the station platform, but no one bothered to answer. Quist ordered the crowd back so the wounded man could get some air. A man came hurrying from the rear of the Warbonnet, carrying a lighted lantern and a flask of whisky. Quist turned Sloan over, and held some whisky to his mouth. Red froth bubbled from the pallid lips. All the color had fled from the fellow's face; his partially closed eyes held a glassy look that Quist didn't like.

Doc Ingram's voice was heard as he pushed through the crowd. Quist said, "Lord, Doc, you got here fast. We just sent a man —"

"He won't find me home then," Ingram said brusquely. "I was over on the next street when I heard the shots. Figured I might be needed. What have we got here?"

He knelt in the light of the lantern and examined the unconscious man. Quist and the others stood watching. Arbuckle plugged out two empty shells and replaced them with fresh cartridges from his gun-belt. Ingram said finally, "Hell, I'm not much use here. This man is almost gone now. If he lived another hour I'd be surprised and he may go any minute. Who shot him?"

Ingram was given brief details. Quist said irritably, "Well, are you just going to wait here while the man dies in the middle of the road?"

"What can I do?" Ingram asked.

"Bring him around. I want to talk to him, learn why he was gunning for me."

"He won't last long enough," Ingram said, then as Quist started to protest, Ingram reached into his bag and took out a hypodermic. After a minute he spoke to a man in the crowd. "Get a wagon from the livery. Tell 'em to throw plenty horse blankets in. We'll take this man to my place. I may help him hang on to live a spell longer, but there's damn little chance of him regaining consciousness."

The hours passed slowly at Doc Ingram's place; one room fitted up as his "hospital room," held the unconscious Dural Sloan's unconscious form stretched on a cot. Lish Corliss had arrived as the man was being lifted to the wagon, and had accompanied Ingram, Quist and Arbuckle to the doctor's house. The four men sat around a table, smoking. Ingram had produced a bottle of *Old Crow* and a pitcher of water and glasses. About once an hour, the doctor would enter the "hospital" and examine Sloan.

It was about four in the morning, when

he emerged from the hospital, shaking his head. "I'm going to bed," he stated. "My housekeeper is upstairs. I'll wake her and have her sit here. You men might as well get along to your blankets."

"You figure he won't regain consciousness, Doc?" Quist asked.

Ingram said irritably, "His pulse gets slower every time I examine him. It's thin, thready. Hell, he hasn't enough vitality left to regain consciousness with. Nope, Sloan is a gone duck."

The sheriff, Quist and Arbuckle left the house, heading toward Main Street. Arbuckle said moodily, "I sure hate to kill a man that way. Figured I'd aimed lower, but in that gloom —"

"As I see it," Lish put in, "you saved Quist from getting shot — could be you saved his life."

"It was almost unconscious on my part," Arbuckle said earnestly. "I saw Sloan lift his gun toward Quist. The next instant I'd yanked my own Colt's and fired twice. At least, I think I spoiled Sloan's aim. Just the same, I hate to kill a man —"

"He's not dead yet," Quist pointed out.

"Might as well be," Arbuckle said. "You heard what Doc said." They reached Lamar Street and Arbuckle added, "I turn here for my boarding house. See you *mañana,* hombres."

Quist and Corliss said good-night and continued on toward Main Street. Corliss said, "Fred seems to take that shooting sort of hard."

"Yeah," Quist said absent-mindedly, deep in other thoughts. They reached Main, and Corliss headed for the cot in his office. Quist continued on toward his hotel and wearily climbed the stairs to his room. Here, he again examined the six-shooter he'd picked from the earth near Sloan's outstretched fingers. It was an old gun, in poor shape. There were two empty shells in the cylinder, one of which was corroded in place and had likely been used only to rest the hammer on. Then Quist noted something he'd not seen previously. Stamped in the bottom of the walnut butt, were tiny letters that read L-Bar-D. The gun apparently had once belonged to Judd Lombardy.

[XIX]
Clean-Up

Quist had been asleep only a couple of hours, when a knock on his door awakened him. He sprang from the bed, fully clothed and opened his door, scrutinizing his visitor in the light of early morning. It was Jay Fletcher. "What the devil you doing here?" Quist asked. He seemed a trifle disappointed.

"What sort of welcome is that, Greg?" Fletcher asked. He looked weary but there was a certain light of elation in his eyes.

"I was half hoping to hear from Doc Ingram that a certain man had regained consciousness —" Quist broke off, trying to make amends for his greeting. "It's good to see you, Jay, of course, but I don't understand —"

"There was too much to put in a wire, Greg. I caught the train that gets here at 6:18. I'll be heading back to El Paso on the 7:12, so I've just got a minute. . . ."

Quist had been splashing cold water on his face while Fletcher talked. He combed his hair, rolled up the shades at the windows to allow the early morning sun to enter, then sat down on the bed across from Fletcher's chair. Fletcher said: "Greg, you've really done a fine job this time. I was a bit dubious at first, but when your wire said to have the 'consignor and consignee' arrested on narcotic smuggling charges, I at once got in touch with the Federal authorities at Washington. Since then the wires have been burning up between Washington,

Chicago, San Francisco and my office. Our investigators have helped too. It's fine publicity for the T.N. & A.S., great thing for the road. The public will realize we furnish a real public service —"

"Don't go into a speech, Jay," Quist interrupted. "Remember, you have to get your train back in about half an hour."

Fletcher nodded. "I'll cut the story short. The government agents arrested two men at Uhlmann's first. There were only two men in the company, Uhlmann and his brother. They caved fast and confessed to distributing narcotics. They implicated others, as well, including Drumm & Tidwell out in 'Frisco. Government agents swooped down there next. Drumm & Tidwell just had a small canning plant, with a single canning machine, operated by hand. Agents found a lot of half-rotten fruit there, but little attempt at honest canning. Drumm & Tidwell's preserve company was just a front. They were really canning and shipping raw opium, under the guise of jam and preserves, so as to get it out of California. Once they heard the things Uhlmann had told about them, they were only too anxious to confess. And they implicated others. It seems the opium was being brought up from Mexico in fishing boats, landed on some spot of lonely coast. Then Drumm & Tidwell took over."

"Figured it was something of the sort," Quist said. "I found two cans of that damned strawberry jam you were blowing up about. Learned it was opium. That's when I wired you to get busy and have arrests made."

"Lord Almighty, the government works fast. They've kept me out of bed with their telegrams, night and day, They made a real clean-up, with one or two exceptions. Both the Chicago crooks and the scoundrels in San Francisco say they had an accomplice named Mead Leftwick stationed in this district. And Leftwick's right hand man was Lloyd Porter, Kate's husband. Well, Porter's dead, but to make the clean-up complete, Washington wants you to do all possible to find Leftwick. The Customs Bureau is sending a couple of men here to help you —"

"They may be too late," Quist grunted.

"You know anything about Leftwick?" Fletcher asked.

"Maybe —"

"And of course," Fletcher rushed on, "the government would like to get trace of those missing cans of strawberry jam — er — opium, Greg. Now if you'll just throw yourself into the job, I'm sure —"

A knock came at the door. Quist opened it to the sleepy-eyed night clerk. "Sorry to disturb you, Mr. Quist, but Doc Ingram sent word if you can get there right away —"

"I'm on my way," Quist jerked out, rushing back into the room to don his sombrero and shrug shoulders into his coat after strapping on his underarm gun. He paused a moment to shake Fletcher's hand. "Sorry to have to leave like this, Jay, but you'll be gone before I get back. Don't miss your train —"

"But, Greg, you haven't told me —"

"I'll bring a complete report to El Paso —" Quist was already passing through the doorway on the way to the staircase.

"Greg," Fletcher called after him. "The government's offering a nice reward if you can —"

"I want it split with a Mexican in Ventoso, named Diego Cubero, Jay," Quist's tones carried back above the sound of his descending feet. "I also want the company reward increased for Cubero. . . ."

The words died to silence. Fletcher heard the hotel door slam.

Quist walked swiftly along Main, wishing he had a horse under him. His gaze flitted along the hitchracks. Not a pony in sight yet. A few men passed, looked curiously after him noting his haste. A few stores were being opened. The morning sun was bright, shining directly along Main from the east. Quist turned at San Antonio, and broke into a run until he'd reached Houston Street where the doctor's home was located. Ingram was standing in his open doorway when Quist appeared, an anxious look on his face.

Quist came bounding up to the doctor's front porch. "He's conscious, Doc?" he demanded eagerly.

Ingram nodded. "I was wrong, Greg. Never did think he'd regain consciousness. But he's slipping fast. He asked to talk to you. I sent for you right off. You'll have to hurry. He can't last much longer. If necessary I'll give him a shot to delay death, but it won't be for long —"

But Quist didn't wait to hear more. He was already brushing past the doctor and heading for the "hospital room." Ingram hurried after him, saying, "What Sloan's got to say, had better be said fast."

It was something over an hour later that Lish Corliss, dropping into the Chinese restaurant for his breakfast, found Quist ahead of him, just finishing off his coffee and a plate of pancakes, smothered in butter and syrup. "Jeepers," the sheriff exclaimed, "I never expected to see you up this early, after we sat up most of the night with Sloan."

Quist gave him a thin mocking smile. "It's even more of a surprise to see a man on the state payroll getting on the job at this hour. However, I suppose there are a good many honest men elected to public office. Only we don't hear of them frequently enough —"

"But, Greg, what gets you out so early?"

"Doc Ingram sent for me."

Corliss' eyes widened as he sat down and gave his order to the restaurant proprietor, then swung back to Quist. "You mean to say that Sloan recovered consciousness after all?" Quist nodded. Corliss asked, "Did he talk — ?"

"He talked plenty." Quist sounded somewhat grim. "Before dying."

"Feel like telling me about it?"

Quist shook his head and rose. "No time now, Lish. I'm on my way. You'll get the details later. See you again. *Adios!*"

"But where are you heading now?"

"Out to the Rocking-T. You got any message to send Kate?"

Corliss colored and said no, he guessed not.

Quist nodded, left the restaurant and headed for the White Star Livery. A few minutes later he had saddled up the buckskin and was loping out of Clarion City.

[XX]
A Certain Hunch

After crossing the plank bridge over the Rio Clarín, Quist turned his horse north, traveling at an easy gait, to follow the creek, which was flanked on either side by tall cottonwoods. Here was all gently undulating grass lands. As he proceeded, Quist began to see small bunches of Herefords, branded on the left ribs with the Rocking-T iron, either just leaving or heading toward the stream. The cows increased as the horse loped steadily on. Eventually the creek made a wide bend to the northeast, away from the well-traveled road Quist had been following. He continued on until the hoof-chopped and wagon-rutted trail carried him in a wide turn to the northwest, bringing him within sight of the Thornton ranch buildings. Here he pulled the pony to a walk, looking about as he approached. It wasn't yet quite ten o'clock, and the morning sun was giving off considerable heat. Almost directly ahead of Quist now was the

Devil's Drum, its rounded side rising sheer against the vast expanse of cobalt sky, where a few clouds announced the presence of the huge thunderheads building farther north.

Kate Porter was seated on the wide gallery of the ranch house when Quist rode in. The man's gaze widened a little as it fell on the girl. Here was no stiff traveling costume, with violeted bonnet, nor yet riding togs. The girl wore a loose white blouse, cut low at the neck to reveal well-shaped tanned shoulders. Her arms were bare, as were her legs; her feet were covered with Mexican sandals, and she wore a wide colored-striped skirt that Quist judged had come from south of the border, as well. Her blond hair was gathered high in a knot at the back of her head. She had been, Quist noted with some amazement, doing some sewing.

"It's nice to see you, Mr. Quist," the girl said, as Quist swung down from the saddle at the edge of the gallery and dropped his reins over the pony's head.

"It's nice to see *you*," Quist said meaningly, his topaz eyes frank with admiration. "I didn't know —" He paused.

"You didn't know I ever dressed like this?" The girl indicated a seat at her side and laughed self-consciously. "I don't often. These are old things I wore long ago, but it was so muggy and warm I wanted something cooler. There's generally a breeze here under the gallery roof. For once there was nothing much to do. Gene's shirt needed mending." She paused, saying tartly, "I don't know why I'm saying all this. You're not interested in what I wear."

"I think perhaps I am," Quist said slowly, seating himself. "It's all very becoming —"

Kate broke in caustically, "The butterfly emerging from the chrysalis after the long sleep, I suppose. Enough of such nonsense, Mr. Quist —"

"And I'm not sure," Quist put in, "that it was a sleep."

The girl said abruptly, "Dad's down to the bunkhouse chewing the rag with Chan Yount, if you want him. I'm not sure where Gene is, someplace back of the buildings. I saw him head down that way with his painting equipment. He said something about early morning light —"

"I came here to see you, Mrs. Porter —"

"I've decided to resume my Thornton name," Kate cut in.

"You're sure your hus— that is, Lloyd Porter is dead?"

"Yes, aren't you?"

"In spite of Ferris' testimony?" Quist asked.

285

The girl didn't answer that. "Just what brings you here?"

Quist replied, "I'm making a ride to the Devil's Drum, and I stopped to ask you a few questions, if you don't mind?"

"Perhaps I do mind," Kate said tersely. "I'm getting tired of being questioned. I had nothing to do with my husband's death, as I testified on the inquest stand. I feel that should be sufficient." Her voice softened a moment. "Not that we're not all grateful to you, for helping Ellen see things in a clearer light. It's made a difference to Gene too. But you can see why I want to resume my own name."

Quist smiled, " 'A rose by any other name —' " he commenced.

Kate's lips tightened. "Mr. Quist, I've heard quite enough flattery in my life to last me a lifetime. I've no intention —"

"Of being flattered into making a fool of yourself again?" Quist finished.

The girl's face went crimson with anger. With an effort she controlled her voice. "If you've anything important to say, Mr. Quist, please get it off your chest, then go down and see Gene or Dad or go to the devil —"

"Devil's Drum," Quist supplied. "Look here, you're showing about the same lack of sense Gene did at first. To date, you've no

286

occasion to scrap with me." He held up one hand for attention as the girl started some sort of protest. "No, you listen to me. What I'm trying to find out is, how much did you know of Porter's smuggling activities?"

The girl's brown eyes widened. She sank back in her chair. "Smuggling?" — unbelievingly.

"Smuggling opium, to be exact," Quist stated.

"Believe me, not a thing," she said in a half-whisper. "I never suspected anything of that kind. Oh, there were times when I felt almost sure some of the deals he talked of weren't on the level. And at times he'd have sizable sums of money — which he gambled away at once. But, you've got to believe me, I never dreamed —"

"All right," Quist sounded a trifle disappointed. "I'd hoped you'd be able to give me some sort of tip to back up an idea I have."

"Smuggling opium," Kate repeated. She sounded dumbfounded.

"You heard about those missing cans of strawberry jam that were stolen. They contained opium."

"And Lloyd was doing that — ?"

"He was assistant to a man named Leftwick —"

Kate slowly shook her head. "Believe me, Mr. Quist, I knew nothing about it."

Quist rose from his seat. "Well, thanks, anyway. I'll be getting along." He hesitated at the edge of the gallery.

The girl also rose. "I'm sorry I couldn't give you the tip you were looking for. If there's anything else that you have to ask that I could make clear . . ."

Quist swung around facing her. "Yes, I think there is, something that will satisfy my personal curiosity. You're a beautiful woman, Kate Thornton, and you could have had your choice of several men, including Lish Corliss whom —"

"Mr. Quist! I don't have to listen to this," Kate flared.

"You're going to listen to it," Quist snapped, "whether you like it or not. I've talked to people around town. Lloyd Porter was the lowest sort of a skunk, and yet you married him. Why?"

"That's none of your business!"

"All right, I'm sticking my nose in where it's not welcome, then. But it's about time somebody told you a few things before you ruin your own life. This hard mannish attitude of yours doesn't fool me. It's all a poise and a damn' bad one. You got sore at the town, and like the idiot you are, you married Porter thinking to spite your enemies and because you'd quarreled with Lish Corliss —"

"I refuse to listen!" Kate was furious, breathing hard.

"Get into the house then," Quist half snarled. "Go ahead, continue as you've been doing, riding roughshod over everyone who disagrees with you. Keep up that fool pretence of being as hard as nails and of having no truck with womanly sentiment. Drive on in your hardheaded, damn' fool way — and ride to the fall you've got coming. The trouble with you, Kate, is that you need a man, and you won't admit —"

"Quist!" The girl's breast was heaving, her face crimson. "You get on your horse and ride to blazes off this ranch, or —"

"— and you won't admit it," Quist finished scornfully.

Kate's arm flashed up and she swung hard, her right hand landing resoundingly against Quist's face. He felt her fingers burn against his skin, as reflex action brought his own hand up to describe a swift arc that fell just short of returning her blow. Instead Quist's right hand landed on her left shoulder. His other hand came up, gripping hard the other shoulder. The girl fought to get free, but Quist shook her savagely.

"You should — be spanked — like a — disobedient child." He grunted, putting considerable vigor into his actions. "Sure — I know no gentleman — ever lays hands — on a lady. But, by God — you haven't — been acting — like a lady. I've lost all — patience with this — hard-boiled poise — of yours. If you insist — on being hard — you deserve the — rough treatment — you get —"

The girl's blond head was snapping back and forth. The lovely yellow hair came tumbling down. Hairpins showered the gallery floor. For a moment, Quist, himself, had been almost angry. Now he stopped shaking the girl and looked at her. To his amazement, Kate's eyes were brimming with tears. Quist said tentatively, "Kate —" and then felt her arms come up and tighten about his shoulders. A tear dropped from the long lashes, and he drew her close, feeling her form warm against his own and her lips pressing against his mouth.

For moments he held her like that, then abruptly she was fighting like a wildcat to release herself, eyes again blazing, in anger at herself. "Go away from here, Greg Quist," she stormed. "I hate you — hate you —"

Turning, she rushed inside the house.

Quist stood gazing at the empty doorway

a moment, then, scowling, he went to his horse, mounted and turned it away from the house in a swift lope.

Once away from the house, he slacked to a slower gait. He glanced up once. The Devil's Drum seemed nearer now, almost towering overhead. He'd not been riding more than three-quarters of an hour, before he caught the sound of rapidly-beating hoofs from the rear. Twisting in the saddle he glanced back, and saw Kate riding hard and fast to overtake him. The girl was bent low over the saddle, the quirt on her right wrist, swinging methodically from right to left and back again to flick the pony into swifter ground-devouring strides. Dust boiled up at her rear and traced a long curving arc on the range behind until swept away by the wind.

Quist slowed to a walk to allow the girl to catch up to him, thinking, "Lord, she must have changed fast." Again the girl wore the divided corduroy skirt and boots, the mannish flannel shirt with bandanna at the throat, the stiff, broad-brimmed flat-crowned sombrero. There was a holstered six-shooter at her right hip. The panting pony drew even with Quist's horse. Kate said harshly, "Thought I'd better come along and show you the way up to Devil's

Drum. There aren't many know it. You'd waste all day getting up there."

Quist said, "Thanks."

They walked the ponies side by side, neither speaking. Kate finally said, "Greg, I'm sorry. You were right. I said I hated you. I don't. I don't love you either — that is" — glancing sidewise at Quist — "I don't think I do. It was just — well, for a moment all bars were down —"

"I think I understand," Quist said gravely.

"I'm not regretting it either," she said. "Maybe I'm glad — I *know* I am. You made me realize — well, gosh, Greg, if there are any more questions you want to ask —"

"I think you've answered most of them," Quist said dryly. There ensued another long silence, while the ponies forged ahead. Quist said irritably, "But I'm still wondering why you ever married Porter, instead of Corliss."

"I don't think I knew my own mind," Kate said. "I'd been going with Lish. I thought I liked him a lot. He was steady — maybe that was the trouble. He talked of his prospects and of how he'd saved. He was planning for years ahead for us, and it was all very secure and safe — and it seemed a bit dull. A girl wants more when she's — well, then Lloyd Porter came along and he had certain ways about him, was full of fun, and had a smooth line of talk. He made a girl think of romance. And then I went on a drive to deliver some cows, with three of the hands. There was talk —"

"I heard something about that."

"Lish thought he could stop the talk by marrying me at once. I didn't like the thought of letting the town run my life. I refused him. We quarreled. Then Porter asked me to marry him. I was just mad enough — and fool enough — to say yes. I knew I'd made a mistake, even before we were married, but —"

"You'd given your word and went through with it."

"Something like that." More silence, then, "Greg, we'd better speed up these ponies. It's quite a ride up to Devil's Drum."

The horses were sent into a swift lope and within a short time they were through the foothills, with Devil's Drum rising precipitously above their heads. Kate led the way to one side and drove her horse up a stiff incline. Quist followed. The ponies' hoofs scrabbled and slipped on gravelly soil, slid back, dug forward again. Finally, breathing hard, they emerged on relatively level terrain. Here the riders paused to rest the mounts. Kate said, "A mile farther on there's an easier way to get up here — even a wagon and team could make it — but this way saves time."

Quist glanced around. Ahead, curving up around the Devil's Drum, lay more steep grades. He said, "Looks like we got our work cut out for us." To the right ran a long straight ridge. "Too bad," he laughed, "that we're not headed in that direction."

"That's the way we go," Kate said.

"But that ridge leads directly away from the Drum," Quist pointed out.

Kate nodded calmly. "I know. But it swings in a big curve, back to the Drum and climbs higher. Oh, a horse can make the steeper way all right, but it's a job, as you thought. Most people don't know the easier way. Naturally, they're not inclined to swing away from the Drum. The way I'm taking you now, a team and wagon could make it, though it's a hard pull in places."

"Ah," Quist put in, "it's beginning to fit." Kate asked a question. Quist explained, "A certain hunch I had about the Devil's Drum. Did you ever take Lloyd Porter up here?"

Kate nodded. "One time when we were first married. There's a big cave up there and any number of smaller ones. Tunnels have been carved through the rock — I don't know whether by some prehistoric people, or if they're due to a freak of nature. What's your hunch, Greg?"

"I've picked up information here and there. Those missing cans of 'strawberry jam' contain opium. Somebody killed two teamsters to steal the cans. Whoever it was, needed a place to hide the cans until the storm blew over. He didn't dare drive the wagon into town. I couldn't think of a better place to hide anything like that than the Devil's Drum. Lish Corliss had already told me about the caves and tunnels."

"The idea seems reasonable," Kate agreed. "Whoever took the opium had to get it to a hiding place fast. If he'd headed for another town or some other ranch, he might have been caught, for all he knew. And no matter where he went, he was on Rocking-T holdings over this way, and there was always a chance he might be discovered by someone from our place. So actually the Devil's Drum was the closest hiding place." She paused. "And you think the man who killed the teamsters and stole the cans of opium was Lloyd Porter?"

Quist nodded. "I'm fairly sure of that."

Kate sighed. "I'm not surprised in a way. He was always a schemer. And the Devil's Drum would be convenient. He wouldn't have to haul the whole load down at once.

Living at our house he could make trips up here from time to time and just bring a few cans back with him. I understand opium is really quite valuable."

Quist nodded. "Porter was playing for big stakes. Well, these ponies have rested about enough. Ready to show me more of the route?" Kate nodded and they spurred their mounts along the wide high ridge to the right. For the most part the footing was gravelly sandstone of a greyish-yellow color, spotted here and there with stunted brush and cactus, whose roots clung with stubborn tenacity to cracks in the sandy earth. Now and then the horses were swerved aside to avoid small boulders and outcroppings of rock. The wind blew steadily warmer. Quist glanced at the sky. Tumbled clouds were piling high in the north. His gaze was continually on the girl riding ahead, admiring the erect back and good shoulders tapering to waistband of her riding skirt. Like an Indian arrowhead, Quist mused.

The route ascended gradually. On either side of the ridge, far below, were blind canyons and lower ridges, choked with scrub oak and scraggly cedar. From this high vantage point he could look across a sea of canyons and tumbled rock, some of which had been eroded by centuries of rain and wind, to queer formations, appearing at a distance to be spires and castles. By this time they were nearly to the level of the Devil's Drum which now was situated east of the riders. Once or twice Quist had wanted to take ridges running more directly toward the big Drum, but Kate vetoed that.

"You'll only get into trouble that way and find yourself at a dropping-off spot with no where else to go. This whole section is criss-crossed with canyons and ridges, and it's mighty deceiving if you don't know the way. Golly, it's hot, but there isn't much farther to go. Looks like a rain making up too. Suppose it came on to storm and we had to spend the night in a cave?"

"I can imagine worse situations," Quist chuckled. The girl made no reply.

The sky was completely overclouded now, and the wind was lifting. Quist could look back and see that the ridge they followed had described a great arc and was once again heading directly toward Devil's Drum. The gravelly soil had taken on a reddish hue now, and the way became marked with wide patches of rock, streaked with brownish red. Quist was remembering now the red strata that patterned the surface of the Devil's Drum. He remembered also the bit of red earth caked to the edge of Porter's boot-sole he'd seen at the undertaker's.

And then, quite suddenly, they had arrived on a wide apron of that same colored rock, at the foot of the great cylindrical formation, which showed the way to a cave with a high opening. Quist tilted his head back, gazing upward and saw the whole surface was perforated with openings of various sizes, reminding him of nests of bank-swallows he'd seen in steep sand banks. He and Kate checked their ponies and dismounted on the rock apron several yards from the cave mouth which was some twenty-five feet high and wide. To left and right of the wide apron, the way sloped off to deep gulleys grown with brush, cedar and scrub oak. Somehow a lonely pecan tree had managed to survive and lifted its head above the lower growth.

"Well, here you are," Kate said, as they moved toward the entrance to the cave. "You hadn't figured to go to the top of the Drum, today, had you?"

"That can wait for some other time," Quist said, walking at her side. "Today, I'm just interested in this cave."

"I hope it's cooler in there than out here," Kate commented. "If this weather doesn't bring a storm, I'll be surprised." She whipped off the heavy stiff-brimmed, flat-topped Stetson, and shook out her blond hair. "I should think, Greg, that you'd roast with that coat on."

"It's not as heavy as it looks," Quist said. "I had it made up special to take care of the bulge from my gun harness."

A drop of rain spattered down. By the time they entered the cave at a run, there came a rumble of distant thunder, and the rain increased.

[XXI]
Showdown

The roof of the cave arched up. Plenty of light came in at the entrance. Once inside, they turned and glanced out. The rain was really pelting down now. "We should have brought the horses in too," Quist observed. There came another rumble of thunder, nearer now, and Quist could feel the vibrations run through the rock. He turned to examine the interior of the cave and almost at once saw a stacked pile of wooden boxes against one far wall where the course of the cave appeared to take a turn to the right.

Followed by Kate, he strode swiftly to the boxes. All those on top had been opened. Splintered covers lay about, and Quist judged the boxes in the lower tiers were loose as well. "Kate, I think we've hit it," he exclaimed exultantly. "Look, there's ten boxes. Forty-eight cans to a box —" He broke off. "That one box is badly splintered. That must be the one Pardee dropped."

Kate stood watching him, her heavy Stetson in one hand, still mopping at her face with the bandanna. She laughed softly. "Better make sure it's strawberry jam, Greg."

He pushed aside the splintered pine top of one box and brought out a can, read the label. "Strawberry jam, as sure as you live — so it says. But now you and I know better than to believe labels."

He turned, smiling, away from the boxes, and looked about. There were many footprints on the dusty floor of the cave, and at one point they were so jumbled as to indicate some sort of scuffle had taken place. Suddenly he moved to the opposite wall which lay in half shadow, stooped down and straightened up again, a double-barreled shotgun in his hands. "Look here, Kate."

The girl came hurrying to his side. She looked over the gun a moment, then said, low-voiced, "That was Lloyd Porter's shotgun." Quist said, "You're sure?" The girl nodded. "I've seen it too many times to be mistaken."

Quist broke the gun and discovered one shell had been fired. He said, "Hmmm . . . one more bit of evidence, I reckon." He stood the weapon against the wall of the cave and glanced back toward the interior, where the cave started to narrow and turn to the right. "Probably," Quist observed, "this cave closes down and turns into a tunnel. Think I'll have a look-see around that shoulder of rock and learn if there's any more evidence to be uncovered. Coming?"

The girl shook her head. "You're right about its being a tunnel though. I followed back there years ago. You won't go far, it narrows considerably."

She stood watching him as the shadows closed in and his form began to fade. Behind her, rain spattered down at the cave mouth. She raised the Stetson in her left hand and began to fan herself. For an instant she took her eyes off the spot where Quist was lost in shadow. Then when she looked again, she saw him backing toward her, hands raised high above his head.

"Take it easy, Kate," he spoke over one shoulder. "I walked right into it." The tones sounded bitter.

What the girl said was lost in another rumble of low thunder. Quist came backing into the light, followed by another man who held a six-shooter level on Quist's middle. Kate uttered a gasp of astonishment as the other figure emerged into better light. "Why — why —" she exclaimed, "it's the Texas Ranger — Fred Arbuckle. What — ?"

"Not Arbuckle," Quist spoke again, voice steady. "The name's Leftwick, Kate — Mead Leftwick, your late husband's pardner in crime."

Arbuckle-Leftwick slowed step so he could watch Kate as well as Quist. "Never mind the name," he said coolly. "Just keep those mitts high. You, Mrs. Porter, lift that gun carefully from your holster, and drop it on the ground."

Kate hesitated. The man spoke again in sharper tones. Quist said, evenly, "Better do as he says, Kate."

Reluctantly, Kate drew the gun from her holster and let it drop, hoping the shock of the fall might explode it, and give her some opportunity. . . . The gun landed in the dust. There was no explosion.

"Want me to drop my gun too?" Quist asked genially, as though trying to co-operate.

Arbuckle-Leftwick chuckled coldly. "It don't work, Quist. I don't want your hand anywhere near that hideout gun. Fold your hands on top of your hat, and keep backing until you've reached the girl. Then stand where I can keep you both covered." He came farther into the light from the opening. Low thunder vibrated through the cave. Rain drummed beyond the entrance.

Quist halted a couple of feet away from the girl, who stood helplessly holding the flat-crowned Stetson in both hands, not even daring now to fan herself.

Arbuckle-Leftwick also halted, several yards away. "Dammit," he said irritably, "why did you have to come snooping here?"

"The question is," Quist said quietly, "how did you know we'd come here?" He was stalling for time, hoping for a break that would allow him to get his gun into action.

"That's easy," Arbuckle-Leftwick said. "I saw Lish Corliss a few minutes after you pulled out. Lish said that Sloan had regained consciousness and talked. Said you were heading for the Rocking-T. I knew the jig was up, if you'd talked to Sloan, so I saddled up and followed you. Wasn't sure if you knew about the Devil's Drum —"

"I guessed that part," Quist put in.

"Anyway, while you were at the Rocking-T, I headed up here — just in case, you know. Hid my pony in one of those brushy gullies beyond the cave mouth. Lucky he didn't make any noise when you arrived. And so I waited for you to stick your nose in where it wasn't wanted. So now you know. You know something else? You're not going back to Clarion City."

Quist nodded. "Thought you might have some such idea about me. But you won't dare shoot a woman."

Arbuckle-Leftwick laughed harshly. "Use your head, Greg. There's only one cache of opium like this. There are other women. Unless perhaps Mrs. Porter cared to make some sort of deal with me." Kate shot him a look of contempt. The man shrugged. "How you could pass me up and at the same time fall for a yellow-belly like Porter —"

"Look here," Quist interrupted, "you haven't got a chance of getting away with this. Your Chicago and San Francisco pardners are under arrest. They talked plenty, and Federal men even now have a warrant out for one Mead Leftwick."

"As to Uhlmann Company and Drumm & Tidwell, well maybe they had it coming. I was through with them sometime ago." The man didn't appear particularly surprised at news of his former pardners' arrest. "They never did kick in with as much money as I should have had. One thing I don't understand — how did you learn I was Leftwick instead of Arbuckle, the ranger man?"

Quist laughed coolly. "When you and Porter and the Lombardy crew were running dope up through Ventoso, a Mexican named Cubero saw a lot of you. Later when you trailed Porter there, he overheard your conversation. He has an excellent memory —"

"But I still don't see —" Leftwick-Arbuckle frowned. Thunder vibrated through the cave.

"Look here," Quist said, "you want information, so do I. Maybe we can make a trade. I'd like to know how right I was figuring things out. Is it a deal?"

"Stalling won't help you, Quist, but go ahead."

"As I see it," Quist started. "You and Porter planned to highjack a shipment of opium. His part was to dynamite Shoulder Bluff and when the two teamsters got certain freight from the stalled train, he killed the teamsters, loaded such 'jam' as he wanted in a wagon and took off. Your part — remember I listened to Sloan's confession — was to get Sloan to send the message, signed with Tyrus Wolcott's name, ordering the stationmaster at Clarion City to hire teamsters to drive out to a stalled train. You promised Sloan money for that job, and then hit him over the head to make it look good. You almost fractured his skull."

"That was an accident," Leftwick growled. "I hit him harder than I intended. Had a hell of a time squaring it with him too, when he came back to work. But I needed him to listen in on the wires and see what was being done about the missing teamsters and freight. I wanted to come to Clarion City, but at first I was a bit leary. Meanwhile, Porter the dirty crook, double-crossed me. He'd promised to meet me in Kingboro with the wagon and cans of stuff. I waited there two days for him, before it come to me that he was trying to keep all the opium for himself. Naturally I wanted to find him. Finally I figured he might have gone to Ventoso. I caught up with him down there —"

"Yes," Quist nodded, "Cubero told me about that. He'd heard your talk, heard what was said when Porter left with you. It's my guess —"

Leftwick broke in. "Mrs. Porter, quit fanning yourself with that Stetson. I don't want any movement from you two, beyond talk."

Kate stopped, and Quist went on, "It's my guess you scared Porter into bringing you up here and showing you where he hid the cans."

"That's right." Leftwick growled. "But I

didn't trust him a minute. When he thought I was looking over the cans, he raised the shotgun to kill me. I'd been expecting that sort of move, so I closed in fast, grappled with him. We struggled around here, and I finally jerked the gun from his grip. He let out a scream that I'd hurt his finger. I reckon it got twisted in the trigger guard somehow, and broken when I ripped the gun away from him." Leftwick paused, shrugged his shoulders, said, "All right, so then I let him have a blast in the face. I was mad."

"So you left the body here and headed back to see if Sloan had heard anything over the wires," Quist prompted. Kate had started fanning herself again. Leftwick scowled at her but didn't say anything.

He went on, "Again you guess right, Quist. Sloan had picked up word that a ranger stationed at Kingboro was to be sent to Clarion City. I didn't want any rangers messing into things. They're dynamite — nigh as bad as you. So I headed for the L-Bar-D, waited on the road until the ranger came riding along, knowing he had to come down from the north on that rail. I stopped him and borrowed the 'makin's.' We talked a few minutes and I learned for sure he was Fred Arbuckle. When he rode on, I shot him in the back —" He broke off, scowling, shrugged again. "All right, so I'm a murderer. After a first killing the next ones come easier —"

"And changed clothing with him and buried him," Quist took up the story. "You took his credentials and left identification with your name on it, in the clothes you dressed him in. Probably some of the L-Bar-D crew helped you. It doesn't matter now. All that mattered to you, Leftwick, was now you could come into town with ranger credentials, and who is in a better position than a ranger to hear what goes on?"

"You hit it right on the nose, Greg," Leftwick sneered. "So there I was, chummy with the sheriff and hearing everything that went on. Folks had begun to wonder where Porter was about that time. I was leary for fear someone might come riding up this way and find the cans. So Porter's body had to be found. I joined a hunt for him, riding by myself of course. Came up here, where I'd left Porter's horse. Porter had turned the team and wagon loose after getting the cans unloaded, so I loaded his body on his horse. The damn' bronc was thirsty I suppose and anxious to get back. He was hard to handle, but I got him down to the foothills all right, then the blasted animal had to take a spill and break his leg. I shot him. Never could stand to see a horse suffer. Humans are different. Loaded the body on my horse and brought it to town. Then you had to show up. I'd heard about you. I didn't like it. Not any —"

Storm and wind swept in through the entrance. There came the sound of heavy thunder. Leftwick shifted uncomfortably.

"Afraid of storms, Leftwick?" Quist asked sarcastically.

"I don't like 'em if that's what you mean," Leftwick snapped, with some irritation. "But to get back to Porter. With his face gone I figured there might be some doubt about identification, so I left his pockets intact. Just took the letter from one envelope, postmarked Albuquerque. It was from a woman over there. Porter had been fool enough to tell her about our business, and she commented on it."

"I've got an idea you had Albuquerque in mind when you put Ferris up to swearing he'd talked to Porter there — when he'd not been anywhere near the town. Right, Leftwick?" Quist flexed the fingers of his hands, clasped over his sombrero.

"Quit it!" Leftwick rasped. His gun barrel moved a trifle. "Don't move your hands." Quist said rather meekly that he was sorry.

Leftwick continued. "You're right, the Albuquerque postmark tied in with Ferris' story. Made it seem true. Trouble was, that dumb Ferris could only fake an address on Ventoso Street. With all the Spanish names there are, he had to think of Ventoso. Anyway, his testimony got everybody confused as to whether Porter was alive or not."

"Not for long," Quist denied. "I figured Ferris lied. But you were getting worried too, Leftwick. You wanted a man named Leftwick considered dead, in case your name got connected with Porter's murder. So you had Deray dig up the body of the real Arbuckle with Leftwick identification papers and bring it to town. And that was supposed to make us all confused and think less about Porter."

"Maybe it didn't work so well," Leftwick conceded carelessly, "but it don't matter now. After I return to town, I'll hang around a spell, and then just leave. When the time's right, I'll slip in some time and get the opium. There's just one thing I want to know. When did you first suspect I wasn't Arbuckle?"

Quist smiled thinly. "I rather doubted it from the first, when you claimed it took five hours to bring in Porter's body. I knew about where you were supposed to have found it, and five hours sounded too long. Again, you claimed you found no 'sign' about. That didn't sound like a real ranger. You tried to patch up things at the inquest by saying it took about three hours to bring in the body. You'd done some more thinking in that direction. I'll admit you had me fooled now and then. You staged a good act when dealing with the Lombardy crowd. One day I listened in on one of your messages to Captain Craig of the Rangers. It sounded right genuine, until it occurred to me any name can be signed to a telegram. I'll bet you never sent any written reports."

"You're pretty smart, Quist, but I —"

"I made a trip to Ventoso, talked to Diego Cubero. He has a fine memory for faces. He made one sketch of a man named Leftwick. So then I knew for sure you were a fake ranger." Leftwick swore harshly. Quist went on, "Meanwhile, Duval Sloan had lost his nerve. He'd heard I was in Clarion City and decided to see me and confess the whole business. He was almighty afraid of you, but even when you saw him, you didn't dare do anything to him, right in town. And he managed to slip away from you and stay hidden until I'd returned. Finally he saw me coming out of the Amber Cup and he followed me to talk to me. Trouble was, you'd been hunting him all day with an extra gun and a scheme to get rid of him and make yourself solid with me at the same time. When he followed me down Railroad Street, in the dark, you shot him and dropped that extra gun near his hand."

"You'd have a hell of a time proving that in a court," Leftwick blustered. "He shot at you and then I plugged him —"

"Why lie at this stage of the game, Leftwick?" Quist said wearily. "When you've heard as many gun reports as I have, you'll learn there's always some slight difference in the sounds of the explosions, even from guns of the same model. You fired once, waited a second, then fired twice more close together. The shots all sounded the same. I picked up that gun you claimed was Sloan's. The barrel was cold. Maybe you overlooked that little detail. Incidentally, if you've wondered what happened to Gilly Deray, I left him down in Ventoso. He got too interested in my business."

Leftwick growled. "You've been a damn' busy man, Quist. Too busy for your own good —"

A tremendous crash of thunder interrupted the words, a splitting rending sound, seeming almost at the cave entrance. It swelled to a deafening roar as the noise rushed through caves and tunnels, shaking the Devil's Drum with vibrations that carried on and on — *brrumph-h-h!* — *brrrummmphh!* — *brruuummph-h-h!* — like the rolling of some huge percussion instrument under gigantic drumsticks, the mighty rumbling shaking the earth beneath the feet of the three.

Leftwick cursed and cast a half-fearful glance toward the cave entrance. And at that moment, Kate with a deft flick of one hand sent her heavy flat-crowned Stetson sailing through the air toward Leftwick. Straight toward the man's body, the sombrero flew, curving upward toward his head. Leftwick snarled something unintelligible and dodged to one side, firing as he moved, but his bullet flew wide and high.

Quist's hands flashed down, his right darting within his coat and emerging again with smooth swift precision. Flame and lead spurted from the muzzle of the Colt .44, the violent impact of the heavy leaden slugs whirling Leftwick off balance, as the man's second shot flew wild. Quist shot him again, even as he was falling, the jolting detonation of the shots blending with the final *brruuummmph!* of thunder.

Dust was shifting down from the cave roof. The acrid odor of burned powder stung eyes and throat and nostrils. A gust of wind and rain swept through the entrance of the cave, clearing the air of swirling smoke. Quist cast a quick glance at Kate and saw she had retrieved her own gun from the floor, and was now lowering it again.

He moved in swift strides across the earth, and stood gazing down on Leftwick who lay stretched on his face. The man's booted toes drummed spasmodically against the ground for a moment, then he lay very still. Quist stood above him, methodically plugging out spent shells and reloading. He said to no one in particular, "These fools who allow themselves to be sucked into a conversation. I'd been dead ten times over, if crooks would shoot first and talk afterward."

He turned back toward Kate, looking steadily at her a moment, until a faint smile touched her lips. "I owe you a lot, girl. And I won't have to worry over you any longer. You're steady, steady as a rock when the showdown comes. . . ."

[XXII]
CONCLUSION

It was night when Quist reached Clarion City. It had ceased raining. Stars shone brightly in the velvety indigo sky above. Yel-

314

low lights from a few buildings were reflected in small puddles along Main Street.
A lamp burned in the sheriff's window.
Quist turned the buckskin in toward the
hitchrack, and lowered his drenched form
to the soaked earth. Corliss appeared in the
doorway, form silhouetted against the light
in his office.

"That you, Greg?" he asked anxiously.

" 'S'me," Quist grunted, rounding the
tierail, and stepped up on the small porch
before the door. Corliss backed inside, eyes
curious. "I've got a job for you, Lish," Quist
said.

"Yes? — Say, where've you been, Greg?
I've been sort of bothered — haven't seen
Fred Arbuckle since early morning, either."
Puzzled excitement showed in the sheriff's
eyes. "Say, there's a Ranger Captain in
town. Jim Craig. He's looked at Leftwick's
body, down to Cromlech's, and he swears
the body is that of one of his rangers, named
Fred Arbuckle. It's a hell of a mix-up. Craig
is waiting at the hotel for you. I tried to tell
him he was bad mistaken, that we knew
Fred —"

"Captain Craig's right, Lish. I sent for him
to come here and identify the body. The
man named Leftwick is dead in a cave up
in Devil's Drum. I had to kill him. You'll

hear the whole story from Kate. She was with me. You'll have to go up there for the body. We brought his horse down —"

"Hell's-bells!" Corliss' eyes were bulging. "What's happened?"

Quist told the story as briefly as possible. The sheriff's jaw sagged. Quist went on, "Now the rest is up to you, Lish. There'll be a couple of government agents arriving to clean things up, but you get into the record with your part. Gather a posse of men you can depend on, ride to the L-Bar-D, and place every man there under arrest. Get busy tonight, when you can catch them all there. Maybe they're not all guilty of smuggling, but I doubt it. Tell 'em Leftwick is finished and they'll give in fast, I'm betting. I doubt you'll have any trouble —"

"But what you aiming to do, Greg?"

"My job here is finished. I've got just about enough time to get to the hotel, find some dry clothing and then catch that 11:43 train to El Paso." He was moving through the doorway while he talked. Corliss was still asking questions. Quist cut him short: "And, Lish, just the first minute you find free, you ride out and see Kate. Ask her again to marry you. And don't make the mistake of telling her how much money

316

you've saved, or how much you intend to have when you're fifty years old, or of the position you hope to attain in politics. Just tell her you love her. I think that's all she'll want to hear."

He returned to the hitchrack, got the buckskin and left it at the livery stable, then started at a swift walk toward the hotel. In the hotel lobby he found Captain Jim Craig of the Rangers, talked to him about ten minutes, then shook hands and wearily mounted the stairway to his room.

A short time later he was repacking his satchel. With his belongings stowed away, he cast a last glance around the room. Lamplight shone on a brown bonnet covered with artificial purple violets, which lay abandoned on the table. Quist picked it up, studied it a moment, then dropped it into his open satchel.

A wry smile curved his lips. "Souvenir," he said softly. "A souvenir of a very courageous lady. . . ."

ABOUT THE AUTHOR

(Allan) William Colt MacDonald was born in Detroit, Michigan in 1891. His formal education concluded after his first three months of high school when he went to work as a lathe operator for Dodge Brothers' Motor Company. His first commercial writing consisted of advertising copy and articles for trade publications. While working in the advertising industry, MacDonald began contributing stories of varying lengths to pulp magazines and his first novel, a Western story, was published by Clayton House in *Ace-high Magazine* in 1925. MacDonald later commented that when this first novel appeared in book form as *Restless Guns* in 1929, 'I quit my job cold.' From the time of that decision on, MacDonald's career became a long string of successes in pulp magazines, hardcover books, films, and eventually original and reprint paperback editions. The Three Mesquiteers, MacDonald's most famous characters, were introduced in 1933 in *Law of the Forty-fives.* His other most famous character creation was Gregory Quist, a railroad detective. Some of MacDonald's finest work occurs outside his series, especially the well researched *Stir Up The Dust* which was published first in a British edition in 1950 and *The Mad Marshal* in 1958. MacDonald's only son, Wallace, recalled how much fun his father had writing Western fiction. It is an apt observation since countless readers have enjoyed his stories now for nearly three quarters of a century.

We hope you have enjoyed this Large Print book. Other Thorndike, Wheeler, Kennebec, and Chivers Press Large Print books are available at your library or directly from the publishers.

For information about current and upcoming titles, please call or write, without obligation, to:

Publisher
Thorndike Press
295 Kennedy Memorial Drive
Waterville, ME 04901
Tel. (800) 223-1244

or visit our Web site at:

http://gale.cengage.com/thorndike

OR

Chivers Large Print
published by AudioGO Ltd
St James House, The Square
Lower Bristol Road
Bath BA2 3BH
England
Tel. +44(0) 800 136919
email: info@audiogo.co.uk
www.audiogo.co.uk

All our Large Print titles are designed for easy reading, and all our books are made to last.